Charlotte Cooper is a freelance writer who lives in the East End of London. Her background is in small-press publishing – for years she produced her own queer grrly sex zine, *Kink*. She has also worked as a porn-packer in the seedy world of swingers' contact magazines. Charlotte's non-fiction book, *Fat and Proud: The Politics of Size*, was published in 1998 by the Women's Press. She likes loud rock 'n' roll and dirty-mouthed bitches.

visit **www.charlottecooper.net**

Cherry

CHARLOTTE COOPER

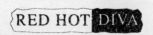

First published 2002 by Red Hot Diva/Diva Books,
an imprint of Millivres Prowler Limited, part of the Millivres Prowler Group,
Worldwide House, 116-134 Bayham Street, London NW1 0BA
www.divamag.co.uk

A catalogue record for this book is available from the British Library

ISBN 1-873741-73-1

Printed and bound in Finland by WS Bookwell

Distributed in the UK and Europe by Airlift Book Company,
8 The Arena, Mollison Avenue,
Enfield, Middlesex EN3 7NJ
Telephone: 020 8804 0400
Distributed in North America by Consortium,
1045 Westgate Drive, St Paul, MN 55114-1065
Telephone: 1 800 283 3572
Distributed in Australia by Bulldog Books,
PO Box 300, Beaconsfield, NSW 2014

Acknowledgements

Thank you for helping: "Anything Could Happen" by The Clean, the Coopers, Diva Blue Rooms, every great rock 'n' roll record I've ever danced to, everyone I've ever fancied or shagged, Helen, Iain, Jason, Kim, Lora, Libertas, Lukas, RainbowNetwork.com, The Ramones, Santa Pod Raceway, Stewart, Stratford, Tamsin, Therme Vals, Tracey, Vikki, Xtina.

Special thanks to Kathleen for her insight and support.

Extra big thanks to Simon for cooking my dinners, being potty-mouthed, scratching my feet, buying me sweets, making me laugh until I pop, playing my favourite records and being super-fucking-fine.

*For my girlfriend Kay Frances Hyatt
and her naughty dog, The Bean*

The summer before I shaved my head was a motherfucker. It was so hot your knickers would be sticking to you with ten minutes of leaving the house. My hair felt like a wig. Even the fake Blu-Tack that stuck hookers' cards to phone boxes along Charing Cross Road was starting to melt. Everything felt rotten and the city stank.

A good day back then would be spent strolling over to the post office, cashing my giro and then coming home to my room to paint my toenails and read trashy magazines all afternoon.

A good night would go like this: I'd pull on my best vintage frock and kitten heels. I had a bra that made my tits into a kind of big bosomy shelf that turned heads; I liked that then, and I like it now too. I'd get a one-way ride into town or sometimes I'd sneak in behind a salaryman as he put his season ticket through the automatic gates. I'd amuse myself on the train by winking at couples sitting demurely. I was what my dad used to call a saucepot.

I remember this power I felt when I was walking down the stinking summer street. I was the kind of woman that makes dirty men suck their teeth as they imagine sticking it in me, and uptight witches sneer at the flesh on my arse. My hips would get loose, there'd be some song in my head, and I'd go striding away down the road. On this kind of good night people would step out of my path because they knew they'd better. If I were in 70s New York or 60s Detroit, I would step through steam rising from manhole covers but in London you don't get those film-set moments. Still, there I'd be, trying to pimp-roll down the street like John Travolta in *Saturday Night Fever*. I know all this makes me sound like an arsehole, in real life I try not to fuck people over, you know, do as you would be done by, but life wasn't real back then.

I try not to make a habit of talking about the weather, but heat and humidity are the best kind of background for a nightclub. You really feel as though you've had a proper outing when you wake up naked with skin glowing from a night of sweat and your clothes a foul pile of dampness; it's like being reborn. Pure heaven for me is sauntering down a red velvet-lined staircase, feeling the heat rise and pretending that you're entering hell, which is funny because that's what this place was called.

A good night in Hell would involve propping up the bar with my Hellmates and not paying for anything as we positioned ourselves there like fruit for the monkeys. God, we were hot. At that point Hell was starting to be featured in the style mags, which meant that the old guard was becoming infiltrated by a few faker wannabes who thought they were slumming it big time by mixing with the likes of us and falling over drunk on the sticky floor. We didn't care, it just meant that there was more cock to rip off, more sweat condensing on the walls, more free drinks to be guzzled and more sneering to be done.

Like half the punters there, my main Hellfriend supplemented her admin assistant day job with a little bit of sulphate dealing. We'd start by having a tiny taste, just a nip from the end of our fingertips and later on we'd be off chewing the insides of our mouths and yakking about nothing at all. My pal had a beautiful boyfriend who was a Bowie-style bisexual; I doubt he had ever done it with a guy in his life, but he loved to boast and speculate about sissy-fucking endlessly. He was into it because he knew the ladies loved it, and they did, you know.

On this one night the Bowie boyfriend brought a friend along with him. If I was a teen magazine I would have to say that he was, like, a total cutie-pie in a fucked-up, degraded junked-out way. He was skinny and white; he had a waist that I could put my arm right around and then back on itself. His clothes hung off him and his eyes were like glass. Heroin chic is a look that I find very appealing, let me tell you, and you know what's coming now.

I leant over and whispered "I want to do you," clearly, so there could be no mistaking my intentions. He looked at me and smiled vacantly. Moments like these still make my heart flutter. I took Junkieboy out into an alley behind the club, my hand in his, striding ahead of him. He would have gone anywhere with me, he was so compliant. Now I know that heroin is supposed to kill your libido, but I've never had any problems with that particular theory. We were out in this place all alone save for the rats hiding under the grating and, well, we jumped on each other.

The thing I liked about this man was that he looked really fucking young and yet he had these skinny arms that were surprisingly strong and tough enough to push me up against the wall. I felt honoured to be the subject of such passion from a person so passive. As if to thank him, I bit at his face and his lovely soft mouth, and the patchy stubble on his cheeks scratched me and felt good. His hands, cool despite the heat, grabbed at my tits through my frock. "Go on, lick them, eat them," I said, so he got them out and sucked at them like a hungry baby hitting paydirt. I raised my arms above my head and rolled back my head. Up above us were planes flying low along their landing path; they looked like UFOs to me.

I ran my hands over his head, getting my fingers tangled in his greasy hair and yanking it so that he could look me in the eye. He smelled of smoke. His own fingers were creeping up my dress and reaching into my pants. I was a slippery wet girl inside.

J-boy pulled down my knickers and I stood there awkwardly with them tangled round my legs before I kicked them off and forgot about them for good. He had his face pressed up against my cunt and I could hear and feel him humming with pleasure. Droplets of sweat slid down the backs of my knees, and then he dug in, slurping and licking me out. He shook with pleasure. He ate me out like a greedy boy with an ice cream. My juices covered his chops as I stood shoulders propped against the wall with my hips thrust forwards, riding his face, flexing my thighs. He had his hands on my arse and his mouth clamped on me, holding tight so I wouldn't wriggle away. As if.

Inside Hell, the house band was rocking out loud, and baby, I was warming up.

I was hot and sticky and dirty out in that alley. My clothes were plastered to me and tangled up good. We were a mess of sex already but I wanted a good fuck; I wanted some real filth.

"Stand up, sweetheart."

He did. He was out of breath, his cock was big in his scummy jeans, his lips were full and red. I pulled his cock out and played with the pre-come around the tip of his dick before jamming on a condom. I turned my back, pulled up my dress and rubbed my arse against him. His cock felt strong and hard; it was twitching. He made for my tits but I bent over, out of his reach. My snatch was big and ready, so I slid myself very slowly on to his dick.

I told him to fuck me, and he did. With a hand on each of my hips he started slamming it in. Some girls like it slow and gentle, but not I. I like the hardness inside, I like feeling rearranged, the peace of my body disturbed. I steadied myself with my fingertips on a step. J-boy was grunting like an animal and we started to get into our rhythm of rocking and slamming together, connected only by cunt and cock.

In the olden days I loved the moment that hot sperm shot inside me then cooled and dribbled down my leg. Being filled up and feeling liquid was all I've ever wanted from a lover. I loved the consistency of a man's come, sometimes like soup, or snot, or melted ice cream. I miss those days. Yeah yeah, but these days I have other pleasures.

Like voyeurism. The alley behind Hell was not a private spot. A guy in a sports jacket walked right up to us and asked very politely if he could watch.

"Fuck off, you dirty fucker," we replied in unison with voices over-loud and distorted from tiredness and sweat. He scuttled away but we knew we'd have to reach our destination soon.

4

Junkieboy said, "I wanna come."

"Not yet."

"I wanna come."

"I said not yet, you cunt."

"I want to come." It's funny how desperation makes people enunciate more clearly.

"Not. Yet. Me. First."

With my spare hand I started the familiar rub on and around my sticky wet clit, his cock still fucking me hard, sliding and pounding, until the warmth got hotter and the sweat dripped faster and my head turned into a great big zero and there it was, I was groaning and coming, and I beat him; I won the race.

"Get out of me now." I stepped away, leaving him looking sorry and confused with a handful of soggy latex.

"Did I do something wrong?" he asked.

"No baby, it was very adequate," I pouted as he rolled off the condom and stuffed himself back into his trousers.

The part that still makes me laugh is that he wanted to see me again. He even pecked me on the cheek, almost tearful. "Aw, come here and give me a hug," I commiserated as I reached round and lifted the wallet from his back pocket. Even junkies have something you can steal from them.

What a bad girl eh? That poor lad! In my room, I laughed to myself as I counted out J-boy's small change and examined the tatty photo of the pet dog he kept in a hidden compartment.

I had a secret too, something nobody knew except me. Can you guess? You must have some idea, you can't have been taken in by the front.

My secret was contained in the shelves of books that lined my room. Let's open one up and have a read.

"Rain bucked her hips as Meg held her close and sang forth a crygasm, their bodies fitting together so naturally…"

No, before then, start at the good bit.

"The womyn's voices were soft outside as Rain and Meg entered the bathroom.

'Show me how you do it,' said Rain. Meg worked at the healthcare collective and had promised to teach Rain how to do breast self-examinations.

'Well, we'd better take off our tops,' answered Meg.

The two womyn helped each other off with their soft work-shirts. Their skin glistened from the hours they had spent in the sun, tending to the farm's vegetable patch, although they did not stop to admire each other's strong, muscular frames.

Meg intuited that Rain was nervous. 'Let me put on some music, it'll help us get started,' she said, as she rewound the cassette that sat in the dusty old tape recorder.

'The first thing you have to do is to really look at your breasts. You need to get a good understanding of what they are like, so that you will be able

to notice any changes in them,' said Meg. 'Look at my breasts – they are very round and firm; look at the nipples – they are tight like little raspberries. If I squeeze them, there is no discharge.'

Rain looked down on her own breasts. They were loose; her nipples were flat and wide, with fine hairs growing around the areola.

'Now then, let me get a little closer,' continued Meg. She took up her position behind Rain, who was standing in front of the large chipped mirror.

'Raise up your right arm.'

Rain complied, and Meg held her wrist aloft.

'Now, use the flat of your left hand to roll your right breast. You are feeling for unusual thickenings, or lumps. It's changes that you need to look out for.'

Rain felt embarrassed. Her breasts tightened at the thought of her husband, whom she had left back in Tucson, seeing her now, standing half naked in a bathroom with a womon to whom she was incredibly attracted. Rain's nipples started to become erect at the thought of Meg's strong fingers restraining her wrist, but she did as she was told, and began to circle her right breast as though she were a virgin, feeling it for the first time.

'You seem a little lost,' said Meg, 'perhaps I could show you how?'

'Uh yeah, please,' stammered Rain.

Meg cupped Rain's breast in her hand, squeezing and rubbing her with strong fingers and thumbs. Meg licked her lips as Rain leant back into her, the better to smell the clean muskiness of her teacher. She sighed with pleasure as Meg ran her hand, from fingertip to wrist, lightly over her increasingly hard nipples. Meg's own breasts were engorging and quivering from the sheer wonder of touching another womon so intimately.

'Shouldn't we check the other side?' asked Rain, already lifting her arm to accommodate Meg's reach.

'Yes, but let me show you a trick that'll help you do the examination more easily,' answered Meg, taking a bar of soap and lathering up her hands until they dripped with white froth. She rubbed the slippery mess on to Rain's breasts, whispering in her ear, 'You'll find that a good wetting agent will speed up the process nicely.'

Meg's hands slid over Rain's breasts, squeezing and pulling at her nipples, lifting then dropping the whole of their weight, playing with the slippery wet flesh and rolling them around. Meg mashed Rain's smooth breasts tightly against her ribcage, creating two half-moons of cleavage high up on her chest – like Queen Elizabeth tightly laced into a corset, thought Rain, guiltily.

'You're very good at this,' muttered Rain.

'It's because you have beautiful, rich, womonly breasts,' came the reply.

Rain's breathing was shallow and hot as she looked out of the window to see the other womyn talking in the yard. She pulled against Meg, allowing her breasts to smear against her teacher's arms. 'Let me kiss you.' Their mouths met hungrily; the womyn devoured each other, pressed up against the mirror.

Meg whispered: 'Open your legs, I want to make love to you.'

Rain leant back, supporting herself on the sink, whilst Meg crammed her muscular thigh in between her lover's legs. Throwing back her head, Rain felt herself go weak as she began to rub and grind. Meg herself stood astride the womon's leg, thrusting her hips and riding her hard. Both let out gasps of pleasure as they shook and pressed themselves together, steadying themselves by clinging to each other's belt-loops. Faster and faster they rode as they lurched about the room, knocking over a pile of feminist magazines, and hitting their heads against the thin walls. It was only a matter of moments before Rain bucked her hips and let the heat spread through her vagina and thighs, filling her completely and so satisfyingly, as Meg held her close and sang forth a crygasm, their bodies fitting together so naturally.

Coming round after their powerful lovemaking, Rain wondered aloud to her partner spooning against her back: 'How can something that feels this good be considered so wrong?'"

Okay, so it's not *Macho Sluts*, but that didn't matter to me; I was a hungry woman and long before Meg and Rain, whoever they were, sorted each other out I would be rocking on my hand, eyes closed tightly, licking my lips and humming "pussy pussy pussy" to myself like some holy mantra.

It's easy to laugh at this now, but at the time it was terrible. I wanted a woman, it was as simple as that. I'd never had one and I wanted one. I wanted a face full of tits; I wanted to feel inside a woman; I wanted to get my hands on a fat wet gash; I wanted to let her in right under my skin. It had never happened – don't ask me why – but I wanted it so fucking much.

It wasn't that I was ashamed of wanting to fuck women, I was no closet-case loser, on the contrary I thought dykes were the coolest people on the planet and I often said so until I was challenged with the inevitable "So why don't you be one then?" There was no ready answer for that. It was the fact that I was a slutty virgin wanting something that was out of my reach that bothered me so much. Boys were so easy for me, but it was the girls I needed and none had ever paid me the time of day, let alone sat on my face. I could suck a hundred dicks but nothing could take away the sorry truth that I wanted something I didn't know how to get.

I kept my secret lesbian cherry to myself because I had a façade to maintain, propped up on my kitten heels at Hell, and no way was I letting everybody in on this little piece of truth that would have left me too open and vulnerable had it got out. Me, a baby dyke? Forget it!

Being a dyke is a ticket to freedom; you can behave appallingly whilst maxing out your credit card on shopping trips to New York and claiming bona fide oppressed-minority status. How perfect is that? Not surprisingly, these bitches are protective of their turf. I still think that it's easier for a woman to become a freemason than to be accepted into the lesbian scene in London. Lesbians are a secret society accompanied by weird codes of behaviour that mean nothing to the non-dyke passer-by. Not only do you have to wear the right clothes, you have to get the haircut, go to the right places, say the right things, fuck the right women and like the same things as other lesbians if you want to stick with these particular kind of scene-lezzies – I was going to say "if you want to be welcomed into the fold", but that's a little too strong. There are a lot of lesbians out there who are inherently suspicious of outsiders – they could be men or, worse still, bisexuals. And if you break the rules, they will kick you out of the club without the slightest hint of mercy. Weep for me brothers and sisters, if only I had known this then.

My lesbian cherry was dripping with desire and need. I had to sort myself out; I needed to learn the ropes fast, but how was it ever going to happen? I needed a way in. A lightbulb clicked on in my head: I would find a lesbian to get me through the door.

My little black book was full of names that had been crossed out. Fuckers. I kept flicking, knowing that there had to be a number I could use. More little shits. A couple of dead people. Johnny.

Johnny was my first boyfriend and, miracle of miracles, though we rarely got it on now that he had discovered monogamy, we had stuck together and remained friends.

The last time I saw Johnny was when he came sobbing to me the night that his girlfriend made a bonfire of his porn stash. You would have wept too if you were him, because Johnny had the biggest porno collection I'd ever seen. He started buying when he grew out of trainspotting and it wasn't long before he'd built up quite a library that filled pretty much the whole of his bedroom.

Johnny didn't discriminate; all porn was good porn to him. He had everything, from frightful pretentious guides to *The Art and Science of Lovemaking*, to swingers' directories filled with deeply unsexy Readers' Wives, beautiful vintage gentlemen's magazines and even fetish catalogues.

Back in the old days we would spend a lot of time drinking vodka, flicking through the endless pages, and sharing our favourites.

"Hey, look at this."

He'd show me stuff like a picture of a woman dressed like a nurse sitting on a man's knee, holding up her skirt with one hand and pulling her G-string tight over her snatch lips with the other, staring right into the camera, so available.

"Oh my god."

Following that, Johnny showed me an extreme close-up of a cock stuffed into an arsehole. The men's pubes were all shaved away and frothy white come dribbled out of the hole. The bulging flesh squeezed tightly together; you could see the cock forcing its way in, and you could almost feel the thrust and the hard movement. The photograph looked like some strange abstract painting. It was very good.

"Don't they use condoms?" No answer.

I held up a centrespread of some manga chicks licking each other out. One was tied to something that looked like a medieval rack, her over-big eyes a pastiche of terror, whilst the other one got to work, leaning over so that you could see the fine penlines of her neat little slit. The page was littered with characters I couldn't understand, with occasional English thrown in at random: "Fucky-sex", "Oh! Beautiful Love!", "Pussy Sugar". Cartoon sweat pinged off the women's faces as they rolled their heads in ecstasy, and cutesy animals frolicked around.

I remember how Johnny had licked his lips, adding: "Sort me out, will you?"

"Only if you do me, too."

Johnny shifted over next to me and unzipped his jeans so that I could reach inside. His cock felt warm and smooth beneath the tangle of pubic hair which snagged my fingers. He sighed and whistled softly to himself, eyes closed. I started jerking him off. His balls were tight and hard. I made a tight circle of my hand and Johnny fucked it. The skin on his dick pulled back and then released. He was shuffling and humping next to me faster, making little blowing sounds with his mouth, holding his breath until he could not hold it any more and the dryness in my hand turned sticky and wet. And all the while he stared at those Japanese women eating and sucking each other.

I found a picture of a woman sucking off another woman with a strap-on dick. She was on her knees with her eyes closed, her hands tied and her head back. She had pretty much the whole thing in her face, deep-throating it. I thought of her gagging as the standing woman held the back of her head and shoved more of it into her. The standing woman looked so kind. It made my pupils dilate.

Johnny made a fist inside my pants. I wanted something that I could grind against and adjusted his arm so that his knuckle was held against my hole just so. I liked to think that he was about to punch his fist inside me. I got my hands down there and opened up my lips so that my clit lay hard against the back of Johnny's hand. I started twisting and shifting against him. I thought about that rubber dick in my mouth, the woman's soft hand on my head, I imagined her saying "Go on Ramona, take it deeper for me, take it deeper for your Daddy." I wanted that woman to call me a good girl. Johnny jerked his hand

13

around as I ground harder and wetter, the friction felt divine. He twisted his fist up against my hole and thought of that rubber dick in there, really big, really tight, barely accommodated in my cunt, and that thought is what made me come like electrical sparks through my thighs and clit.

We sat in silence, staring blankly at the walls.

Johnny loved his girlfriend, but she had some funny ideas and she'd made him choose between her and his beloved smut.

"But baby, please!" he'd cried, begging her not to make him decide.

"If you really loved me, you'd do the right thing," she'd answered, opening the box of firelighters. What a witch.

The flames had started small but soon grew tall and hot. Johnny had watched lipsticked faces and money shots turn into ash as the heat evaporated the tears on his face.

But let's get back to the story. Years of collecting porn had made Johnny some good contacts, and he made some money on the side organising models for amateur photo shoots. Recently he'd told me that he'd worked on a set for a dyke porn shoot.

"None of that long fingernail stuff," he said, "this is the real thing. Some of these birds look like geezers!"

I called Johnny, and within three minutes I had the phone number of one of those birds, and within five minutes I had arranged to meet her for coffee and -- ahem – a "chat".

Jackie was late. She sat down and ordered an espresso before sparking up a fag and asking: "So, what is it you want?"

Already Jackie had made me nervous and twitchy. She didn't do niceties; she wore leather despite the heat, and she looked at me as though she already knew what it was that I wanted. I felt naked. Jackie had a tattoo of a 50s-style pin-up girl on her forearm. Later, she showed me how she could move a muscle to make it look as though the pretty lady was shaking her booty. It was cute.

"I'm going to be blunt," I said, "I want to fuck a woman."

"Is that how you impress a gal?" She laughed.

"No, I'm serious. Johnny said that you might know someone who could help me."

"I might." She smirked. "Tell me more."

I shifted in my seat and said: "I want to hold a woman's hot stinking pussy in my hand. I want to feel her skin. I want to make her come and I want her to shake fifty orgasms out of me. I want to see her on her back groaning and wriggling in front of me because of the things I can do to her."

Jackie chuckled. "Yeah, you and every other dyke on the planet."

I cleared my throat: "I have a problem in realising my ambition. I don't know where to start. I need help. I want to know where to go to find women who will let me do dirty things to them. "

"Well, that's all we need," said Jackie sarcastically, "more wannabe lesbos hanging around and getting in the way. What's up, did you read about it in a mag? Thought you'd give yourself and your boyfriend a thrill?"

I cleared my throat. "I'm not a tourist," I said, "this is for real. Listen sister," I leant over the table to be closer to her, "we could have some good fun together."

Jackie's eyebrows shot up.

"You could teach me –"

"Stop right now," she interrupted. "Firstly, I don't do chicken. Secondly, I'm not your sister."

I sobered up.

"My heart bleeds for you, it really does, and I don't envy you, but I'm not the one to help you right now. If you want to fuck women you have to go out and do it yourself. No one is going to sort it out for you. I had to do it, everyone has to do it, it's how it is."

I was chastened.

"I'm sorry." She leaned over and said under her breath, "You are hot stuff, just put yourself out there and you'll have women swarming all over you in no time."

Jackie drained her cup, gathered her things together, and left with an "Excuse me, I've got to go".

She left a matchbook on the table. It was printed with the name of a club: Girlina's.

Oh boy oh boy oh boy. That Saturday night took far too long to come around. By the time I was shimmying into my sluttiest outfit I had developed quite a little fantasy about how the evening was going to proceed. I would have women queuing up to buy me drinks, they'd laugh their arses off at my stunning wit, I'd have my pick of the hottest, feel them up on the dance-floor and then we would fuck all night. I was very excited at the prospect of losing my cherry at last.

Only it didn't quite work out like that.

"Sorry love, it's for lesbians only," said the mean-faced woman on the door. She stood across the entrance, blocking my way with her arms out.

"And what makes you think that I am not a lesbian?" I said boldly. No answer.

Fuck. Inside myself I was quaking, but I refused to be stopped by this idiot goon. Quickly I stammered, "I'm a friend of Jackie's." At these magic words, the door fascist stood aside and down I went.

Of course I was there way too early, so I had to sit and wait for the place to fill up for a while. This meant that I had to buy my own booze. Shit. So I sat and played with my drink and watched the women arrive.

A couple of girls dressed in sparkly bikinis danced on platforms nonchalantly. The light danced off their arses as they gyrated and chewed gum. Everybody looked as though they were there with their friends or lovers; I was the only person who came alone.

A tiny woman walked over and sat next to me. She was wearing a miniskirt, a glittery belt, black stockings, heels and a top with straps that kept falling off her shoulders. There was a pack of fags tucked in by her tits. She had black curly hair, sort of Mediterranean-looking, and soft round cleavage.

I looked at her and looked away, play acting. She was so slight. Too small for me – I wanted someone who was going to be strong enough to match my own heftiness. That didn't stop her, though; she homed in on me fast. Told me her name was Natalia and that she was a nurse, as though her profession were a come-on. She was drunk, even though it was early in the evening.

She made me laugh with her chit-chat because her questions were so obvious and direct. "Are you waiting for someone?"

"No."

"Do you have a girlfriend?"

"No."

"No?! But you are so beautiful!"

"Thank you."

"I am a lesbian; are you a lesbian?"

"No."

"Are you straight? Are you bi?"

"No, I don't know what I am."

"Do you want to be a man?"

"No."

"You are so beautiful. Do you like me?"

"You're funny, but you're not my type."

"Will you give me a chance?"

"We can be friends, but I don't fancy you."

"I don't want to be friends; I want to be with you," she sulked.

Although I didn't want her, I was loving the attention. I'd never been spoken to in this way by a woman before. She was aggressive and I liked that. It made me twitchy and fidgety, which only encouraged Natalia more.

She came and pulled up my skirt and stood between my legs. She put her soft little hand on my thigh and began to rub. She was a champion flirter, walking off and looking at me over her shoulder, then coming back to dance in front of me. She leant over and tried to kiss me; she sat as close as she could get and scratched the back of my neck, at which point I nearly gave in, because I love being scratched there – sometimes more than life itself.

I wasn't into her, but in retrospect I don't know why. She was hot; I just couldn't see that at the time. I had this cherry like a millstone around my neck but – and you can call it a Catholic upbringing, conservative brainwashing, general cringiness or whatever you like – I wanted to give it up with the right kind of someone, not a silly little scrap of a girl. Natalia was definitely somebody's fantasy, just not mine. She left eventually, but I could see that she still had an eye on me.

She flirted like a pro, I thought. Oh, it dawned on me, she probably was a pro. Sure enough, I looked round and saw clusters of women motioning towards me, mouthing the name Natalia, rolling their eyes and laughing at a tired old joke.

I felt the panic rising within me; I was wheezing and sweating and I wanted to cry. I felt myself whooshing backwards in time, the fat kid in the playground, evil mocking teens saying that no one would ever want me. I marched to a toilet stall for a moment of privacy and took some deep breaths. Shit, people can tell, I thought, and my cherry felt more like a burden than ever.

I knew I couldn't give up, I wouldn't allow myself to be intimidated, and the joke had passed by the time that I re-entered the main room. I didn't understand the pecking order at Girlina's; it was confusing; I felt so new because I didn't know what was and wasn't cool. I didn't know where I fitted into the club's hierarchy, although I suspected it was somewhere very low down with the other single-cell organisms.

I stood and watched the women dancing and cheered myself up by imagining what it would be like to fuck some of them. A woman dressed in long boots would roll her head around as she came. Her friend would like to be done like a dog. That over there with the curly hair would be my slave and let me piss in her mouth.

One group of women stood out, primarily because of the bottles of champagne they were waving at each other. This group was definitely at the top of the food chain. They were a real rabble, falling all over each other, interrupting, shouting into their mobiles, waving money about. One wore a T-shirt that said "Player" on the front of it in large glamorous letters. Most looked like teenaged boys overdressed in expensive Soho gaylad fashion. There was a lot of bleach and tattooed biceps and hair product going on. I was transfixed; I wanted to be with them; they had the moves and every single last one of them looked insanely confident.

Jackie was there. She ignored me completely.

One was a beauty. She had long messy hair; she had a bit of the androgyny going on in her as well as some good-looking meat on her bones. She wore a tight top and loose trousers which sat low on her hips. She had boots on. I wanted to be near her, but I couldn't handle more rejection. She was dancing as though she loved the music, so I copied her moves and tried to get into it, too.

I watched the Player say something in her ear and she broke into a smile. Player said something again and she smiled harder. Then she did this dance: she opened her legs and surrounded the Player with her body, very close, then she leant back, raised her hands and arms over her head, swung her hair out and dry-fucked her friend hard and fast.

My jaw hung open and I began to dribble. I had to get out of there; it was too much; I was out of my depth.

As I left, I saw Natalia sitting by herself with her head in her hands. She looked small and crumpled. I felt responsible, but I didn't want to approach her.

I dreamt about the woman with the long messy hair.

This is how I met the Dipper.

A long time ago, before I became gloriously and resolutely unemployed, I worked on a series of shit jobs. One of these below-minimum-wage deals was as a private security guard in a department store on Oxford Street. I was sacked on my second day for filling the pockets of my scratchy uniform with hand-made chocolate truffles. On the first day, I met Dipper.

Maybe her clothes were too expensive, her hair too primped, her shoes slightly too high and too big, whatever, but there was something about her that made me suspicious. She minced around the cosmetics and costume-jewellery hall carrying a very large bunch of flowers. She must have squirted herself with at least fifteen different perfumes and when no one was looking she'd drop a fancy atomiser, some expensive nail polish, tiny gold and silver accessories, whatever came near to her thieving hands, into the bouquet where her swag was hidden away out of sight. She was oblivious to me. I watched her steal eyeshadows, bangles, purses left on counters whilst their wealthy owners got made-over by orange-faced beauticians. She was impressive in her audacity.

I sneaked up behind her and made her jump. "Let me help you with your flowers, Miss, they look terribly heavy," I said with a smile. She knew the game was up, but played along.

I could have taken her to the airless questioning room that was reserved for shoplifters. If I wanted to be seen as promotion material I could have made an example of her, emptying out the results of her work in front of my neanderthal supervisor in return for an extra star on my nametag. I didn't. Instead I walked her to the main entrance, helped her through the revolving doors and told her to have a fucking great day.

Six months later, we became friends at an end-of-tour party for some mutual acquaintances who were in a moderately successful band.

The party was being held at the suburban home of the drummers' parents, who were on holiday in Malta and who would have died of shock if they could have seen their son's friends pissing on the lawn and threatening the neighbours. They wouldn't have been too happy either to see two couples fucking frantically on their twin beds. I was underneath the singer and another woman was getting done by the guitarist. My heels tore up the pink bedspread and the carpet was stained with beer and cheap wine. The men's white arses rose and fell over us as we hooked up our legs, the better to accommodate them. There was a lot of huffing and grunting going on, not the least from some poor sod rapidly passing out on the floor, and another one going through the guests' coat pockets for souvenirs. I was sweating and fucking my man as best I could after a night of vodka, lifting up my hips to meet his thrusts, trying to get him in deeper, trying to get off as fast as I could. He wanted to kiss me but his breath stank of stale beer, and I turned my head aside so that he would catch my cheek instead.

Well, who should be getting fucked on the next bed but the Dipper herself, still recognisable with her tits hanging out and her hair loose and wild. Sensing that something had happened, she looked over at me too, shrugged off the sex blur and recognised me immediately. We both started laughing hyaena-style.

Our men made puzzled sounds, so we resumed our fucking to shut them up. I reached out my hand across the divide between the beds, she took it, and we squeezed each others fingers tightly, our arms jerking haphazardly as we laughed our way through two happy orgasms, then swapped over men for a few more. You've got to stay friends with someone after that, right?

We had some brilliant times together. Dipper could shoplift anything, she stole a whole set of saucepans and a microwave oven as wedding presents for her brother (he was thrilled), she could steal televisions to order and she would dump her grubby trainers and walk out of exclusive shoe shops in brand new high heeled mules without once opening her purse. She stole computer equipment, glossy coffee table art books, even a settee. She was truly gifted.

One sunny afternoon Dipper came round with a special present. From out of her loose sleeves fell two big fat massage wands.

"I've never tried one before,' she grinned sheepishly, "I saw them and I couldn't resist. I thought we could have a go, so I got one for you too."

I plugged one in to the wall and switched it on. It hummed and throbbed impressively.

"I know where I'm putting that," I said.

"Dirty bitch!"

We propped ourselves against the wall with our knees up.

Dipper said, "You go first, let me watch."

I switched it on and ran it up and down my thighs.

"It's good," I said.

"Stop teasing!"

I held the massager against my crotch and let it buzz against me. Dipper noticed that I had become quiet.

"Feel anything yet?"

I answered, "It's nice, it feels warm."

It felt fantastic but I wasn't going to show myself up in front of my friend. The nerve endings around my clit started to dance away; I felt myself get a girl-erection and warmth and wetness spread inside my pants.

Dipper interrupted: "Let me have a go." She tried to grab it from me. I held on to it tightly.

"Fuck off, get your own."

She plugged in and got settled. Two minutes of quiet humming passed. "I see what you mean," she said. I peeked at her; her eyes were closed tight in concentration and she was rocking gently.

"Careful, you'll crush it," I sniggered.

"It's alright, I know what I'm doing," replied Dipper haughtily.

Our breathing got heavier.

"They're very disappointing."

"Not good at all," I panted.

"Maybe they'd work better if we took off our pants."

I said, "That's just what I was thinking."

Both of us semi-naked now, I spread my lips and held the head of the thing up against my clit. The buzzing was intense. I let the feeling fill me up, then rubbed the soft head against myself to increase the friction.

Dipper had hers switched up to full power and her head lolled behind her.

I felt it growing in my belly like the beginnings of a sneeze. I wanted to come but I didn't want to do it too loudly in front of Dipper – I dunno, I felt shy or something. I rode that thing, but held myself back; I let the vibrations pass through me; it felt as though I was going to fall over the edge.

"Oh fuck it," huffed Dipper, as she groaned her way through a series of sizeable orgasms, shaking her hips so violently that the wand flew across the room and made me stare.

"Don't stop on my account," said Dipper, all mussed hair and red-faced. She came over and held me in her arms as I finally let myself slide into my favourite hot, wet, tantalising place and came loudly.

Sitting up, dazed, I smirked. "These things are shit; you should take them back."

Not long after that Dipper reverted to her real name of Suzanne so as not to confuse the baby. She told me that the night she got pregnant was the best fuck of her life. She always wanted a kid. I wish that

I could have put a bun in her oven myself, but that's another story.

I loved that girl, but if I could have made her child disappear without it upsetting her, I would have done so in an instant.

It's not just that Billy was a demanding little kid, nor even that he was always crying. It wasn't the fact that he was covered with eczema that transformed him into a horrible itchy blotchy bundle of scream. The problem with Billy was that his presence had made my beautiful, wild, funny and courageous friend transform into a sorry drudge who stank of baby puke and sterilising fluid.

Suzanne's parents were born-again Christians who worshipped their grandchild like a false idol. They saw Suzanne's motherhood as divine intervention for her previous sinfulness. Because of their own life of pleasure-free thriftiness, Suzanne was set to inherit some money when they died, so she just did the best she could to keep them sweet.

Billy's grandparents had already filled so many photo albums with images of the boy you could have made flicker books with them. Each new development was minutely documented. These loons even took a photo of baby's first shit. The boy was growing up in a bubble, the focus of what a popular television psychologist might have termed "severe familial dysfunctionality". Left alone with Billy, I would promise to buy him some therapy as soon as he was old enough to say his own name, and then we'd practise: "Bill-y, Bill-eee, Billy."

My heart sank as I saw the light disappear from my friend's eyes. One day she showed me her stash of Prozac.

"Gimme some," I joked.

Suzanne answered sternly, "Don't fuck around with my head Ramona, this is serious."

Although we inevitably made up, the mood had changed. "Okay," I answered, "I won't fuck around with you at all any more, I'll go and do it by myself." So I did.

Six weeks later – today, actually – I was knocking on her door.

Suzanne greeted me with, "I knew you'd be crawling back. What do you want? Are you in trouble?"

I ignored her and launched into it: "If you were a woman, would you want to fuck me?"

"I am a woman, you spazz."

"You know what I mean. If you were a dyke, would you want to do me?"

"What sort of question is that?"

"I've decided that I want to shag birds."

"Well, that's a surprise," she replied sarcastically.

"Don't be mean."

"So you're a lesbian now?"

"Sort of. Maybe. I don't know. I haven't been very successful so far."

"You don't look like one. No lez in her right mind would fuck you looking like you do. You need sorting out."

Suzanne ran her clippers over my head and I watched my shoulder-length hair fall to the floor. She shaved me a mullet and we both laughed until we pissed ourselves.

"That's better, now you're a proper les-be-friend."

"Fuck you, gimme them." I snatched away the clippers and finished off the job myself. When I looked in the mirror, I was thrilled by the transformation. My head felt like velvet. My eyes were as big as Billy's. I imagined a woman looking into my face and wanting to kiss my lips and for once it did not seem like such an outlandish idea. I wanted to try out my look immediately.

I took Suzanne's advice to "Go to Hackney, that's where they all live." I'd put away my going-out dresses and had gone for some boy clothes instead, although there was no hope in disguising my tits, belly and arse, all of which stuck out rudely.

When I told her about Girlina's, Suzanne had said: "Be a tough girl. Nobody is going to give you a free fuck. I've seen you toughen up with the boys. Don't be intimidated, try it on the girls too – they'll go for it, I'm sure."

Some horrible flaky lesbian goddess must have taken pity on me that night, because I found a dyke bar without even trying. Standing outside, underneath a tatty old rainbow flag, I felt like a debutante at her coming out ball. I don't believe in God or magic or anything, but it seemed like there were scores of dykes out on the street enjoying the warm night air. They looked at me as I passed by like they were trying to work me out, as I did with them. I was trying to be tough but I couldn't help but crack the occasional smile and yes, some smiled back. I had stopped being invisible.

It was a proud Ramona who walked into that place, took her rightful position up at the bar, ordered a large vodka and paid for it in coppers.

I didn't find out her name until later but Chrissie took one look at me and said, "You're new, I can smell it." She was propped up on a stool next to me. Chrissie's belly hung over her belt and she had arms that looked as though they could mash me into the ground. She wore a silver pinkie ring and motorcycle boots.

"I love new girls," she winked at me," you're all pliable, you've got no history, and you listen because you want to learn fast."

"A tasty chicken needs a good teacher." I smiled.

"Yes, yes. The sound of cherries popping in my bed is music to my ears. Nothing makes me hornier than a fresh young thing curled up under my covers. Chicken is so willing, you tell them to kneel and they'll kneel willingly, there's no arguments about who knelt last time, or whose knees are the most decrepit and in need of rest. You ask them to fuck you as though you're the queen of the universe and they'll do it like a princess."

She made me blush, but I tried not to show it.

"Chicken doesn't see ugliness, they don't care if your tits sag or your cunt reeks, age is a blessing, they are grateful to have it, and they just wonder and marvel at the brilliance of it all."

I felt Chrissie's hot breath on my ear: "Sometimes chicken misbehaves and pisses in the proverbial bed, sometimes they get scared, but believe me it's worth it to enjoy something as delicious as clumsy fingers on your cunt and a frightened face at your breast. All you have to do is say 'That's right sweetheart, that's good,' and you can have whatever you want. Chicken is so easy to use; get them to hold up their fist and you can pretend the rest of them isn't there; tell them to shut up and they will, and you'll still feel like a king in his castle.

"But you know what I like best about chicken? It's those tight, wet, fresh little holes they have. Those one-finger cunts that have to learn to be stretched to two fingers, then three or more until tightness is just an old memory."

I swallowed.

Chrissie continued, "It's a shame you're not ginger or I'd have you."

She bought me another drink, and one after that too. I started to feel as though I had something someone might want after all. I felt loose. I needed to piss.

There were women fucking in the bogs. The thin stall walls rattled and thumped as though someone was being repeatedly slammed up against them. Two women went "Uh... uh... uh," punctuated by groans that were deep like the bass cranked up in a car. Their clothes rustled. At the bottom of the stall partition, I could see a pair of feet spaced apart and teetering on tiptoes. One murmured hoarsely "Get it in, get it in."

I wiped myself and noticed thick sex goo on the paper and in my underwear, then I put my finger inside and felt the rich wetness. Having sex so close was like visiting a dreamworld. I sat and listened to those women shifting and humping in the hot damp toilet.

The sounds were getting faster as their voices became more breathless. One of the women hissed, "Shit, shit, shit," through gritted teeth and gave out a moan which sounded as though her larynx was imploding.

The quiet that followed brought me round. I was ashamed; I knew they knew they had an audience.

"You go out," I heard one mouth to the other.

"No, you go first, she'll know if we leave together."

I stepped out of the cubicle and went to wash my pussy-stink fingers.

Someone fumbled with the lock on the other toilet door and two women spilled out. One, short and bleached, made a run for the door, head down. The other came and stood at the sink with me.

We didn't look at each other directly, but I saw all in my peripheral vision. The woman was tall with short hair cut like a man's. She had biceps which peeked out of her short sleeves. Her clothes, sports labels, looked expensive. She was the latest in a long line of immaculate butches whose doppelgängers I had seen in 1920s book jackets, in bar scene photos of the 50s, and on 60s pulp novel covers.

She took off her silver rings and washed them one by one before rinsing her fingers. Her hands were strong and broad. She leaned over and splashed her face, then rearranged her hair in the mirror. She looked very cool. She glanced over at me and stared.

"Did you like it?"

What could I do? I laughed nervously, nodded and stammered out the first thing that came into my head: "God, you're sexy!"

"Come here," she said, unfazed.

"Huh?"

"Come here, I want to tell you something."

I stepped forward until I was an arm's length away. She reached out and pulled me by the waistband of my jeans until we stood hip to hip, her face in mine.

I was close enough to smell her perfume and to see the way her clothes sat on the body beneath, like a shell. I imagined being small enough to climb inside her top. I thought about her breasts and the place between her legs.

She leant in and rubbed my earlobe with her nose, like she was an animal checking me out. I stood numb. She had her hands on my waist now and held me steady and upright as though I were her doll. I was glad of this when she licked my neck. Oh, oh, oh, oh, was all I could think. She nibbled my neck with her soft lips, then worked her way round to my jaw and up until she was kissing my mouth.

It was pure Mills and Boon. I felt like a fly captured on a spider's web, but I did not struggle. My mouth was open to her as I saw a ghost of myself standing away from us, equally open-jawed. My tongue was inside her, and she was in me. She was soft, it felt good, and I let her reach right in and have me.

Her name was Nicky and I went home that night with her phone number written on my arm.

When you get someone's number, there's a whole waiting and calling ritual that you have to perform to show that you're not the desperate one. I'd done this dating dance many times before, but I'd never been as humiliated as I was when I did it with Nicky.

"Hi there, it's me, Ramona."

"Who?"

"We met three nights ago."

"Oh yeah," warmth oozed into her voice, "blonde, right?"

"No, I was the dark-haired one."

"Oh." The friendliness evaporated.

"Remember? The one after the blonde."

"Oh yeah, sorry, I'd forgotten you."

I laughed nervously. What a bitch. "I think you're very special and, um, I'd like to see you again."

"Okay."

"Really?"

"Yeah, what do you want to do?"

"Do you want to come over?"

She did, and I gave her my address. I had a date; it was easy.

I never invited anyone back to my place. For a start it was tiny, barely big enough for me and my stuff, let alone anyone else. Neither did I want people in my own little private world. Don't get me wrong, I'm not a serial killer with a fridge full of human heads hidden away; I'm just what you call a private person. I live modestly by myself and I like it that way.

The night before our date I slept badly and dreamt of nothing but sex. I awoke feeling anxious and set about cleaning my place like a madwoman.

My anxiety increased. I found an illustration of a cunt in an old sex education book. It looked terrifying. The words felt wrong. I was worried that I wouldn't know what to do. I got a mirror and looked at myself, as I had done many times before, but this time the landscape seemed alien.

I went out and spent the last of my giro on some wine and chocolate cake. Then I had a long bath, cut my nails, and plucked and primped myself for two hours in readiness.

She was due at 7.30. I gave her until 8.15 before I started to get jumpy. By 9.00 I had drunk half the wine and by 9.45 the cake was eaten. I considered crying at 10.00 but gave up and jacked off over some of Johnny's rescued porn instead. Then I watched the late film – some crap with Bruce Willis, the last person with whom I'd ever want a date – and went to bed grinding my teeth.

I got as far as two days without her, but Nicky was like a scab that needed to be picked so I called again.

"Hi, it's Ramona."

"Who?"

"Ramona. We had a date. You missed it."

"Oh shit. Ramona, I'm sorry. I remember."

I softened. "Are you okay? Did something happen?"

"No, I just got caught up with something. Do you want to reschedule?"

"That would be great." I was a sucker and I didn't even know it.

"Listen, I need to get my diary. Can I call you back in two minutes?"

Yeah, like she was ever going to call. I waited for two hours and then went over to see Suzanne to bitch about it.

It's not as though I'm admitting something you don't already know but, frankly, I was very uncool. You would have been too if you were as hungry as I was. For the whiff of promise that she'd given me, I would have waded through an ocean of shit for a chance at Nicky's snatch; she knew it, she was playing with me, and it just made me more ravenous.

I called again when I got home. It was late and I was fired up from several hours of quality bitching with Suzanne.

I yelled into the mouthpiece: "Don't fuck me around."

"Hi Ramona, it's lovely to hear from you."

"Do you want to see me or not?"

"What are you doing tomorrow?"

"I'm busy," I sulked.

"Great, I'll be over at midday. We'll have some fun. See you!"

If I'd had any self-respect, I would have refused to answer the bell when she called round. But the sight of the picnic basket on the back seat of her car somehow eroded away any feelings of self-preservation I might have had.

Nicky drove too fast, which was no surprise, and cut up countless innocent motorists along the way. I didn't care – she had her hand on my thigh and she'd squeeze at my leg whenever she wasn't using it to steer and that was all that mattered to me.

"Are you checking to see how ripe I am?" I asked.

"Yep, and I think that you're more than ready to eat."

My snatch throbbed whilst the blood rushed to my face. I felt like her bitch.

Twenty minutes from the motorway we pulled down a quiet road where the Tarmac gave way to sand and deserted dunes, a big fresh sky and the twinkling blue sea. How perfect is this? I asked myself.

Not so perfect. I felt self-conscious again. I was nervous. What was I going to do with this woman? I worried that nothing I had or did could impress her. In my experience, men would be happy with whatever you threw them because they could still get off on the fact of a woman being different to them. But I wouldn't be able to use any of my boy-tricks on Nicky; there'd be no faking, no twisting it around on my part. She'd seen it all before and I was definitely not the one in charge this time.

I fiddled with our supplies, trying to be casual whilst my knees shook. Nicky came up behind me and ran her hands over my arse as though she was sizing me up and liked what she had found. Bending over, I braced myself with my hands on my knees. She reached between my legs and rubbed her hard hand against me. It felt good through my jeans, I rolled my hips and tried to relax and be blank so that I could go with it.

"Oh yes, that's good," said Nicky.

Because dyke sex books and magazines had been just about the only things that I ever read, I already felt like an expert. It never occurred to me that the theory might be different to the reality but now, like smack to my head, the truth hit me. I got stage fright. The panic wouldn't leave me. I was scared. I knew I was going to fuck up. Nicky would know that I wasn't a real girlfucker because I wouldn't be able to do it right. We had come all this way and it was going to be a disaster. Then afterwards I'd never get to fuck anyone again. I had been wrong; I should have stuck to what I knew; I shouldn't have taken this risk. I saw myself as others must have seen me: an idiot. I thought I was going to be sick. I was trying not to cry.

And then I ran.

I'm not a particularly fast runner but, when the adrenaline kicks in, I can shoot away like a dragster accelerating up a strip at three hundred miles per hour. I ran up and across the sand as though I was being carried by the wind. Dune grass whipped my legs.

"Hey!" shouted Nicky behind me. She sounded angry, although it was hard to tell, maybe she was faking it.

I kept going. I ran until my legs started to crumple beneath me. Nicky was closing in. I ran further. I was afraid. She caught up with me and pushed me to the ground and sat on top of me.

"What the fuck are you doing?" She was laughing at me, not angry at all.

I couldn't say anything, just looked up at her with sorry eyes.

"We'll get sand everywhere if we stay here," she said, wagging her finger at me, fake angry. "C'mon, let's go back, you naughty runaway."

Nicky picked up the heels of my jeans and dragged me by the ankles back down the dune to our private spot. I felt better, happy and you could even say excited.

And so we got back to our spot, and we started again, and this time it was good and my fear melted away.

Nicky pulled off my top and bra. I worried that my body would not be good enough for her, that she would be grossed out by my awful, shameful stretchmarks or my tits sliding east and west.

Nicky looked at me; she really took me in. I cringed like a slave. "You're a sexy fucker," is all she said, whilst pushing me back and climbing on top of me. She held down my legs with hers and pinned down my wrists above my head with one strong hand. She kissed me violently. I pretended to struggle, just for the pleasure of feeling her wriggling on top of me. She was heavy; her hips ground into mine.

She fought her way out of her shirt.

I was nervous about touching her. My sweaty hands stuck to her intensely soft skin. I kept moving and stroking her; that felt like the right thing; she didn't moan with pleasure though, like women do in porn. I felt Nicky's back and arse and legs. She was muscular and solid but smooth and neat, too.

I wanted to feel her tits, but couldn't bring myself to do so. It felt unallowed. Up until now I had spent my life restraining my desire to touch another woman's breasts or apologising if I knocked someone accidentally. Nicky evaporated my social conditioning with one small impatient movement; she grabbed my hand and placed it on her right tit. It felt lovely moving underneath her bra. I just held it, feeling the weight in my hand, squeezing her flesh and running my hand over her hard nipple. I tried to undo her bra, but fumbled like a drunken teenager, so I just pulled it off over her head and tossed the tangled mess aside.

Nicky reached her hands down below and unzipped my jeans. She yanked down my pants expertly, rolled back and threw the rest of my clothes aside. I felt extremely vulnerable lying there naked as she towered over me and my legs twisted round together like a shy little girl.

Nicky looked like a hungry wolf ready to devour me. She pushed open my legs – I did not resist – and manoeuvred herself between them.

My hands flew up to cover my face.

I peeked through my fingers and saw her running one finger along the whole of my slit, like someone testing cake mixture. I was oozing dampness. Nicky said, "You're so wet, you bad girl," and I squirmed with pleasure.

"Do you want me to fuck you?"

"Oh yes," I replied eagerly.

"Are you sure?"

"Yes!"

"Shall I fuck you now?"

"Please please fuck me." I was serious.

"It's your first time, isn't it?"

I shuddered at my own obviousness and nodded that yes, it was.

"Are you ready?"

"I'm ready."

And then she was in.

Nicky had one finger inside. It was cool and long along the walls of my cunt. I exhaled and felt as though a spell had been broken.

Her finger twisted, exploring, turning upside down then the right way up, round and round. She'd tease it out slowly and then plunge it back in. I raised my hips to meet it as she pushed it into me.

"Want more?" she asked.

"Yes!" I replied, my voice coming out high and desperate.

Nicky put two fingers inside me and rubbed them in and out. She was building up a rhythm, chopping and changing it whenever it became too predictable, whenever I anticipated it, she'd change it again, always one step ahead of me. She was cool. It was good and hard. Her knuckles nuzzled the opening of my cunt and I pushed myself down on them to meet her fingers, now right in me.

She shuffled down and got her face close to my hole. Leaning on her elbow, she brought her free hand round and laid her wrist on my belly.

Nicky held two fingers either side of my clit. I looked down along my body to see her concentrating. Still fucking she licked at my clit, which was popped up between her fingers and hard as a nail. It felt as though it was glowing. It felt huge. Fireworks, explosions and earthquakes are nothing compared to how Nicky made me feel with her tongue.

"Oh fuck, oh God, oh fuck, Jesus fuck," I was gibbering. I could hear some unearthly noise not far away from us and realised just in time that it was coming from me. I felt as though I was flying out of my body. It was heavenly.

Nicky pushed more fingers inside. I felt stretched tight around her. It hurt, but in a good way. I was gasping for air. I wanted more of the pain she was giving me. My legs spasmed out of control and I was scared that I was going to piss and shit everywhere, but I didn't care.

I started to feel as though I was the one fucking her. My hips thumped against her and Nicky looked as though she was holding on to me like a rodeo star on a bucking bronco. Her tits were shaking all over the place. Her arm muscles were tense, like she was using all her girl-might to fuck. She looked up to meet my eyes and smiled; my cunt juice was plastered around her mouth. It was the sexiest thing I'd ever seen and it stayed in my mind as I screwed up my eyes and came like thunder cracking on a hot summer night.

Almost immediately afterwards, my anxiety returned. Although I felt as though I'd been beaten to a pulp with a cartoon mallet, I had to get it together to do her.

"What about you?" I could barely speak. The words felt like big unwieldy lumps in my mouth.

"Don't worry about it, I'm fine," she said, flopping backwards.

Nicky had brought champagne and fancy breads for us to eat. We guzzled artichoke hearts and roasted peppers. Oil dripped down my face and Nicky licked it away. I fed her fingers full of cream and popped sticky red cherries in her mouth, then I lay naked and full under the late afternoon sun.

It was late by the time that we got back to my place. She wanted to come in and crash in my bed with me, but I said no. I needed time to doze and think about the day. She looked so sorry when I sent her away that I took pity and said, "Come round tomorrow night, I want to see more of you." She even perked up when I added, "And listen bitch, don't you stand me up again," all fake angry.

The truth was that I wasn't certain she wouldn't back out at the last minute, so I didn't waste my time sprucing up my home for her.

She called at seven o'clock exactly. I was painting my toenails, just slagging around in a T-shirt and pants and watching the soaps. Nicky stood in the doorway with flowers and a toothbrush.

"Is that some kind of lesbian sex thing I should know about?" I laughed. She looked away and I whistled through my teeth. This girl meant business!

She was dressed in leathers tonight and looked like a young Elvis. I licked my lips.

I liked the way that she sat on my chair. There was no apology in her stance; it was as though the chair should feel lucky to serve her.

I climbed on Nicky's lap and said simply: "I want to do you tonight." She gave me a sideways smile. "What's up?"

"A chicken fuck – I'm supposed to be excited about that?"

"I'm not so chicken now."

I came close to kiss her then pulled away at the last second so that her face was left hanging in the air with a goofed-up expression on it. I tugged at her leather trousers but the belt was too tight and I couldn't get in. She sat there smugly.

"Okay, be like that then," I flounced away and stood with my back to her then looked round, winked and flashed my arse from under my T-shirt. "So I wouldn't know what to do?" I pouted, turning round and feeling my tits through my top and running my hands over my body. "How hard can it be?" I flashed myself at her again then ran my hands underneath my clothes, feeling myself, out of sight.

"Wanna look?" I teased. She nodded.

Standing in front of her, I lifted my right leg and rested my foot on Nicky's shoulder, rubbing her cheek with my toe. She got a good eyeful.

I had my hands down my pants and was rubbing at my clit with my middle finger. I used my other hand to pull my underwear tight against me so that she could see everything pressing through the delicate fabric. It felt good too. I was getting very wet and gradually a damp stain spread across the material.

I bent my knee so that my cunt was inches from her face. "Smell good?" I asked. Her face flushed.

"Tell me what you want and I'll do it."

Nicky shrugged my leg off her shoulder and undid her trousers. She reached inside herself, hooked her hand round my neck to draw me close then stuck three wet fingers in my mouth.

She looked me in the eye and said, "It's high time you learned how to fist a woman."

We were soon naked together on my bed and I can barely begin to tell you how good she looked lying there in front of me. Out of her boy-drag she had surprisingly feminine hips, large and heavy they were – motherly, you could even say. I loved the feel of our skin together, she was smooth and soft, like no man I had ever fucked.

Nicky sighed quietly the first time I entered her. It was the sound of relief. I watched my fingers disappear inside her big cunt. I was a little bit afraid; this thing looked so greedy and I wondered if I had the right ingredients with which to feed it. There seemed so much of it, the thick fleshy lips and delicate lace of her labia within. She had a dirty wet hole that you could lose yourself in, so it felt to me at the time. Her pubic hair was soaking and formed little ringlets.

Nicky could take four of my fingers easily. I was on my knees between her legs, sliding them in and out, twisting my hand so that she could feel the hardness changing inside her.

I am fucking a woman, I thought, this is what dykes do.

Nicky saw my loss of concentration and hissed, "Get the lube." I had some by my bed and squeezed a big dollop into my hand, working it around over the knuckles.

"Push it in me, get it in!" She was ordering me and I liked it.

Her cunt was big, I reasoned, but surely not big enough for my whole hand. I made a point with my fingers and fucked her with that, forcing as much in as I dared. I was afraid of hurting or ripping her open.

"Get it in me!" She sounded angry and I started to panic.

"I can't! It won't fit! My hand is too big."

Nicky reached down, grabbed my wrist and pulled my whole hand into her with a big fat groan. My fingers curled round inside her snatch and formed a fist.

"Fucking hell!" I'd really lost my cool this time.

The inside of Nicky's cunt felt smooth like silk, hot, tight and claustrophobic. I was frightened to move my fist in case it damaged her, but she insisted I fuck her, that she liked it. I made slight movements that made her gasp with pleasure. Emboldened, I turned my fist around slowly so that my wrist was skywards. Then I fucked her, using small and indistinct movements at first, growing into faster and harder thrusts.

Nicky commanded, "Do it more, I want to feel it," so I fucked as hard as I could and it felt as though I was punching her.

Not that she cared. Her hips were flailing madly, like she was using her cunt to shake my hand. She was on my bed, leaning on her elbows,

43

head back, neck arched, jawline taut. Her belly flexed and twitched whilst her cunt clamped down on me. Inside my knuckles were bashing up against her cervix and I could feel her muscles gripping my hand.

Nicky's hands were jammed down on her clit, she was jerking herself off furiously.

"Jeesus! Jeesus!" she spat through gritted teeth. "Uh, uh, uh. I'm coming now, I'm coming, oh baby, yes, that's good. Fuck it! Fuck it harder, ohhh, oh yes!"

I stayed inside her until she was still, then pulled out my hand slowly and gingerly. I was in shock.

Nicky sat up and pulled me on to her. She spent the next twenty minutes decorating my breasts and thighs with lovebites, then she let me fist her again, and a couple more times after that too.

She was too fucked to make her way home so I let her stay over and in the morning she brushed her teeth with her own toothbrush. I noticed that she didn't take it away with her when she left. In fact, I noticed that it took her a long time to go at all.

"Don't you have a job or something to go to?"

"I'll call in sick."

She was all lovey, all "Let me stay with you." It was unsettling, but I was secretly flattered. I had to kick her out in the end with a lie that I was going to visit my auntie. Auntie Dipper, more like. The only thing that placated her was the promise of another date.

There was a suspicious bulge at the crotch of Nicky's jeans when I answered the door to her two days later. It was the kind of bulge that most nice girls don't cultivate.

"My, that's a nice looking package you've got for me, mister," I crooned in fake southern belle. Nicky stood and let me admire her – what a peacock. "Won't ch'all come in and let me get acquainted?"

As soon as we got inside, Nicky threw me on to the bed and climbed on top of me. She forced open my legs with hers and started dry-humping me. I fought her off with all my strength, slapping at her.

"What the fuck are you doing?"

"I thought that's what you wanted," she replied gingerly. I thought she was going to cry.

"I'm sorry, c'mere."

She came and sat next to me on the bed and rested her head on my shoulder.

"Poor baby," I cooed. "Let me tell you what I want," I said rubbing and patting her erection. "This is what I want."

I love feeling a hard dick through tight jeans, all good, nice, sexy. I love to run my hand up and down that thick shaft, feeling it respond to me, knowing that it's one of the few times that the man I'm fucking has really stopped to take notice of me. I had Nicky's cock in my hand; I was holding it through her jeans and she was leaning into it, letting the base press against her; it must have felt hot.

"You've got a lovely cock."

"Mm, hmm." She was becoming hypnotised as I stroked and worked that thing.

"It feels so big and hard; I'd really like to fuck it."

Nicky smiled saucily. "You're such a straight girl," she teased. I put my finger to her lips and shook my head.

"You're wrong. I'm not talking about straight-girl pussy, I'm going to fuck you with my mancunt. I'm going to suck you in and shit you out again. You want to be a man? Then be one, be a big fucking man, Mr Tom of Finland."

Nicky was astonished by the speed at which I got her cock out of her pants and into my mouth. Practice makes perfect, I guess. She had a good-looking dick, anatomically correct in every way if you happen to be a giant made of black rubber. It was a pleasure to suck.

I held the cock against my cheek then pulled it round and into my mouth. I played with it, licking it along the whole of its length then swooping down on it with my mouth. I grabbed the base of the dick in my fist like a lolly and teased the end with my tongue. I could tell by the little grunts she made that Nicky enjoyed that very much. I opened my throat and went down on it as far as I could, forcing more of it into me, then drew back my head and let my lips leave a wet trail along the cock's length.

Nicky's hand rested lightly on the back of my head – it felt as though she was blessing me; it was a fatherly gesture, as though we were doing something holy together.

She began fucking my face. Saliva oozed out and dribbled down my chin. Sometimes she'd miss her stroke and make me gag or catch my teeth. I didn't care as long as her safe hand was holding my head steady, making it feel like a precious and sacred skull. I looked up into her eyes and she looked down on me, mesmerised. As my eyes watered, I wished she could know how grateful I felt.

We arranged ourselves so that Nicky's cock lay between my breasts. I held them together and let her pump at them. It felt simultaneously tawdry and comical. It took a lot of balance and effort for her. I traced patterns with my finger in the sweat which formed in the small of her back.

"I bet that makes you feel like a real man," I sneered.

"Yes, yes," she puffed breathlessly, unaware of my sarcasm.

"I'm just a pair of tits to you, cock-boy."

She didn't hear me, or chose not to show it if she did.

"Who's the straight one now?" I said loudly.

She pulled out, leapt up and grabbed me by the face, mashing my cheeks together.

I said, "Do me, Daddy," but it came out all distorted and she threw my face away in disgust.

"What are you then? Some kind of hustler?" I spat in her face defiantly.

"Yeah, actually I am."

"Only you're off duty." She nodded. "I see, and you've come home to me for a bit of arse."

"That's right."

I went on: "And it's not tits that you want."

"No, sir."

"It's my dirty shithole, you filthy cocksucker." She nodded.

I ordered: "Help me off with my trousers." She pulled them down and I stepped out. I turned and stood with my back to her, doing a little Betty Grable hip sway.

"You like sissy boys? Or something a bit more macho?"

"Any way is good by me."

She came up and stood close behind me, smoothing her hands over my big fleshy arse and smooching my neck and ears. I ground myself against her cock; I knew she liked that.

She pushed me over so that I was bent in front of her with my hands braced on my knees. Nicky knelt down behind me and continued to feel my arse cheeks as though they were some kind of ripe fruit. She put her face in there and I heard her sniff hard. I knew I stank, but I didn't care. She started in with tiny baby licks, like a cat lapping milk. She was methodical, working her way around the whole area, then forcing her tongue up against my hole. It felt like I was shitting a big squirmy delicious wriggly thing. Nicky was going "Mmm, mmm," and my cunt was dripping with sex juice.

Her thumb closed in on my arsehole, feeling and pressing, waiting for something to give.

She pulled away and put on a latex glove. There was lube by my bed; she squeezed a blob on to her hand and spread some around my arse.

I murmured, "Oh, you big dirty man," and she slapped my arse with a loud thwack.

"Hold still for me."

My arsehole prickled and contracted; it was like a closed door and as far as I was concerned, there was nothing heading in there.

Nicky teased me with her fingers, she circled my a-hole and eased it open with her index finger. I panicked and shifted away, but her fingers were insistent. Soon she had sneaked her thumb inside and was easing it in and out slowly, the rubber and lube making it feel like a long smooth tube. My arse was unlocked, I could feel myself letting go, and I relaxed on to her fingers.

"Good boy," she said, standing up and placing the blunt tip of her cock against my arse. Where her fingers had felt dainty, her dick felt impossibly big. "Trust me," she whispered, pushing it into me whilst I leaned backwards on to it.

"Stop, ouch, go slowly," I whined.

"Shut up, fucker, and smell this." Nicky fumbled a bottle under my nose and I inhaled a lungful of poppers.

I got an instant head rush, like slamming into a wall then turning inside out and upside down. I felt as though I was tumbling backwards with pure dizziness and pleasure, like being shot into space on the front of a rocket. In that precious moment where all was loose, Nicky thrust the last few inches in my arse, pulled out slowly and then slammed it in again.

We were now attached to each other and I lost the ability to speak. I had no breath; she was fucking it out. I croaked and took another hit from the bottle, my belly and tits shaking from the force of getting fucked so hard.

Nicky's cock made my eyes water. I coughed up mucus and goo. It was so big that I felt invaded, violated even. It was appalling and dirty to feel so powerless. I was merely a receptacle for her cock. She made me feel as though I was nothing but arse. I was so high that I said it out loud.

"That's right, you are nothing but arse to me, don't forget it," she replied, lovingly.

I felt weirdly emotional, but I wasn't going to lose face. I demanded: "Fuck me, you filthy fuck pig. Fuck it up my arse." She complied. "Harder, fuck me harder." I wanted her to know that I could take whatever she dished out.

Nicky slapped my arse again, and hissed, "Shut up, you little weasel – Daddy's working."

She had me impaled and was poking me as hard and as fast as she could. Our wet bodies slapped together as they met. She had one hand under my chin and the other holding the base of her cock to make sure it didn't fall out of me. She was so strong, bouncing me around like a rag doll with her fucking hips, off in a world of her own, in a place where she was the stud of the century, where guys were only too ready to bend over for her big fat cock.

She was fucking me fast now, like a piston. I wanted to get myself off but it was too much for me, too overwhelming, too big, too exhausting; there was no way that I was going to come like this; I gave up wanting anything for myself and just let her have me.

If I could have twisted and turned myself around to face Nicky, I would have seen her with her fingers jammed down between the base of her cock and her clit. I would have seen that she was holding open her lips so that the dick bashed up against it every time she shoved it inside me and that she would follow it in by rubbing and shaking her cunt to add to the friction. I would have seen that this is what it took to make her come; that her head was thrown back and that she was going "Uhh, uh, uhhhh, uh, uhh," with dead unfocussed eyes.

If Nicky could have read my mind as we both lay shivering and twitching together, she would have known that I was dancing around and laughing inside my head, so pleased was I with the beginnings of my girl-fucking career.

Later that night, after I'd finished washing myself clean of all the sex dirt that had accumulated on and in my body, I found Nicky hanging up some of her own clothes with mine. She'd also made a little bit of space in one of my drawers for a neat pile of her clean underwear. I didn't know what to say.

"It's more convenient this way," she shrugged. I laughed, but I didn't know why.

My hair was staring to grow a little bit too long and girly so I hot-tailed it over to Suzanne's place to get a shave. Billy cooed and kicked in his bouncer in the corner of the kitchen whilst my hair fell to the floor.

On my way to Suzanne's some drunk guys had yelled "Fat Dyke!" at me from across the street. I was filled with pride, so I gave them a royal wave and smiled: "Howdy!"

Suz thought this was hilarious when I told her. She said, "So, apart from revelling in the kind of attention that would make most people gnash their teeth, what have you been up to? I haven't seen you for a while."

For a few moments it was hard to find an answer because I was pre-occupied by the vision of my friend's tits as she stood close with the clippers. Two big wet milky patches had seeped through her bra and on to her T-shirt.

"Er, I think you're leaking."

She looked down. "Oh fuck, it'll have to wait," she answered dis-tractedly, then jabbed my scalp accidentally on purpose and laughed. "And what the fuck were you doing checking out my headlamps? You dirty homo-girl!"

Luckily she was too busy to see me blushing.

I changed the subject quickly. "Okay, okay, let me think, what *have* I been doing lately... Do you know what fisting is?"

"Duh! Of course I do. Next!"

"Um, I've met this girl, I mean, woman."

"And?"

"Well, we've been playing around a bit."

Suzanne hugged my head to her belly. "Oh my God, my baby bust her hymen! Well done sweetie, at long fucking last, eh?"

"Thank you for your support, I couldn't have done it without you, really I couldn't," I slipped into luvvie-speak.

"Ah, shaddup. Was it as good as you'd hoped?"

"Yes," I said quietly.

"So are you going to tell your momma Suzanne the details?"

"You're not my mother."

She pulled a face. "Don't be like that."

"Okay, I'm sorry." I softened. "Yesterday I nearly died when Nicky fucked me in her car."

"She's that good?"

"No, yes. I mean that I nearly died because we were doing a ton up the motorway whilst she was fucking me."

"Don't shit me."

"I'm not shitting you."

"Nicky's pretty wealthy."

"That's the best news I've heard in a long time."

"Don't interrupt. She has a lot of money and she has quite a flash car. I don't know anything about cars, but it's some low-slung sports car type affair. Anyway, she was there beeping her horn outside my window, going, 'I've come to take you for a ride in the country.' The weather was beautiful. I had nothing to do. How could I resist?"

"You couldn't, that's your problem."

"Shut your smart mouth. So we're cruising up the motorway, we had the windows wound right down and we were listening to something loud. I love the roar of the wind around my head on a summer's day. She had her hand on my thigh and was stroking my leg."

This is where I stopped giving Suzanne the details. I was still a bit too shy to tell her everything. I let her think that we nearly crashed because I was getting my leg felt up, but this is what really happened:

Nicky was feeling me up like she did on our first date; she had one hand on the steering wheel and the other on my thigh. It was good; she made me feel like a sexy motherfucker.

She said, "Play with yourself."

I wasn't sure if I'd heard her correctly.

She repeated: "Play with yourself."

I stared at her blankly. "Are you joking?"

"No, I want to see you play with yourself."

"Shouldn't you be keeping your eyes on the road?"

"Shut up," she said, "and do it."

I was shocked. Even though I'd been through a lot with this woman, I didn't want her to see me so nakedly. I didn't want to perform for her; it was too much to ask.

"Go on," she said.

But I couldn't turn into a prude and risk fucking up. I knew I had to go along with the game, so I pretended not to be shy and I put on a mental mask so that I could do this thing. I remembered my mantra: "Put yourself out there."

I tried to zone out; to leave my self-consciousness behind and get in the mood. Out of the window, I saw the hard shoulder zooming by. There were families crammed into crappy old hatchbacks; I didn't envy them one bit. I saw grumpy wives reading maps, bickering couples, truck drivers singing along to the radio. I looked up and saw the hot blue sky, then sank down into my seat.

I ran my hand over my belly and tits to wake them up, and to let my body know that there was work to be done. I pushed off my jeans and let them concertina down my shins. I stroked my thighs. I stroked my pubic hair and let it tickle. I warmed up my cunt with the flat of my hand, holding it there and grinding against it softly. I pushed my middle finger between my lips and felt the beginnings of wetness. It was thin and watery at first, then became thick and viscous as I dipped my finger into my sex hole and wet the rest of my cunt with the juice. I teased my clit and felt it harden and protrude. It was too tender to touch directly, so I rubbed at it through my clit hood. More wetness oozed from my hole; I spread it around until my whole pussy was wet through.

Nicky had her hand on my leg, she was stroking me firmly and I undulated under her touch. She got close to my cunt; I wanted her to touch me there, and she knew it. She held off so I shifted down and forced her to feel. I was grateful when she held it in her hand, and more so when she slid her finger inside. It must have been awkward for her, twisting her hand round so that it fitted, and I felt satisfied to think that I must have been irresistible to her.

Neither of us said a word.

We were accelerating up the fast lane, weaving in and out of cars to keep overtaking, always ahead of the others. Doppler-effect horns trailed off behind us, and I realised I was scared.

"Nicky, why don't you slow down a little?"

There was no answer. She had her foot flat on the pedal, the needle showed 95 and counting. I don't know how to describe the look on her face.

Nicky's fingers were still inside; she was still fucking me.

"Stop," I said nervously.

She dug her fingers in deeper and the car swerved noticeably. I could feel myself going cold. She knew I was sobering up fast.

"I want you to come, then I'll stop," she shouted above the noise.

We swerved a little. "Fuck you! Keep your eyes on the road," I screamed, my voice sounding high and afraid.

"Just come for me, then we'll pull over."

Despite my fear, the truth of it was that it was not hard to come in these circumstances. I had only to get the right pressure on my clit and I was there feeling electricity running through me, my nerves dancing inside, screaming like a fucked-up siren.

Nicky wiped her wet hand on my thigh as I shuffled back into my pants.

"There, that wasn't so difficult," she said, patronising me.

We were slowing down. She took her eye off the road again and, when she looked back, the configuration of road, speed, car and traffic was slightly altered for her. A second's confusion was all it took for Nicky to slam on the brake. Cars dodged around us as we spun three hundred and sixty degrees. Inside it felt as graceful as a slow waltz, albeit one danced to a soundtrack of screaming.

We came to a halt in the slow lane with the whole of the motorway stopped behind us. Everything was still. People got out of their cars to run over and help. All I could hear was the sound of blood rushing around my head, two women breathing heavily, and two hearts thumping around in our chests.

We exploded into laughter as the shock kicked in. Nicky twisted the key in the ignition, revved it up and we shot off before any do-gooder could remember our numberplate details.

"You silly sods," said Suzanne, after I told her only that Nicky had felt up my leg, "that's pure fucking bravado. I bet you really wanted to shit yourself, and I bet you haven't told me everything either." The voice of reason continued: "You could have killed yourselves, and other people too." I was ashamed. "Nicky sounds like a cunt." She grabbed my chin and made me look into her eyes; I struggled to avoid her gaze, but she was serious. "If she ever hurt you, I would kill her."

I was silent.

Suzanne held it for a beat, then perked up. She blew the hair from the clippers and smoothed her hand over my newly shorn head. "You look handsome," she said.

I beamed up at her.

"Heartbreaker," she snorted.

After the car episode, I decided that I wanted to take a little bit more control when I had sex with Nicky. Well, actually a lot more control.

"Tonight you are going to call me Mistress Ramona," I said in a big, deep grim voice.

Nicky saw my corset and high heels and brightened up. "Okay!"

I stood over her and slapped her face. "'Yes ma'am', is how you address me."

She looked at me with surprise and admiration. "Yes ma'am."

I sat in the easy chair and ordered her to take off her clothes. She was hesitant at first, but speeded up when I shouted at her. She looked vulnerable undressed.

"Lie down." Nicky started towards the bed. "Not on the bed, on the floor." She got on the floor. "Not that bit of floor; I want you over there." She moved with a "yes ma'am".

I stood over her and looked down. She was grinning like a fool. "Stop that!" I commanded, and she stifled her smile unconvincingly.

I squatted over her face. I could feel her gentle breath on my snatch. I lowered myself closer and felt the tip of her tongue straining out of her mouth, trying to reach me. I pulled away before she made contact, then teased her again. Nicky sighed with exasperation and I sunk to my knees and landed on her. She got a big face full of my fat wet pussy – ha fucking ha.

She ate me out like a pro as I rode her face. I rubbed myself all over her nose and mouth; she had her tongue right up in my snatch, and her lips and teeth ate and sucked at me.

I shut out the reality of the scene, the fact that I was glad she couldn't see my arms windmilling as I tried to keep my balance. Instead I imagined myself as the hottest, bitchiest witch in the whole history of fuckdom. In my head I was the most capable and experienced top. I could do up a woman in full body bondage with the merest flick of a wrist; I could twirl whips and floggers around my head like a majorette; I could play the most devious and saucy headgames on my bottoms.

I am ashamed to say that it is these delusions of grandeur which made me come as I thrust against Nicky's face. The final piece of mental cinema which tipped me over the edge was the thought of some delicate beauty showing me her arse, pulling down her pants and trusting me enough to beat the shit out of her – in a safe, sane and consensual way, of course.

That was as far as my fantasy had gone, but Nicky was still raring to go. I didn't know what to do to stay in control of the scene, especially since I was still spaced out from my own recent little cunt-sized earthquake. I had to maintain my Mistress Ramona decorum, but I needed some time to decide what next to do.

I told my charge to "Lie still and shut up," whilst I went to the kitchen to find some props.

"Yes ma'am."

I hoped that she could not hear me ransacking the cupboards; it wasn't a dignified sound. I pulled the place apart trying to find something I could use and ended up with some clothesline.

I used the clothesline to tie Nicky up to my bed. I didn't do it very well. It took me an excruciating fumbling age to get the knots secure enough to hold her, nothing like a bondage fantasy at all. She lay there passive but, thankfully, did some mock struggling now and again in order to encourage me. I was hoping that the line would hold her spreadeagled. But my bed wasn't big enough for her tall frame, so her limbs hung over the edge awkwardly.

Holding the wall for support as I wobbled along the bed, I stood over her again and pressed the sole of my boot to her mouth.

"Kiss my boots."

Silence.

"I said, kiss my boots."

Nicky looked embarrassed and muttered, "No, ma'am."

"Kiss them!"

"No."

Her defiance confused me and I dropped the Mistress Ramona act. "Go on," I pleaded, "just kiss them, you don't have to use your tongue."

"No." Her voice was firm and adamant.

I knew I wasn't going to win so I backed down, humiliated.

I needed to control her before she gave me any more lip. It was exciting having to think so quickly, in such a charged atmosphere.

I soon found what I was looking for as I poked around under the pile of her clothes and grubby undies that Nicky kept by the side of my bed. I wondered if she hoped I was going to wash and iron that lot for her like a little wifey.

Nicky's dick was still sticky from its last outing. I took my time washing it and digging out a condom; Nicky would just have to wait for me.

I held up her harness and wrinkled my brow. Nicky was a lot smaller than me and I didn't know if I would be able to squeeze into that thing. Again I was glad she couldn't see me as I pulled and heaved at the straps, trying to make them stretch an inch further the better to accommodate me. I was worried that I was never going to get it on, but soon there I was looking at myself for the first time as a dyke with a dick.

The angle of my hard-on looked all weird; it was too horizontal; it just stuck out like a branch on a tree; it was nothing like a real cock. I started fretting about how I was going to get it into Nicky without looking like a freak, or how I would know that she had it in her. I wondered what it would be like to fuck her with this thing – good probably, but weird too.

I tried not to worry about it, the idea that I was getting perform-
ance anxiety over a fake penis seemed too stupid to humour. Instead
I focused on how the thing felt. I liked how the harness held me in se-
curely, and later when I took it off I liked seeing all the little buckle
marks left on my skin like some kind of proof that I had really fucked
her.

"What took you so long?" whined Nicky as I re-entered the room.

"Aw, shut up, you ungrateful cow."

"Me want fuck!" she cried.

I stood over her face and slapped her cheek with the side of the
dick. "You're going to get a fuck," I sneered.

She was lying there with her legs wide open to me, the unmistak-
able darkness and redness between her legs as available as I wanted her
to be.

I could see she wasn't wet enough so I blobbed a gloopy handful
of lube on the dick and smeared the rest around her cunt hole.

My mind was still buzzing on angle, entry points and various random mathematical equations. I knelt between her legs and held the
end of the dick up to her hole.

"You've made your Mistress very angry," I declared coolly, "and
now I'm going to fuck some manners into you."

Below me, Nicky's cunt looked as flushed and ready as her face.
Her legs strained as though she was trying to rise up from the bed,
hips first, and I realised she was making herself open for me. I teased
her until I could no longer maintain my balance in the peculiar
crouching position I was holding over her, so I just stuck it in.

Whatever it is that's inside you, and no matter how many times
you fuck or are fucked, that first poke is always the best. Nicky
thought so anyway, because she just about threw herself on the dick
and started to hump it.

I held back a little, partly to tease her and partly so that I could see
the cock sliding in and out, appearing then disappearing into her
body like the ultimate porn shot. This cheap rubber schlong made me

feel unexpectedly intimate with Nicky; I couldn't help but wonder what it would be like to have my own real cock inside her, the warmth and wetness of her cunt all around me, making me come, creating the fantasy that we could orgasm together.

I lay down on top of her and thrusted and pumped for all I was worth. It was exhausting, though I liked grinding myself into her, feeling the pressure of the dick's base against my own cunt. I fell out a couple of times; I found myself fucking thin air and jabbing some unidentified piece of Nicky's body. She went, "Ow! Ramona!" and I eased it back in again sheepishly.

The fucking made me ache, I was unused to moving in this way, so I pushed my thumb against Nicky's clit as I fucked her and got her off as soon as I could. I pulled out, her eyes were staring and vacant, so I must have done okay. Actually, I liked having a dick; it was a pleasure I could really get used to.

The harness was easier to yank off than it had been to get on, and soon it was back on the pile of clothes by the bed.

Nicky was coming back to earth, but I hadn't finished yet; I really wanted to push her to her limit, and she clearly wanted that too.

I spanked her legs and arse a little and gradually built it up until I was slapping her with considerable ferocity. My hands made a satisfying sound and tingled pleasantly. Nicky's skin grew hot and red, and marks started to appear down her thighs.

Nicky cleared her throat and asked, "Ma'am, will you hit me harder, please?"

"I beg your pardon?" I thundered.

"Something harder please, ma'am?" she squeaked.

I felt like a pantomime dame hamming it up as I stomped off in a mock rage over someone daring to defy my authority. It was fun. Soon I returned to the scene with one of Nicky's heavy leather belts flexing in my hands.

"You want hard? Try this for hard." I slapped her arse with all my strength. I repeated the gesture four more times, shouting, "Count along with me... one... two... three," before I noticed that Nicky could not speak. I thought she was acting up, so I hit her some more. The edge of the belt sliced her skin. The leather wrapped around her side and left stinging marks.

It was only when Nicky started crying that I realised that I had fucked up. In a panic, I dropped the belt and tried to undo the knots that attached her to the bed. She was heaving big disturbing sobs. I had to chop the line off with a vegetable knife in the end, my hands shaking and panicking. She recovered, thank fuck, but I couldn't apologise enough.

Later that evening, as we were getting ready to go out, Nicky turned to me and broke the silence with, "You know this afternoon?"

I cringed. "Yes, what about it?"

"This is hard for me to say," she continued.

I was expecting to get what I deserved for being so incompetent. "Go on," I encouraged her magnanimously.

"It was fantastic," she replied like an overly enthusiastic puppy, "really horny." She hugged me and kissed my ear, "When can we do it again?"

If I had been a cartoon at that point there would have been a giant exclamation mark drawn above my head. As it was, I just looked at Nicky and thought, "Who the fuck is this woman?"

Our outing was a special deal for me; it was the first time that Nicky had introduced me to her friends. I didn't even know that she had any friends because she seemed to spend every spare hour round at my place. Anyway, I was quite excited at the idea of hanging out with a group of real live lesbians.

"Oh, I can't wait for you to meet Terry. She's so funny; you'll love her," bounced Nicky as we drove up Wardour Street for the fifth time trying to find a parking space.

"Who else is going to be there?"

"She might still be seeing Kat, I think she's an artist or something, very good-looking girl anyway. Kat's friend Sam is coming too; she's just got a job at a production company; she's very hot."

Our way to the Nås Bar took us by the gates of Hell.

The club's psychotic bouncer whistled at me as I walked passed. "Hi Ramona," he breezed, "I haven't seen you for ages – what's up?"

What could I do? I smiled at him blankly and kept walking. It was strange feeling my two worlds meeting, the old and the new. I couldn't handle it tonight.

Nicky stared at me, "Do you know that man?"

I tried to look innocent, "Me? Naah."

Nås Bar has long since changed hands and gone out of business, but in those days it was pretty hip in a gay-boy, media-whore type way. All the money honeys went there. It had had a great write up for its – frankly bizarre – Scandinavian-Cajun fusion menu in the usual London rags, and the décor was the right kind of cutting edge for a season or two.

Nicky managed to get us through the door without us having to wait in the queue that wormed down the road. She shouted at me over her shoulder, "I love it here; it's like my local."

Jackie – the woman who inadvertently introduced me to Girlina's – she was there too with her friends. She ignored me, I knew she would, I didn't even bother to wave or nod in her direction.

We squeezed through the crowded room to a booth at the back of the room where Terry, Kat and Sam were sitting around a table littered with wallets, mobiles, torn Silk Cut packets and empty cocktail glasses. All were smoking furiously.

"Nicky!" Terry climbed over the table and ran to her friend. The others followed. There was a big show of hugging and kissing, picking each other up and squealing – "You look gorgeous!" "Give us a snog!" "Where have you been?" – all rolled into one. Nicky was jumping up and down, obviously loving the attention. I stood aside to give them space and knocked over a drink between a couple behind me. They glared.

A special place was cleared for Nicky. There wasn't enough room for me in the booth so I went and found a chair. Everyone was deep in conversation when I got back and sat at the end.

Kat, tall and thin, with a severely fashionable haircut, made everybody fall on the floor with in-joke catchphrases she'd picked up. Whenever there was a lull in the chat she'd throw one over in a faux northern accent and they'd all be off again, some trying to copy her but none really succeeding.

Terry shushed everybody to be quiet whilst she shared her exciting news: she namedropped about how she sat in the same chair as some ultra-Z-list celebrity, and about how she might be getting her own column in some poncy new queer rag. Her pals were impressed.

The attention turned to me. Sam asked Nicky, "Is this her?"

I said "Hi," and tried to look friendly.

"What do you do?" said Sam.

I answered: "I am proud to say that I have a long and unblemished record as an unemployed person."

Sam replied: "Oh, I'm sorry to hear that; I hope you find a job soon."

Terry interrupted: "They're looking for someone to work in the mailroom at my office, maybe you could go for that? I could put in a good word for you."

I smiled. "That's kind, but I'm not looking for a job."

The information did not compute; there was a major malfunction as the table went silent. Nicky fiddled with a cigarette; I could tell that I had embarrassed her.

"Oh, okay," replied Sam.

Kat pulled a comedy face and everyone collapsed with laughter.

Terry pulled Nicky over and whispered something; they both looked at me and giggled.

Sam looked over to them, said, "What? What?" and Terry passed it on to her too.

"Jesus fuck," I muttered, smiling politely. Fade to black.

A few days later, after I had recovered my composure, I told Suzanne about my exciting night out at the Nås Bar.

"They sound hideous," she said.

"But they're her best friends, I've got to be nice to them."

"Why?"

I ignored that question and continued, "I haven't told you the worst bit."

"What's that?"

"As we were leaving, Nicky invited them over to 'our place'."

"What do you mean 'our place'? You haven't got an 'our place', it's 'your place'."

"I know, there's more. She fucking said 'the wife's a great cook'."

Suzanne and I screamed. I tried to kill it with a laugh, but Suz was still screaming.

"That's not funny," she said, "where did she get that from? Have you been feeding her up?"

"I made her scrambled eggs on toast last Sunday."

"And now she thinks you're a great cook."

"Correction lady," I interjected, "now she thinks I'm her fucking wife."

"Oh fuck, you've got to leave her," said Suzanne.

"Oh fuck," I echoed.

The best thing about being unemployed is being able to sleep whenever you want. Take an afternoon nap if you like; you won't get a chance to have another one until you win the lottery or become a pensioner. Get up at midday and eat your leisurely breakfast whilst the rest of London's population is sweating at their desks. At its best, unemployment offers halcyon days spent however the fuck you like, your rent's paid and you can live for the moment.

There are lots of worst things about being unemployed, though, and always being poor is the least of them. Signing-on day always brings mixed feelings with it – you can relax because you know St Giro's Day isn't far off, but you also have to face the gatekeepers whose job it is to prevent you from claiming your rightful state cash. Sometimes it's possible to get in to the Jobcentre, sign and run out without any problems. This day was not that day.

Before he would let me sign, the bloodless Jobcentre guy motioned me over to a cubicle.

I knew most of the right answers to his questions. He asked: "Are you actively looking for work?"

"Yes," I lied innocently.

"What kind of work will you do?"

Before I could say "I don't know," he interrupted: "I'll put admin and secretarial." He continued, "Do you have proof that you're looking for work?"

"Yes, but I haven't brought it with me."

"How long have you been a jobseeker?"

The trick question. In truth it was years, but I couldn't say that without getting into trouble, so I answered vaguely, "I'm not sure, it's been a while."

The guy pushed up the sleeves on his nasty suit. "Let's get down to business," he said in creepy management speak. "I think you deserve a bit of help. I'm going to sign you up for a place on one of our Jobquest™ courses. They're very good; you'll get lots of good help and advice there that will be useful for getting back to work."

I was horrified. This was my worst nightmare.

The man continued: "You'll be developing interview skills with lots of role-playing exercises, you'll get help in writing your CV, there'll be a team-building component and a good proportion of the day will be spent doing supervised jobchasing."

"No thanks."

"I don't think you understand," he fought for my gaze, "your benefit will be affected if you do not attend; you don't want to lose out on that, do you?"

"No."

"The course starts at 9.00am on Wednesday."

By 9.20am on Wednesday I knew that I had to kill everyone in the room, paying particular attention to Pat, the slimy facilitator, and by 10.00am I wanted to kill myself before any more of my precious life slipped away in this dump.

I doodled with my biro, changing the wording on my Jobquest™ handouts to read Jobshame, Jobdodge and Jobshit.

Supervised Jobchase was planned for after the lunch break, during which we were not allowed to leave the building in case we didn't return.

Pat looked at me kindly and read out my name badge. "Ramona," he said, "have you used a computer before?"

Mistaking the way I bristled at his overfamiliarity for shyness, he went on gently, "It's not difficult. In fact, it's a bit like a typewriter. Would you like to come and learn how to jobchase with a computer?"

Like I had any choice.

"We've got all afternoon and the rest of the week, so it doesn't matter if you're a slow typist; you might even improve your keyboard skills." He chuckled.

East London, where I live, has a high population of unemployed people. Lord knows why, but my area has been picked as some kind of a base for a programme of social experimentation, and lot of money has been made available for work creation schemes. During my unemployment career, the local Jobcentre metamorphosed from a glorified shed to a specially built state-of-the-art office block. Staff woolly jumpers were replaced with ill-fitting businesswear, nametags and quota systems. Task forces were recruited and money was found for their generous expense accounts. Unusually, some of that money found its way to Jobquest™, which meant that within a week the faceless organisers had been able to replace the room full of high-end computers that some bad kids had stolen with an identical set. Luckily for me, they had not yet installed any sex-site blocking software.

Why am I telling you this? Whilst Pat was giving his "Introduction to Online Jobchasing" talk, telling everyone about the exciting world of mouses and clicking and websites and jobquesting, I had positioned myself at a terminal at the back of the room.

Pat wrote INTERNET in block capitals and JOB on his flipchart in different colour marker pens. "Have you used the Internet before?" he asked without waiting for an answer, "it's a wonderful place to jobchase."

Meanwhile, I was roaming around some of the less wholesome areas of the web, doing a different kind of chasing.

It took a while to find someone.

<You are in WetLesbianPussy. Monkey521 has a message for you>
Monkey521: ASL?
>20, f, london
Monkey521: pic?
>No. sorry

Monkey521: Too bad

<Monkey521 has left the room>

I tried again, with a bit of genderfuck thrown in.

<You are in Butch_Heaven. lavndrjan has a message for you>

lavndrjan: Age sex location?

>25, m, london, u?

lavndrjan: get lost you prick, it's women only in here

>Oh, sorry I am a woman. Still wanna play?

Lavndrjan: fuck off loser

Then, bingo.

<You are in Dyke_Fuck. Btch_qn has a message for you>

Btch_qn: asl?

>24, f, london

Btch_qn: pic?

>No, u?

Btch_qn: 28, f, wisconsin. Do you wanna cybr?

>Ok

Btch_qn: Just ok?

>Yeah, I wanna cyber

Btch_qn: What are you wearing?

> What do you want me to be wearing?

Btch_qn: I imagine you'd look good in some lingerie, something lacy.

> Well, it's funny you should say that because I'm sitting here in my bra and panties. My bra is very tight, it pushes up my lovely big soft tits, and my panties are tiny, you can almost see everything. I'm wearing stockings and suspenders that are tied with soft black ribbons.

Btch_qn: Are you wearing heels too?

> Yes, my heels are very high and mean. They hurt my feet but I don't care because they look so hot. Do you like high heels?

Btch_qn: Yes, I do.

> What would you like me to do to you in my heels?

Btch_qn: I'd like you to just let me touch them.

> I'm standing here in front of you, just get down on your knees and you can touch them. What do they feel like?

Btch_qn: They're hard and shiny, you have beautiful ankles, may I kiss them?

> Yes, you may. Do I taste good?

Btch_qn: You taste delicious.

> Do you want me to tease you with my heels?

Btch_qn: Yes, I am opening my legs for you.

> Your cunt looks very wet to me, have I done that to you?

Btch_qn: Yes, you have. I am wet and ready for you.

> I'm holding my six inch heel against your cunt.

Btch_qn: I'm rubbing myself up against it. I'm pushing my clit against the black leather.

> You look very sexy. I'm sliding my heel inside you now.

Btch_qn: oh god, that feels so good. It's long and sharp. I'm afraid that you might tear me but I want it anyway.

> Don't worry, I'll be gentle with you.

Btch_qn: I'm fucking your shoe.

> I'm letting you. I'm moving it gently. I'm watching the heel slip inside you. I'm standing over you and I have the other heel in your mouth.

Btch_qn: I'm sucking it gratefully, even though the position isn't physically possible.

> It's a fantasy Btch_qn, I can do what I like! I'm taking my heel out of you and now I'm kneeling between your legs.

Btch_qn: I want you inside me now.

> I'm fucking you with my hand.

Btch_qn: I'm kissing your heavenly face.

> No kissing, too intimate.

Btch_qn: Oops, sorry.

> That's ok. I'm sliding my hand inside you, I have my whole fist in your cunt. It's big and wet for me, it feels unbelievably good.

Btch_qn: I'm riding your hand, I want you to push it into me more.

> I'm fucking you fast, my hand is like a fist punching you.

Btch_qn: I'm loving it. I'm holding my legs open for you so that you can fuck me harder and deeper.

> I've got my mouth on your clit. It's very big and hard, it feels like a cock.

Btch_qn: Suck it.

> I'm sucking it hard, I'm running my tongue around it. It tastes good, you dirty girl.

Btch_qn: Lick it hard and make me cum.

> I'm licking you so fucking hard, and loving the taste of your hot cunt in my mouth as I fuck you with all my strength.

Btch_qn: Oh god, that's good. But now I've switched positions and I'm fucking you.

> Naughty naughty.

Btch_qn: I'm pulling your lace panties aside, I'm opening your cunt wide with my fingers and sticking my tongue deep inside you.

> Yes, do it more.

Btch_qn: I'm stretching you open, I'm eating you out.

> That hurts but I love it, don't stop.

Btch_qn: You're so big and wet and ready for more.

> Yes.

Btch_qn: I'm putting my big toe inside you.

> Your what?

Btch_qn: My big toe, now I have the rest of my toes in your big wet cunt and I'm wriggling them about.

> Ow, it feels too big, it's too tight!

Btch_qn: I don't care, I'm pushing the whole of my foot up there now.

> I'm grinding on it, it feels enormous, it feels amazing.

Btch_qn: I'm easing it in and out gently.

> I like that. I want to come, can I come?

Btch_qn: I wanna cum too.

> Oh god, don't keep me waiting.

Btch_qn: You look so fucking sexy. I'm cumming now. Ohhhh yesssss.

> Uh uh uh uh. I'm coming. Oh god, I'm going to come again.

Btch_qn: Do it, I'm watching you.

> Aaaah, yesss, shit, yes.

Btch_qn: You sexy fucker.

> And you!

Btch_qn: So, can I see you again some time?

>Maybe, do you come here often? Oh, shit, hang on a second, I've got to go.

<ramona has left the room>

Btch_qn: wait… I haven't finished.

Pat was standing behind me; he had been there for a while. I smiled at him sheepishly.

"I think you'd better leave," he said.

It had been only been a month since I first heard Nicky fucking in the bogs and she had more or less moved in with me. She had her own place, to which I had never been invited, but instead chose to spend her time at my pokey dump. I can't say that I was happy about the way this had turned out. I was frisky as fuck and already I felt tied down, afraid that I was about to become Suzanne. There was so little going on with Nicky. As a fantasy she was fabulous, but in real life? No. Sex, hair, rings, leathers, and car were all she meant to me. Her friends were universally awful; it was a trial going to see them; I didn't want them to be a regular part of my life, and I questioned her own attitude towards them – she didn't even seem to like them that much. I was creeped out by Nicky a lot of the time – her desperation appalled me, but I admitted it to no one. At first this was because the sex made up for a lot of things, but it wasn't long until that began to unravel as well.

Some nights I felt as though we were a sitcom couple, sitting up in bed chastely, drinking cocoa. Okay, so I'm exaggerating, but it wasn't far off the truth.

Nicky would climb on top of me and kiss me hard. I liked feeling her body pinning me down, the fact that I could support her weight made me feel strong, but vulnerable too, and it would make me wet. She'd put her hand down and slide two fingers into my cunt. I would look at the ceiling, try and get turned on, attempt to go blank, just let my imaginary flickerbook of sex images play in my head. Nicky would fuck me fast, sometimes slow, sometimes a random mixture that was always predictable. It was nice, I won't deny it, but it wasn't what I

77

needed to get me to the money shot. Getting fucked like this was like not being able to stretch enough, like being cramped in a box, or not being able to breathe deeply when you need to catch your breath. It felt as though I was constantly trying to reach something slightly out of my range. Sometimes I faked it to get her off me a bit faster. She never said anything, I still wonder if she knew.

Then Nicky would roll over. I'd slap her a bit and tell her what a big, strong, gorgeous and sexy gay man she was. She loved that, she told me that it felt really naughty to her. I didn't think it was that perverse. Anyway, it would get her going enough to flip over on to all fours, point her dirty wet snatch at my face and allow me to sink my fist right inside her. She liked me to fist her for ages; I grew quite a bicep during the time that we were together and sometimes I'd swap hands because I was afraid of becoming like one of those weird-looking crabs that scuttle about with one enormous overdeveloped claw and one tiny weakling.

As Nicky was coming back down to earth, twitching and shivering under the covers, I'd nip out of bed to get the kettle on.

The more bored I became, the more in love with me Nicky seemed. She was full of shit, but I didn't want to hurt her. Even though it was boring, the sex was still sex, I was still fucking a woman, something that I'd always wanted. Nicky meant well. I went along with her more than I should have. I needed her money. I knew the end was coming.

It came on one stifling afternoon. I had been to the Jobcentre to plead for some more cash.

I stepped through the front door in a murderous mood. I ate a couple of paracetomol to calm my thunderous headache, then I went to lie down to wait for the pain to go away.

In my peripheral vision I saw something new hanging above me, something that hadn't been there before. It looked sinister.

"What the fuck?" I leapt up. In my dopeyness I thought there was a giant spider sitting above me in its web. My heart was beating wildly.

I took some deep breaths to calm down and refocused on the Native American dream-catcher that was hanging there.

"Nicky," I said simply.

I sat with that dream-catcher in my lap until long evening shadows appeared and Nicky returned and stuck her head round the door with an ironic "Hi honey, I'm home!"

I was deadpan. "What is this?"

"It's a Native American dream-catcher," she replied perkily.

"What's it doing here?"

"I put it up; everyone has one; it's a dyke thing. I thought you'd like it."

"You didn't ask me."

"I didn't think I had to."

"Well you did, this is my place."

"I thought it was our home."

I could feel myself looping out. "Are you insane?" My voice rose. "I hardly know you! Don't make out to me that you've always been into Native American culture because I bet you don't have a fucking clue. And when was the last time you had any fucking dreams to catch anyway? You're always out like a light and snoring your head off." It was time to say it: "I want you gone. I've had enough."

Nicky put her arms around me, pinning my own hands to my sides and immobilising me with her hug.

She said, "Don't be like this; this is nothing; it's just a lovers' tiff; let's be friends again."

Her little talk was making me more angry – I thought I felt tiny blood vessels exploding in my eyes.

Nicky whispered conspiratorially, "You look so sexy when you're angry."

The rage that had built up inside finally exploded.

"You stupid pathetic fuck!" I was screaming. My face was turning purple; I must have looked like one of the World's Strongest Men that you see on television at Christmas, all gurning chops and popping veins.

I struggled free from her and walked away sharply. Then I spun around, charged at her legs and bowled her over. She hit her head on something, I heard the hollow knock, but she laughed it off.

I was so angry, I was on the verge of a nosebleed. Like the donkey in that 70s cartoon who turns into a tornado when his tail is pulled, all my remaining powers of self-restraint flew out of the window. "I live alone!" I shouted in her face.

I was a berserker on a battlefield. I stomped the dream-catcher into the floor, then stamped on the pieces some more. "This is my place," I hissed, "stay away from me."

"Oh my god," Nicky was suddenly sober, "you're not playing, are you?"

"Get out now," I said, calmly.

"Jesus, you're a mess." Her words meant nothing to me.

"Go."

She went, shouting "Fuck you!" back at me in a pathetic high voice. Later that afternoon I gave my landlord a blowjob and within two days the locks had been changed.

I went and got very drunk.

I got hit on by a man drinking next to me. He said: "Can I buy you another one? Maybe a lemonade?"

"As long as it's got gin in it, I don't care," I answered.

He had a handsome young face, delicate features, pretty eyes. I couldn't work out how old he was, sometimes he looked prepubescent, other times in his early thirties. There were just the two of us leaning against the deserted bar. I had already left a neat pile of puke outside which had sobered me up enough to want to drink some more.

"You look like someone just broke your heart," he said gently.

I snapped back, "Who the fuck are you, mother hen?"

"You're funny."

"Thank you."

"You're a good-looking woman too."

"Are you on the make?"

"Maybe."

"You like rebounds, do you?"

He smiled. "You should sober up a bit."

"Why?"

"Because."

I hate it when people say that. "Because what?"

"Because I'd like you to be at least semi-conscious when I fuck you."

The hairs on my neck stood up in alarm. The idea of someone else wanting me was very alluring, not to mention another pair of broad shoulders to hold on to as they bore down on me. This guy was good – after all, I reasoned, I could do with a break from women; Nicky had been enough to put me off pussy for a good long time.

There was something I had to say. "I don't mean to be rude, but there's something I don't understand about you."

"What's that?"

"I don't know."

"It is because I look a bit like a girl?"

"Er, yeah, maybe," I faltered.

"There's a good reason for that."

"What's that then?"

"I used to be a girl."

Oh. "Ah." Silence, then: "I'll shut up, I'm being a twat."

"Thank you."

"That's okay."

There was a moment of emptiness between us.

"You still want to fuck me?" I had to ask.

"Yeah," he said shyly.

"Good."

More silence. We sipped our drinks.

"How do you want to fuck me?" I was pushing it.

"Come here," he motioned, "I don't want everybody to hear this."

"Why is that? Is this a line you're going to spin me?"

"Maybe." He thought again. "No, it isn't actually."

I smiled indulgently.

He said beneath his breath: "I want to make you laugh because you've got a sexy mouth. I want to fill you with penny sweets and eat them from your cunt whilst you wriggle and giggle, then I want to see you grinding and moaning and performing for me. If you'll let me, I want to whip the bullshit out of you and leave my mark on your skin. I want to get right inside you, under your nails, I want to be closer than close."

I winked at him clumsily, slurring, "I don't care if it is all a line, I still like the sound of you," as I slipped off the chair and on to the floor.

Alex took me home with him.

I was fucked; it was all I could do to lie on the floor of his flat to stop the room spinning around me.

"Are you going to stay there all night?" he asked.

"Mmpph," I mumbled in reply. This would have translated as: "I really like you, I want to fuck you but I'm trashed right now, can we save it until the morning?"

He must have understood because he made a bed around me of cushions and blankets. He even left a bowl and some water nearby for my inevitable hangover.

I was instantly asleep. I dreamed that I was swimming. In my dream, I could breathe underneath the deep clear water. There was a shadowy thing circling below me, intangible, it was stalking me. The thing followed my moves as I swam this way, then that, supple like a seal, turning in on myself, stretching out, perpetually moving like a shark or a gymnast's ribbon. I called its bluff by making myself still. Everything was static, then the shadow shot up between my legs like a rocket and there was nothing I could do to stop it.

I was suddenly awake; it was suddenly morning. I opened one eye and surveyed the scene. Some funny-looking guy was staring right back at me. Immediately I closed my eye again.

Alex asked: "Are you asleep?"

"Yeah," I said, trying to sound nonchalant.

"Can I put my hands on you?" he asked.

"Yeah."

"Can I put my lips on you?"

"Yeah," I peeped.

"Can I fuck you?"

"Yeah."

"Is 'yeah' all you're going to say?"

"Yeah."

"Yeah," he echoed with a rich warm voice.

I kept quiet and still, as though I was sleeping.

He pulled the covers off me, but I didn't feel cold. I was naked. My legs were spread.

He was concentrating hard on me, watching my cunt intently for clues. He was very sexy, his beautiful round muscled Action Man shoulders had tattoos of bluebirds and flowers spilling over them. His mastectomy scars were faded, like shiny silver ropes across his chest. He had a slight beer belly that was covered with soft hair, and the bum-fluff on his face tickled me as he kissed my thigh.

I could feel my stink filling the room, stale booze reeking from my pores, my armpits smelling rotten. I was ashamed, but too far gone to stop and wash.

I felt so calm, like the way that people say they feel when they think their death is inevitable. Alex was off in a world of his own, opening me up and easing himself into my cunt.

"You're so tight and fresh," he mumbled to himself. He was already up to his knuckles. He was twisting and turning his hand, trying to find a bit of space in my cunt that would give and allow him to inch in a little bit further.

Alex was fisting me.

I didn't think I could take any more. He got some lube and poured a measure of it down the channel made by his curled up palm. He was wearing a latex glove; it made him feel extra-slippery.

I still felt as though I was dreaming. I was excited, but the emotion was removed as though I was being hypnotised. Although I had been in her many times, Nicky had never managed to fist me; she complained that my snatch was too small and I had believed her.

But now Alex's knuckles were forced up against the mouth of my cunt. It was intense. I know this is what people say when they are fisted, but it's true. It was as though I was nothing but a hole. My legs were open as far as they would go. Electricity ran through my central nervous system, making me at once rigid and relaxed. I truly felt made of muscles and blood.

Alex's whole fist squeezed into me. My cunt dilated at the right point; he slid it in and immediately there was the relief that I had let him past the most difficult part, mixed with anxiety that he would tear up my insides with his hand. If felt as though I was at breaking point. He opened his hand slightly and I thought I was going to tear, like a mouth splitting and dislocating around something clearly too big for it.

"Beautiful," he said as I tried to arrange myself around his omnipresent fist.

He began to pull it out and push it in; it was like moving slowly through treacle. I wasn't much help, grinding against his hand and feeling my clit, now hard and ready. I brushed my fingers gently across my pussy lips, as though the soft tickle would cancel out the hardness within.

I reached down further and felt Alex's wrist and hand disappearing inside my hole. The muscles in his forearm tightened and contracted. He was getting deeper, pushing inside against my cervix. I was widening and stretching to give him more room, I don't know how I did it, it just happened. He was so deep, I was frightened that he would fuck me up for good.

"Hold it still," I gasped.

He did.

"Hold it, hold it!" I was panicking.

"I'm holding it. Don't clam up; just ride along; I won't hurt you."

Alex shook his fist inside me, small vibrations at first, then stronger. He was shaking my cunt, then he was shaking me as though I was a glove puppet.

I needed to piss and shit. My body was going into shock and I needed to dump all the extra internal crap to cope with the fist rearranging my insides. I was losing my grip, I felt wild, like I was flying somewhere. The throbbing fist was overwhelming; Alex bent down and licked at my clit and I was gone. He didn't give up then, but rubbed around my clit with his thumb and I came again, flailing and groaning.

Alex whispered: "Do it to yourself, I want you to come one last time." So I put my fingers either side of my clit and worked that thing. I was exhausted; my cunt hurt; it was painful getting off, but so fucking good. I shook my head with each spasm, sweat flying off my hair, using all of my strength to squeeze one last fucking shot of pleasure out of myself.

"Oh fuck," I felt something wet spraying out of me. I must have pissed on him. "Oh fuck, I'm sorry." I shat Alex's fist out through my cunt as though I was giving birth to a baby. The wet patch on the bed horrified me.

Alex looked pleased with himself. "That's not piss," he laughed, "you've just shot your load!"

He was turned on.

"What do you want?"

"Just hold me," he said, placing himself in my shivering arms.

Alex put his hands down his pants and worked away at himself, pulling and teasing at his cock whilst I licked and sucked his neck.

"Will you come for me, baby?" I had my hands on the buckles that held the rubber cock in place against his hormone-enlarged clit. I wanted to fuck his girl-hole, he looked so good, but I didn't know if it was off-limits and I didn't want to spoil the moment.

"Yeah," he said with his eyes tight, concentrating hard, neck stretched away, "I'm going to come; I'm going to do it now."

Alex's breathing was shallow and he shook and came, his head resting back on my shoulder, body all tense, my arms holding him tight across his chest.

We shared a bath and went to a café for some breakfast.

"What's your name?" he asked.

I laughed. "It's Ramona."

"Can I see you again?"

"No."

"Why not – didn't you like it?" He looked worried.

"Don't be a fuck, it was amazing." I straightened with him: "I've got a bit of sightseeing to do before I become someone's dingleberry, that's all."

"Well, that's fine with me, just drop by my way now and again, okay?"

"Okay."

Thanks to Alex, my cunt was raw and painful as I lowered myself slowly on to the hard seat at the computer. Most of the other library users were checking out cookery books and taking care of their email. Not me, I had booked a full hour for something dirty. My dad used to tell me sometimes that I had a bit of the devil in me, and I think he was right.

I clicked to enter the room and a box popped up. I shifted to get comfortable, hunkered down behind the computer cubicle partitions and flexed my typing fingers in anticipation. I called myself Ixnay. Yeah, I know it's weird but I liked the sound of it; just don't ask why.

There was only one name sitting in Girlfuck. I clicked on it.

> A,S,L?

Molex: Same as you, alpha male, anywhere you want me to be. And you?

> 30s, girl, London.

Molex: A local lady.

> What do you like, Molex?

Molex: A woman with a lot of imagination.

> Have you got time? Do you wanna play with me?

Molex: Mmmmmaybe. Depends what you want to do.

> I could look pretty for you.

Molex: Pretty-schmitty. What-ever.

> I could tease you a little. Or a lot.

Molex: Go on then sweetheart.

> I'm looking you in the eye and licking my lips.

Molex: I need more than that.

> I'm mouthing "I'm gunna fuck you." I've got every syllable covered.

Molex: Gimme some context.

> Oh shit, I nearly forgot – safeword?

Molex: I prefer not to.

> You're hardcore.

Molex: Some say that, yes.

> I'm not. My safeword is Custard.

Molex: That'll do for me too.

> Where were we?

Molex: Context.

> I'm wearing lipstick, on the bottom of the tube it says its name – Slutty Red. My lips look wet.

Molex: More.

> I'm winking at you, hooking my finger at you giving you the come-on.

Molex: I'm interested.

> I'm pulling up my dress to show you my cunt. I'm naked underneath. My skirts are large and voluminous, they rustle in my hands.

Molex: I can see that you're wet for me, you've got pussy juice smeared down your thighs.

> I want you to fuck me so much.

Molex: I'm going to stride over.

> Yes.

Molex: I'm going to run my hands over your soft thighs.

> Yes.

Molex: I'm going to smear open your pussy lips with my thumbs.

> Yes.

Molex: I'm going to get a good look, I'm going to smell you and I'm going to lick you.

> Yes

Molex: Then I'm going to stick my cock inside you.

> I want that cock fucking me.

Molex: I'm pulling at myself already. I'm hard.

> There's one small problem.

Molex: ?

> I'm not alone now.

Molex: That's not a problem.

> It is. Molex, my father has just arrived.

Molex: You like incest scenes?!

> No, you arse!

Molex: So what's going on?

> Well, to tell you that I'd need to explain a slightly bigger problem.

Molex: Just tell me and then we can fuck.

> I'm with my dad because it's the most special day of my life.

Molex: I don't understand you.

> Dad's holding my arm and telling me how beautiful I look in this dress.

Molex: Stop this, I want to fuck.

> He's lifting my veil and giving me one final peck on the cheek before I become Mrs Ixnay.

Molex: What's going on?

> As I'm walking down the aisle I turn and look at you. I bare my teeth and smile at you.

Molex: I can smell your cunt, I want it badly. I want to fuck you. I'm salivating like a dog.

> Better watch it, I might slip out of your reach.

Molex: Bitch.

> I'm halfway down the aisle. My future husband looks nerdish and nervous at the altar. I turn to look at you and I say, "Chase me and you can have me."

Molex: I'm running already, I don't need any excuse. I leave a ghostly skin of myself that hangs in the air behind me momentarily. I'm going to get you.

> I extricate myself from my father's arm, hoist up my dress and start running. There's shock on the faces of all the wedding guests as I run and run and run.

Molex: I'm gaining on you already. I'm going to pin you down and fuck you in front of everybody.

> I kick off my shoes and run past my fiancé, past the holy guys, I'm heading for a door at the back of the church.

Molex: My cock feels bigger than ever. I've got you in my sights. I will have you.

> Out the door there's a field of poppies and I'm charging through it in the sun, my clothes melt away, my feet scramble on stones underneath.

Molex: I'm ten feet behind you, catching up. The sun's in my eyes. I've never felt stronger or more virile as I close in on you.

> I can feel your breath on my neck. I imagine your mouth between my legs, your hands down there, making me ready for you.

Molex: I can see the dampness oozing down your thighs. I'm grabbing at you.

> I'm out of reach.

Molex: I can feel the fine threads of your hair sweeping out behind you.

> I hold out my arms and they turn into wings that lift me off the ground.

Molex: I have wings now too.

> Flap flap mister. My ankles are fusing together and I've got two jet engines in my heels, I'm a stealth bomber, I'm breaking the sound barrier.

Molex: I'm right behind you.

> I'm thundering over hills, hugging the land.

Molex: I'm aiming myself at a mountain and then pulling up at the last minute.

> I'm flying over the sea.

Molex: Down below us our reflections are fucking hard and

relentlessly, your legs over my shoulders, my cock stuck right in, the expression on your face as tight as your cunt.

> Not so fast big boy.

Molex: The world has become tiny down there because we're moving faster than anything.

> I'm still ahead of you, you can't catch me.

Molex: I'm splitting into a hundred molten clones of myself, separating and regrouping like mercury pushed through a sieve.

> You're surrounding me and you're moving in.

Molex: I'm going to have you.

> I'm throbbing with pleasure, suspended high in the stratosphere, caught in a circle of you, trapped in a dead end. It's a stalemate.

Molex: I'm going to close in on you until you can't move and then I'm going to open your legs.

> Not yet you're not. I'm growing, like a giant, like the attack of the fifty-foot woman, and I'm going to chase you away.

Molex: I can make myself bigger too.

> That's cheating. You'd better run because I'm going to get you now.

Molex: I'm running faster than I've ever run before.

> Your lungs are pumping.

Molex: I feel like a machine, all strong and relentless.

> You look so alive.

Molex: Every vein, every cell is pumping with lust.

> I'm watching you run as fast as you can and it's making me laugh because I catch up with you easily in one giant stride.

Molex: And so here you are, right in front of me, and now I've been caught.

> I'm picking you up by the scruff of your neck and dangling your little body in front of me.

Molex: My cock is still hard. I want to climb inside you, big girl!

> I'm licking the end of your tiny cock with the tip of my massive tongue.

Molex: It's making you shrink back down to regular size!

> You can't wait to get your sweaty hands on me.

Molex: So let me, stop running.

> I've stopped. We're here together now, kind of glowing, floating in outer space. It's beautiful.

Molex: I'm on your clit, on your breasts, in your mind, up your arse, covering your skin, in your mouth, inside you all at once.

> I'm scratching your back, you're making me moan. You smell of sweat. You feel rough.

Molex: You feel pure. Like milk.

> I want you like a man, on the marital bed, making a baby with me, doing it straight, under the covers, lights off, no noise.

Molex: Fuck, and I thought I was perverse.

> I'm lying back on the bed, you can just about make me out in the darkness.

Molex: I'm slipping it in.

> It makes me start. I had no idea it would feel like this.

Molex: My body is closing in on you, you're pinned underneath me, you couldn't move even if you wanted to.

> I don't want to move, I want to feel your weight on top of me.

Molex: I'm thrusting and fucking you. I'm holding your body in my arms, pulling you on to my cock.

> I'm raising my hips to meet you, trying to suck your cock into me more deeply.

Molex: I'm hunched over you. I have one hand on your breast, I'm squeezing it whilst I fuck you.

> I've got my eyes shut tight. I can feel your body grinding against my clit and it makes me want to come.

Molex: You're big and wet and open. I'm going to come.

> You're fucking me as fast as you can, and you're holding your breath, the better to concentrate on your orgasm.

Molex: I'm coming. My body is tight, and then it's slack.

> I can feel your sperm inside me. I've got to jerk off, I can't let this go to waste.

Molex: Come on honey, do it for me.

> It's out of reach, it's out of reach – uh – and now it's done, and I'm there feeling like someone's jabbed me with a dose of bliss.

> Shit.

> Shit.

> Fuck.

> Wow, that was hot.

> Did you like it?

> Molex, are you there?

Molex: Yeah I'm here.

> Why the sudden silence?

Molex: I'm smoking my proverbial post-coital cigarette.

> You're funny.

> I have to ask you something.

Molex: What?

> Be honest with me.

Molex: What?

> Are you a woman?

> Are you?

> Molex, are you there?

Molex: I'm an alpha male.

> In real life, I'm talking real life now.

Molex: What do you think?

> I think yes.

Molex: Think that then.

> I'd like to meet you if you're really in London.

Molex: molex@Girlfuck.com

<Molex has left the room>

Molex told me that she was freaked out, and that no one had ever read her before. Molex's real name is Bonnie; she's American. She doesn't live so far away from me; the internet is weird like that, being both global and local. Bonnie is a poet – in fact, she's just had her first novel published. It's a beautiful tale of women in love.

So I went to a reading and saw her. I knew she was popular with the ladies, judging by the number of dykey-looking fans she had in the audience. She was older than I imagined; her face looked as though it had lived some wild times. She had gapped teeth and grey hair. She was very beautiful. She looked like an orator when she read, or a rock star. Her writing was so moving, she talked about peace, and freedom, and goodness. I felt choked. I saw her afterwards and she asked me to stay with her, so I did.

Sometimes it is easier to talk to strangers than those who know and love you. I told Bonnie about myself, about how I'd always wanted to be with a woman, about Nicky. I told her that I felt lonely, that I didn't know how I was going to continue. I don't know how she could have known this; the coincidence makes me freak, but she said, "Keep going, just keep putting yourself out there." It was like she had reached into my head and pulled out my most private thoughts. I felt full of hope as we walked together.

I would never have known that it was so easy to sleep with women.

Lying naked in her bed, Bonnie was lean and hard compared to me and my softness. "Come closer, Ramona," she said, shifting so that I was wrapped in her arms and she in mine. She kissed me lovingly, licking my lips and using her tongue gently. She spoke softly, "You taste like a wide open sky." Her eyelashes tickled, like moth wings on my cheek. She ran her hands across my head, down my neck and around my breasts. Her movements were fluid, like a dancer. Bonnie held my nipples between her fingers, she squeezed and pulled at them and made goose-pimples appear. I stroked her incredible skin and felt great handfuls of her arse. We both moved our hands between each other's legs. I used the side of my hand as an edge for her to grind against. She cupped the whole of my cunt in hers and let me rub up on the heel of her palm. It felt slow and dreamy. Juice oozed its way out of her, it made the friction smooth and loose. I scratched her back absent-mindedly, feeling slack and light. We held on to each other, talking quietly as we – what, fucked? Was this fucking? Bonnie put pressure on my clit with her middle and forefingers held together like Scout's Honour. I copied her. I clung to her like a baby chimp on its mother.

I came, feeling like something was melting and sparking inside my body. Bonnie's head was back and she laughed as she came too, rocking on my hand, making slight jerks.

"Just call me vanilla girl," she smiled ruefully.

"Yeah, right," I snorted back. "You're nasty."

"No," she corrected, "I just like nasty dyke sex."

We must have been a pretty sight as we dozed together under the covers, Bonnie's cats purring at our feet.

I couldn't say the same for Suzanne, who was definitely not a pretty sight when I saw her next.

"Ramona, where have you been? I've missed you."

"I've been busy getting fucked and making some new friends." I grinned. "Nicky's gone, I bet you're pleased."

She ignored me, angry. "Does your new life include me?"

"Yes, of course it does – it always has and always will."

"When can I meet them?" she pouted.

I tried to placate her. "They're not really the kind of friends you bring home."

"They're not the kind of friends you think would want to meet me, you mean. You're ashamed of me, aren't you?"

"No, you're my best friend." I didn't sound convincing.

Suzanne pointed at me. "You're keeping secrets from me and I don't like it." Jesus, she looked like she was crying.

I went over to hug her, but pulled back. There were wet patches on her top.

"Oh fuck!" she said, "it squirts out when I get upset," she pummelled at her breasts, making more milk come, "fuck this shit, fuck it!"

"Let's calm down, I have to go out now, but I'll talk to you later." I kissed her on the forehead and went round to see Alex.

Alex was watching a nature programme on the TV at the end of his bed. Two lions were fucking lazily. The female had dull disinterested eyes whilst the male pumped at her. He was holding her still, biting her neck to keep her passive. I felt myself go wet thinking about the animal cock sliding in and out of the cunt mechanically and instinctively. The lioness turned round, roared and swatted the lion as he pulled out.

Alex's lips were full and red as he stared at the screen. He was sitting on the bed playing with a small tin of sharp things including scalpel blades of various shapes and sizes, slender needles and pins. He placed them in some unknown order, rearranging his stuff then moving it back into its original configuration. We sat and chain-smoked. In the hot night the blue smoke hung in drifts over the television screen. He reached under the bed to find more stuff with which to play and I looked at his arse hanging there in mid air. Alex had stopped being a person; he was just this big arse in front of me. I could see his clit and pussy folds under his droopy pants. There was a small drop of moisture soaking through, and three small pimples on his arse cheeks that maybe he didn't even know about. I thought about reaching out to touch him as he leant over; I wondered what would happen if I just ran a gentle finger along the line of his cunt.

"Wanna play?" he interrupted my daydream, sitting up again.

"Yeah, sure!"

"I like needles, do you?"

A fear shot through me. "I've never used them."

"Would you like to try?"

I hesitated, then heard some corny echoey internal voice saying "Put yourself out there," so I went "Yeah, okay."

Alex's needles were wrapped in two layers of packaging. They looked benign and safe in their plastic. They were coded according to gauge in primary colours, like toys or sweets. With latex-covered fingers, he popped a hypodermic out of its sheath. It looked extremely sharp in the blue light of the television and I felt irrationally afraid that it might accidentally fly up at me and embed itself in my eye, or that I might easily swallow it in a freak accident.

I was entering that strange spaced-out feeling you get when you are afraid. I remembered getting jabs at school and the fear that took over when you reached the head of the queue and were called in to take your turn.

"It's easy," said Alex, "I'll go first and you can copy, unless you want me to do you?"

"No, I want to do it to myself first."

He swabbed a patch of his skin with rubbing alcohol, then he pinched some loose flesh on his neck. Like a careful student in a sewing class he pushed the needle through. It was smooth, like a hot knife through butter.

The needle sat there, raising the skin it had displaced, reddened at entry and exit points. It looked tender, though not painful. It was gruesome and compelling. Alex got another needle and laid it under his skin about an inch from the first one. He did another one after that. There was no blood; I was mesmerised; I didn't understand how it could appeal to me so much.

"Do you want to do it?" He looked at me.

I put on some latex gloves and closed my eyes briefly to centre myself, not that I believe in that hippy shit, but I needed something to hold on to to get me past my fear. Needles that looked so elegant in Alex's fingers became clumsy in mine. I cleaned a patch of skin with the swab; the smell made me think of the last time I saw my mother in hospital. My insides twisted; the adrenaline was starting to flow.

I pinched the skin on the top of my breast and held the needle perpendicular to it. The end of the hypo was so sharp that I didn't notice it breaking the surface.

"Just push," encouraged Alex, watching me closely.

I pushed. The needle slid into the fold. It felt like nothing but stung slightly as it exited the other side.

I was looking down at a needle in my skin. I knew it was there, I could feel it hard in my flesh. It was such a tiny thing but I was starting to feel high, like my body was reacting to an accident that had not happened.

I looked up to Alex and laughed nervously.

"You know," I remarked, "I've always been so scared of injections and needles."

"Everyone is," he replied, "that's why it's fun to play with them – it's nice to be a little bit afraid of yourself."

"Can I do some more?" I was emboldened, but didn't know if he wanted to share more of his precious surgical steel.

"Sure."

There was a mood of quiet concentration in the room, of a student learning from a teacher. Alex led and I followed, loving his approval.

Soon there were two short flat parallel rows of needles down my breasts. I ran my finger over the ridges of skin raised by the piercings. Some needles slipped out a little and I pushed them back in, feeling them pull underneath.

Alex had made himself a necklace. He held his head high so that the hypo tips would not tangle and embed themselves in him. He was so pretty.

"You look like Jesus." I smiled.

He kissed me; it was like being underwater; I felt high.

Alex took out some thin elastic cords from his play box. He wound a length of it around the exposed heads and tips of my needles, in and out, he wove a dainty pattern.

"I'm going to pull now," he said.

"No, don't." I was scared he might tear me. "Let go, okay?" He looked momentarily disappointed and in a beat I'd changed my mind. "Oh, go on, then."

I relaxed as he pulled the cords slowly and firmly up, then down, then outwards. My skin raised up, like fins, like sharp fingers below the surface trying to break through and escape. It hurt, but I let him continue, amazed that my body could reveal such secrets. It felt as though Alex was giving me a peek through a window to other possibilities. Holding the cord was like holding my hand, like we were there together. I was not afraid any more.

He slackened and let go. My needles were throbbing.

I said "I'd like to take them out now" but felt a return to the panic. How would I do that? He showed me, gripping the base and pulling one out as smoothly as it had gone in. I felt loss, absence as the needle left me.

Alex dropped the hypo in a sharps bin, adding, "You can do the rest yourself."

Someone looking into that room would have seen me with my chin on my chest, looking down, breathing like a kid concentrating on a colouring book as I removed the needles one by one. Three of them left me with tiny droplets of blood, which I let grow and fall, leaving small rivers down my front, like red teardrops. There was some slight bruising, and I felt proud of that.

We sat and smoked a fat spliff.

"That was full-on," I said.

Alex replied, "Yeah, needles are lovely, but cutting's my real thing."

"Cutting?"

"I like to mark skin." He pulled down a large wooden box from a shelf. "Let me show you something."

Inside the box was stuffed with layers of white tissue paper. Gossamer-thin, flimsy and frail, it was like looking into a collection of pieces of sky. Alex pulled out a layer of paper that formed an envelope about the size of a paperback. He placed it on his lap and unfolded the leaves. There was a fine piece of tissue inside with what looked like writing on it, stiff letters like runes. I made out the words blotted in red-brown ink: "I love my Daddy."

"Fuck!" I yelled.

"Don't worry," Alex reassured me, "I'm not a paedo. This was done for Mikey – he's an old geezer who likes to do Daddy scenes; he knew I'm into cutting, so we got it together. I just like to take a souvenir when I slice someone. Sometimes they let me and sometimes they don't."

"So these are all blots of cuts you've made?"

"Yes."

"Can I see more?"

"Yes, but be gentle with them, they're extremely fragile."

I unfolded more tissue envelopes on the bed. It was like looking at somebody's weird photograph album.

There were lots of stars and hearts, a bluebird of happiness, a couple said "property of:". One said "Fuck bitch"; another read "Molex Forever".

"Aah," I said, "I see you've met the charming Molex, too."

"She's a babe," blushed Alex, "that's all I'm saying."

A big one that stretched across a large sheet of tissue said MOTHERFUCKER in capitals.

Another equally large one read PLEEZ KILL ME.

"You know this stuff is illegal," said Alex.

"Is that part of the appeal, bad boy?"

"Yes, I suppose it is."

This next bit is like a scene in a book, but it really happened. At this stage, and after only a couple of months, my life was becoming more like a lurid novel every day. Things were turning upside down, a life that I thought would be so difficult to achieve was dropping into my lap. I was having the adventures I'd always wanted to live, and some I couldn't have guessed at.

I was up on the platform waiting for a train home and it was late. There was a woman standing maybe about twenty feet away from me. She was by herself – the first thing I noticed was that she had long hair, the second was that she was small. How old? I've no idea. I can't remember what she was wearing, something fashionable no doubt, maybe some kind of a skirt, a jacket; I don't remember. The overall impression I got was that she was tiny and neat.

She winked at me. I looked away automatically, a reflex for when something doesn't make sense. I looked back and she licked her lips. She nodded and I knew it was me at whom she was directing these things. She mouthed something, I'm terrible at lipreading, but it looked like she was saying "Mu-cha-cha," whatever that means. She hooked her finger and called me over. I looked away again.

When I looked back, she was there right next to me; it made me jump.

"What's your name, sugar?" she asked.

I looked away.

She grabbed my face and held it to hers, saying, "I asked you a question – what's your name?"

"Let me go," I answered through gritted teeth.

She released me, laughing. She said, "I'm just playing. I know what your name is – it's Ramona."

"Who are you?"

"A friend of Molex. I heard that you met her." She smirked. "Small world." She shrugged.

I tried to reassess this woman. I looked at her properly for the first time and said, "Why are you being so obnoxious?"

"It's just my way," she smiled, "I'm sorry." She changed the subject, brightening up, "Do you want to come and see something special?"

"Are you drunk?"

"Me? No, I never drink."

"Why should I come with you?"

"Why not?" she replied coquettishly.

"You're a loon."

"Yes, so? There are worse things to be. I'm not a murderer or a rapist."

"Where is this special something?"

"Down here, quick."

She jumped down on to the tracks and looked around edgily.

"What are you doing?" I was shocked, "I'm not going down there."

"Quick!" she hissed, "or they'll see us."

"Oh fuck!" I shimmied down inelegantly, twisting my ankle on the shingle. She grabbed me so that I fell sideways into a small cubbyhole down by the track.

"This is it? Your secret den?" I was incredulous.

"Wait, you have to wait," she said, her bright eyes glowing in the darkness.

I waited.

We were crammed up together; my knees were bent the wrong way; it was uncomfortable.

"Lean right back, Ramona – press yourself into the wall, tuck your legs and feet right in or you might lose them."

A rat ran across the track outside.

The metal made strange electrical sounds, like a hollow knock. I could see the tracks vibrating and rumbling.

"I'm Iris, by the way,' said Iris. "It's not my real name," she babbled, "when I was younger I wanted to be like Jodie Foster in *Taxi Driver*. I've seen that film so many times. Most people want to be Travis Bickle," I nodded, "but I wanted to be Jodie, or Iris, so that's my name now."

We shook hands stiffly. "Pleased to meet you."

The thunderous sound was increasing.

"It's the express train," Iris said flatly.

"This is the special thing?"

"You'll see."

The noise was loud now, like a jumbo jet taking off. I could feel the rumble all the way through me, my fillings were dancing in my teeth.

The train flew by in a hurricane of wheels, sparks and dust. The air smelled of oil and grime, but the noise, that noise was the thing, I'll never forget it. It was like crashing a plane, like sticking your head in a speaker on full blast, like a dragster burning nitro, so big, like ground zero, like shutting your eyes against a nuclear bomb and still being able to see the bones in your hand X-rayed in front of you, like being exploded. I expected to be vapourised. It was so loud that I couldn't hear myself screaming.

The train was gone as fast as it came.

"Wow, thanks Iris – that was fucking ace!" I sounded like a geek.

"Want to stay for another? There's one due in two minutes."

We stayed and Iris kissed me hard as the 00.09 sped past, making her hair twirl and fly round my head.

Of course I went home with her.

Iris lived alone in a series of once-grand rooms above a derelict Victorian pub far out to the east of the city.

We started out sipping tea and exchanging niceties.

"What do you do?" I asked politely.

"A bit of this and that," she replied distractedly.

"How long have you lived here?"

"Quite a while."

"How do you know Molex?"

"Ah, La Bonita and I go back together a long way."

We sat in silence for some moments. Iris broke it, saying, "Do you want to have sex with me?'

"Yes."

She put down her cup and took mine from me. "You're dirty," she said, "let me wash you." Iris took my hand and led me to the bathroom. It reminded me of an old Turkish bath with white and green tiles, rusty pipework, a wooden bench and a big enamelled tub.

Iris pointed at my feet. "Strip for me."

Whilst I was taking off my clothes, she prepared a bowl of warm soapy water. I sat on the edge of the bench cringing at myself. I seemed puny compared to her, even though I was much bigger.

Iris stripped to her waist. The neatness I had noticed about her earlier on the train platform extended to her naked body, her small tits and the muscles just visible under her skin. She had the outline of a pair of wings tattooed on her back. She was beautiful and I felt shy looking at her, like I wasn't pretty enough to deserve such eye candy.

She leaned over the bowl and dipped her hair into it, soaping it up into a lather. She then held it like a ponytail in her hand and used the ends to wash my face. It was a maternal gesture, like when a mother spits on a hankie to mop clean her child's jammy chops. It was a peaceful moment; I felt moved and almost tearful whilst Iris hummed quietly to herself. She washed my back and my breasts in this fashion, stopping to rinse me then re-soap her hair. She washed my belly, my cunt, legs and finally my feet. I was so passive watching her working. Suds disappeared down the drain in the middle of the floor. Flies buzzed round the light-bulb. She finished, looked up and smiled, then handed me a towel and helped me dry myself.

"Come on, come through," she said, taking me to her crumbling bedroom. Piles of debris sat in the fireplace; a vase of lilies decorated the mantelpiece. The light was dim, the outside world was shut out by heavy ripped velvet curtains. There were books everywhere and a telly in the corner of the room that was plugged into an overloaded socket. I spied large hooks screwed into the wall.

Iris held my hands and asked, "Can I beat you?"

I would have done anything for this woman at this point. "Sure."

She laughed a little and said, "I mean, can I really beat you?"

"Yeah," I said. How bad could it be? Iris was a lot smaller than me, I was sure I could take whatever she dished out.

"If you say stop," she said, "I'll stop."

I thought she was being overly formal. "Okay," I said, as though I was doing her a favour.

"Can I tie you up?"

"Yeah."

"Will you put on these cuffs? I hope they're not too tight for you."

They fitted just fine. Iris had to stand on a chair to attach the cuffs to the hooks. When she was finished I stood like a capital letter Y up against the mouldering wall.

I couldn't see what she was doing, but I could hear it. Iris was rummaging in a box of implements. I heard her pick out something, maybe a rod of some kind, judging by the scrape it made. I heard a swish, like the air was being cut, then a thwack as she brought down a blow on her bed. She was testing a whip. She was still humming. I heard her throw it aside; it clattered on the floor.

There followed more rattling of various instruments, then a soft "Ah," and some rustling. There was silence then a heavy thud on the bed.

"Here we go," said Iris, "are you ready?"

"Yes."

She came up close behind me and tickled my skin with the soft suede tails of the flogger.

"It's made of baby deer skin," she said, adding, "well, maybe the skins of several baby deer."

"Like Bambi?" I offered naively.

"Yes, just like Bambi."

"So are you Thumper?" It came out before I could stop it.

"Yes sweetheart, I'll be Thumper tonight."

Iris spun the ends round in her hand, making quick little soft splats against my back. It was warm and nice, like lying in the sun. After a couple of minutes she put her hand on my skin. "You're warming up," she said.

The length of time between swing and splat increased, and the blows felt heavier. She was further away from me now, getting more of a swing going. The flogger fell on my arse and backs of my thighs. It felt good, like a strange kind of massage. I was quiet, zoning out into my own world, when – Bang! – the flogger came down heavily on my shoulders, making me jump and start.

Iris laughed. "Wake up, Ramona! I thought you were leaving me! You're not allowed to go off yet."

"Jesus fuck," I muttered.

Bam, another blow came down, then bam-bam-bam, three in a row. They were heavy and smacked hard on my back; the thuds winded me a little. I straightened up to recompose myself whilst Iris alternated sides, hitting me this way and that, getting the flick right for maximum impact. Occasionally she would flog one side more, it would get too much to bear, and I would wriggle away to avoid it, but she'd spot what I was doing and hit me there again.

"Are you ready for some more?" She counted: "One, two, three," then Bam! – down it came. Again she counted, "One, two, three," and the leather smacked hard. A third time she counted, "One, two, three," and there was no blow; she laughed as I braced myself for it then hit me – Bam! – as soon as she saw me relax.

Tired of games, she built up a steady rhythm of whipping me, and I responded by reaching up to meet the flogger as it impacted on my skin, the surface of which was feeling hot. I was giddy with pleasure, not faint, just high. Our two breaths were the loudest sound in the room, save for the swishing of the whip through the air and its hard thud on me. I was drifting off, daydreaming out to sea then swooping up into the sky. It never occurred to me to say stop. Should I say stop now? I asked myself, have I had enough? I promised myself that I'd take one more and then I'd stop, or maybe one more after that.

Iris was panting as she brought Bambi down on me with all her strength.

"I..." she said – Bam! – "Want..." – Bam! – "Your..." – Bam! – "Soul!" My legs were buckling under me; I was dribbling and giggling like a loon. Behind me, out of sight, Iris was twirling and dancing around the room, high as a kite herself, turning like dervish.

"Oooh, that's good," I laughed, oblivious.

Crack. There was lightning, but no storm. I was puzzled before I realised that the lightning was not outside; it was on me. The white heat of pain seared through my arse. Crack, again.

"I'm caning you," said Iris. "Ask me to do it again."

The pain was total, the burn and then the throb afterwards; it was an awesome feeling, so big and so beyond any pain that I'd felt before. Nothing could hurt as much as this; I thought I would be immortal if I lived through more of it.

"Ask me," repeated Iris.

"Please beat me more," I whimpered, "please." Whack-smack-crack! Each strike was like electric shock therapy; my tongue lolled in my mouth and involuntary tears rolled down my face. The pain was sublime and so fierce I thought it would make me hallucinate. It gave me visions, a smooth black stone, a dark valley, the sense of falling. I pulled out and thought about asking her to stop, but I didn't want to give her the pleasure of seeing where my limits ended.

Iris ran the cane across my lips. She stood behind me, up close, and rubbed her tits against my sore back. Her eyes were bright and shining.

She undid me and I slid to the floor with my head back, gasping for air. Iris stood over me and sat her snatch in my open mouth, like she was sitting on my face. I ate her, she was wet and hot and she held my head up against the wall with her hips.

Iris pissed in my mouth; it was hot and salty and overflowed my mouth, running down my front, between my breasts. I swallowed as much as I could without drowning in it. I was digging at myself with my hands, jerking off fast; it didn't take long. I still had my mouth on Iris, her fingers were working her clit and she too came fast and hard, shaking her hair behind her.

She staggered over to the bed and collapsed. The room was dead.

"You should inspect yourself," Iris called over, 'it's quite impressive."

I stood up on the bench to get a better look at myself in the broken mirror over the bathroom sink. I was confused at first because what I saw and what I felt did not tally. I was not feeling pain, just relaxed and worn out, a little achey like I'd run a couple of miles.

There were small flecks of bruising up over my shoulders, like hundreds of tiny lovebites. Further down, I saw stripes and welts on my arse. I stood and looked at it for a long time; it felt wonderful and right.

Rain was pouring down outside, washing away the filth on the streets. Iris opened the curtain a fraction and we sat together watching a lightning storm brew and break over the docks. I couldn't explain it but I felt as though some deep and important schism had happened in me. I felt like I had survived something big, that I had let myself explore another dangerous thing and I was proud of myself, but aware that others might not recognise my bravery.

Iris played a scratchy old record on her fucked-up turntable, some gospel thing that went: "Take me down to the river, down down to the river, down down to the river to pray. Lord please take my soul, please take my soul, please take my soul today." She took my head and tipped me back on the bed, like a Southern preacher baptising a sinner in a muddy creek.

It was around now that I felt as though I had truly crossed over – like Alice through the looking glass, I had become part of an alternative world that had its own strange codes, rituals and beliefs that made perfect sense to those involved, but which bewildered real life people, you know, normal people.

No one looking at me thought I was straight any more. The streets suddenly seemed to be teeming with dykes who would check me out as we passed silently. Men stopped treating me as potential girlfriend material. I could walk into a dyke bar and feel as though I belonged.

I felt sad to leave the old me behind, but excited by the new shinier version of myself. Old Ramona was a tired story, whereas the reinvented me offered exciting possibilities. I knew that losing my cherry meant burning a few bridges, and that was fine if it was what it took to get what I wanted.

I had learnt some tricks in the short time that I had been out on the prowl, I'd made some friends – if you could call them that – and found out a few things about myself. The biggest thing of all was that I had become increasingly confident in my ability to score some pussy, I didn't feel so chicken now.

My cherry had long gone, but it was not yet the end of my story, I had other ambitions now – like a freshly made vampire, I had poisoned blood in my veins and I was ready to rumble. Shall I talk proper? In short I was haunted by those dykes at Girlina's who had laughed at me; I wanted to get in there and sort them out.

I went out for a drink and saw Chrissie again. She was still a skank, greedily eyeing up the newborn trade.

"You ought to be buying me a drink," she said. "Aah," she patted me on the head, "little girl's all grown up now. I feel like a proud mother hen," she added sarcastically. Chrissie looked and acted nothing like a mother hen.

"You're just sorry you didn't get to me when I was fresh," I snorted back.

She gave a comedy "Hurrumph!" and said, "You weren't ginger enough for me."

Now it was my turn to tut.

"And you're not even that switched on," she teased.

"What makes you say that?"

"There's something really obvious that you haven't even noticed."

"Oh yeah?"

"Yeah, tough girl!" said Chrissie. "Shall I tell you what it is or do you want to blunder around like an arse all night?"

I was chastened; it was time to be humble in the face of such bulldagger wisdom. "Go on then,' I replied.

"She fancies you and she'll let you fuck her for nothing."

Chrissie nodded over to a woman who was standing about twenty feet away. The woman had good dyke hair, all greased up, messy and dyed an improbable colour. She wore specs and was smoking a roll-up. She looked in her mid-twenties, but she probably appeared younger than she was. She was not fat, not thin, my height. She was a pretty, standard-issue lesbian who looked a bit broken. She had pigeon toes and weak eyes – it was cute – and she was wearing the usual dyke uniform. She was standing with friends but staring over at me. She smiled and her eyes and mouth transformed into a series of good-looking horizontal planes.

I said to Chrissie, "Watch me now," as I walked away from the bar towards my next shag.

The woman looked happily surprised as I approached her, she hadn't bargained for my directness and was momentarily fazed by the loss of her expectations over how my seduction would play out. There wasn't going to be any extended flirting, no playing footsie under the table, no booze on which to blame the indiscretion.

I took her hand and led her away from her friends, who were indignant. It was not a proper grip; her fingers were only laced in mine. We headed towards the main door. She did not complain about my interruption, nor put up any resistance; she only tripped and skipped lightly behind me.

There was no talking once we were outside; we just kissed.

She had her arms around my neck, she was standing close, pressed up to me, and I could smell the tobacco on her hair. Her face was so soft. When we kissed, her cheeks were tight and hard and I knew she was smiling. She held my head as though it were a precious thing, and stroked my cheek with her little finger.

I ran my hands down her sides, from armpit to hip. She had a classic hourglass shape, which surprised me since I hadn't noticed it before. I rummaged under her clothing to get my hands on her skin; the dip of her waist was very lovely.

She held up her hand against me like a policeman halting traffic, but she wasn't interested in stopping. She didn't push me away; her hand was up like that so that she could feel my breast, full and heavy under my shirt.

There was too much light, too many pedestrians; it was too public for us outside the bar. She came away and led me through a gate round to the back of the building. There, it was quiet and private. I could hear the bar's punters on the other side of a high wall; they had no idea that we were there. The woman put her finger to her lips to indicate that it would remain so. Then she took off her glasses and tucked them away in her pocket. Her face was naked as she blinked in the dim light, unable to get a proper focus on her surroundings.

I pulled up her top and scooped her breasts out of her bra, she held them up for me so that I could get a face full, rubbing and licking and kissing.

I undid her fly and squeezed my hands down into her pants. Her skin was hot and clammy. She stood passively, so I yanked down her trousers and underwear; I wanted to see her body secrets revealed and I liked the way she looked with her clothing all fucked up and her tits and pussy hanging out, very available.

She braced her shoulders against the wall and stuck her hips out. She kept her knees bent so that she could get her legs open enough for me to do what I had to do. I put my fingers in her sulky mouth and enjoyed watching her suck on them saucily, like a blowjob on my hands. What a fucking dyke! She never took her eyes off me once, like she was daring me to go on.

She was wet and swollen; she'd got into that state so quickly. What a dirty girl, I thought, although my sentiment seems rather prim in retrospect. Her cunt goo was thick and rich; I'd say it was like honey if I was one of those womyn-loving-womyn, but I'm not, so I'll compare it to melting engine grease instead. It was musky and aromatic or stinking and foul, depending on your point of view.

I started working at her. Soon I was inside and fucking her up against the wall. I could feel the tension in her legs as I pressed against her, her hot breath on my neck, on my face, and in my mouth.

She came too soon. It was a real effort for her to stay quiet, she was banging her hips and making weird facial casts, like she was doing some silent war chant. She really shook her thing. She shook it too much. I wasn't convinced, no, I wasn't at all convinced that she had really come. It was too neat for one thing, too perfect. I never come from just fucking, I always need a little bit extra, so I decided that's what she would get too. I didn't stop to think about why she might have faked it; I couldn't spare her the brain time; I just did her again.

She tried to hop off me, like a woman dismounting a horse, but I stayed there with my fingers in her cunt. I eased my thumb up inside her tight arsehole and her expression of surprise told me that I may have been her first backdoor visitor. Well, I like to think that I was, anyway. I got down and knelt on her crumpled jeans, which were all tangled, and kept her rooted to the spot like leg irons. She squirmed when I kissed her inner thigh, which was soaking with juice, and she kind of opened up when I sniffed at her like a dirty dog.

I stuck out my tongue and teased her clit delicately. I gave her tiny licks that were barely there, then big long doggie laps. I fucked her whilst I did this, pleased with myself for being such an excellent and dextrous stud! She let me know that she liked it, wriggling and writhing whilst I gave it to her. It wasn't long until she stiffened, held her breath and then choked on the night air, and I knew I had the real thing from her.

I pulled out my hands and wiped them down her thighs. There was nowhere else for her to go, so she teetered momentarily and then slid down the wall until she was a little heap of rumpled clothes and flesh. I collapsed over her and fell to the dirty, gritty floor. She groped around briefly whilst I sat outside her field of vision and watched her regain her dignity with a warm wet stickiness between my legs.

This nameless woman who I had just fucked came crawling over to get me with her tits all loose underneath her and trailing leftover socks and loose sleeves. She moved like a panther and closed in on me like a heat-seeking missile. I was knocked sideways when she pounced on me, almost ripping off my clothes in a quick fierce struggle.

She had her index finger hooked against my clit and was playing with it, circling with slight strokes, then touching it lightly. She was very gentle, moving slowly and deliberately. There was no other contact from her, no kissing, nothing. It felt so clinical. My cunt was made of molten lava. I was burning up and I wanted her to do me, I needed to get off fast and I moved my hips to try and trick her fingers into entering me. She knew what I was wanted and had no intention of giving it away.

I lay on the ground awkwardly, but I didn't care about the discomfort, my mind was focussed on one thing only. I was amazed at how a simple motion could generate such a concentrated feeling. I was so close to orgasm, in some kind of purgatory, grinding for this weird pleasure that was almost more. In my mind I was teetering at the top of a cliff, I was right on the edge of a diving board, I was dancing on the end of a needle. All the bullshit inside was reduced to a thin line, white noise, body, blood, clit.

I could see her smiling at me in the dimness. She gave no warning as she stuck two fingers inside and I came right there; it was like being punched in the gut by a cloud of moths.

We slumped together out there for a while. The woman sat stroking my head whilst I nodded out, thinking of stars and planets.

Eventually we returned to that busy place the same way we had left it, like a video played backwards. I saw the woman out of the corner of my eye interrupt the huddle of her friends; I saw their disapproving looks, the way they straightened her clothes and patted down her hair, and I saw her smiling and glancing over at me foolishly.

Chrissie was still at bar in exactly the same position as I left her.

"What do you want, then?" I asked, slightly out of breath, my clothes askew and my fingers still smelling of cunt.

"Eh?"

"I owe you a drink," I explained, "remember?"

She laughed, "Fucking hell, you're fast," and shook her head. We sat and gassed like old geezers.

Chrissie pulled out something from her back pocket, "Someone gave me this," she said flattening out the card, "maybe you fancy it, I don't." She handed me the glossy over-designed flyer. It was an invitation for Inky's birthday party, whoever she might be, and the address was in east London.

"The kid's got money," sneered Chrissie.

"Innit!" I replied.

"They're trouble," she said, and that was more than enough of an incentive for me.

Adult party locations are rarely signalled by balloons around the front door, jelly and ice cream stains on the pavement, or the sound of "Happy Birthday" being sung in the front room, but I knew that the suburban terrace was where I was supposed to be because it was the only gentrified place on the street. Bland modern blinds hung in the windows, compared to the nylon nets and brushed velvet drapes of its neighbours. There were a couple of sporty cars and motorbikes parked outside. Behind the glass front door, I could see shapes of people moving about. I hoped that Inky herself did not answer when I rang the buzzer so that I could slip in unnoticed.

Some woman in an imported American T-shirt let me in and then walked away. I mooched into the kitchen, which was crowded with women smoking weed and drinking vodka and Diet Coke. Sad little bowls of curled-up crudités sat on the kitchen table and the big pan of rice and vegetables that somebody had so thoughtfully made had remained untouched save for three fag ends stubbed out in it.

I tried not to look too alone and so I smiled and nodded and chuckled along politely to the conversations being played out around me as though I were part of the gang too.

Everyone looked young. Everyone looked rich. Everyone was wearing expensive gayboy high fashion. Everyone was thin. Everyone had the right hair. Everyone knew each other. Everyone was the same. Everyone was an A-Dyke. I took it all in.

One woman was at the centre of things, talking shit. She had dyed black hair and a delicate pointy face. She talked so fast about nothing at all, laughing nervously at her own non-jokes, calling everyone "dar-lin'" and namedropping her scene-famous ex-shags. Her body lan-guage was edgy and busy, but it was just a pose, something to make her appear more interesting and dynamic. I thought she was a thick bitch. She sat and attacked some kids she saw at the club she runs in a fake comedy accent, and it could have been herself she was dissing if she'd had any self awareness. Funny footnote to this aside: a long time after I saw her at that party, someone told me that she'd gone to get her septum rebuilt.

Back in the present, I switched my attention to three women standing over by the window. I worked out that one, a tired dopey-looking butch, was being pursued by another and that the blossoming romance was being mediated through a third friend. The two would-be lovers refused to even look at each other but were wildly animated when they spoke to the friend who shuttled back and forth between them, sharing the knowledge. I was puzzled and didn't understand why they couldn't just talk to each other; why all those hangers-on had to be involved in the drama.

Jackie, that woman I met for coffee at the start of my lesbo career, she was there in the kitchen. She ignored me. As usual.

A fight was breaking out in another part of the house. A generic lesbian ran into the kitchen closely followed by waxy-faced old dyke. She was waving her fists and making a lot of noise. Space opened up behind them as crying lovers and members of the entourage tried to separate the two.

"What was that about?" I asked the woman next to me.

"She's on hormones; she's pretty volatile."

"Don't call him a she," spat one of the lovers at my neighbour and the trouble was over as fast as it had begun.

As the gap closed up again and guests began to mingle, some late arrivals took their seats around the kitchen table. I sucked in my breath – they were Nicky's friends, the same ones that had done such a good job of humiliating and ignoring me. I suddenly had to face the possibility that Nicky might be here too. Worse was the idea that she might make a display of proving how happily she had gotten on with her life whilst I played the pathetic wallflower.

Kat had the same terrible haircut as before, but it was now bleached blonde. She coughed up the same lame lines, snorted and gurned just as she had done when I last saw her. She had bloodshot eyes that rested on me for a moment and then looked away. She chattered about nothing.

I had spent more than four hours of my precious short life with Sam but when I said "Hi," she made out that she had never met me before and looked panicked.

"Is Nicky here?" I had to know.

"Who?"

"Nicky. Your friend, the one who introduced us."

Sam looked at me as though I was mad. She poked Terry, splurted "Nicky!" and they both held each other to steady themselves as they rocked with laughter.

Terry did remember me, kind of. She was "doing the career thing," she said, and had left her business cards lying around for people to take. She sat and chatted with me in a fake friendly way; she smiled and shook my hand firmly. She wanted to know who I was in case I was useful to her. I watched her eyes scanning the crowd behind me, and she moved on as soon as she found out I had nothing to offer.

Ain't sisterhood grand! I thought.

I remembered the books lining my walls at home, books stolen from libraries, rare books that were so needed by me and others who were equally isolated. It made me think of line illustrations of women cradling each other in their arms, and of personal truth-telling, speaking out, naming one's oppression, striving for a better world. In my imagination I could see disintegrating community newspapers with advertisements for menstrual sponges and women's dances long gone. There were accompanying photographs of broad-shouldered dykes who worked the land, wild hair, pot bellies, no one under 35. I thought about the utopian vision of sexuality that unfolded in my reading of such sexless material; about how lesbianism is an exclusive club, the most desirable way to be, indicative of a higher consciousness. I recalled a line in a song saying that lesbianism was so good because there was "no penis between us," that it was magical and pure, and I remembered that purity as an aspiration was never high on my personal agenda anyway.

Looking around at the women in the party, I felt as though I'd been sold a dud.

Terry, Sam, Kat, they weren't alone. I've since found that they did not represent every lesbian, but in honesty I didn't know anything then, I was still very new, like a baby, and I thought the two extremes of old and new were all there was. Although they were obnoxious, these women were the popular ones, the A-dykes. They were the stars of the show, sucking in attention like a black hole sucks in every last speck of living matter around it.

I couldn't understand why they were at the centre of the scene; why so many dykes seemed to look up to them.

At Hell, way back in my distant past, people could be scene royalty and still be arseholes, true, but they had to have something else too, be that a smart mouth, a good supply of sulphate, a band, a way with the ladies. These women, they were just arseholes.

An imaginary lightbulb pinged on above my head and I realised that these dykes were young, they had money, they looked glamorous. It dawned on me that these are the things that people value. Yes, even lesbians. This was the new order of things, completely unlike anything I'd read from my out-of-date private lesbian library.

At that party I realised that if I wanted to get anywhere, to have dykes fawning over me (which I did, more than anything), to be a popular and successful lesbian, I was going to have to make a decision. Should I run a mile from these bitches? Should I let myself be poisoned? Should I jump in and stop caring?

I needed time to think; I had to get out of that place.

As I dug out my coat and headed for the door, a nasty idea came to me and the party became still, like a painted backdrop.

"Fuck 'em," I said out loud, "Fuck 'em all."

I strode upstairs, across the landing and into one of the bedrooms. Scarves and girlish things hanging on the back of the door hung in the air a moment whilst I slammed it behind me. Apart from an over-full ashtray, the room was neat and clean. The double bed in the centre had a suede headboard and crisp sheets. There was a row of very new and expensive-looking trainers under a chest of drawers. Somebody had left a copy of a sportswear catalogue lying open. There were women singer-songwriter CDs by the stereo, the sleeves of which featured earnest-faced white women with guitars and ethnic outfits. Around the room were silver-framed photographs of friends and parents and pets.

Lying on the side were a pair of air tickets to Barcelona. They were useless to me but I stuffed them in my pocket all the same.

And so it began. I hunted through the bedside cabinet and found a curious selection of sticky dildos and cuffs. I found a secret stash of money, a couple of hundred quid, which went straight down my pants. I discovered an emergency bag of coke too, which got blown away from my palm in one big puff, like I was extinguishing birthday candles.

I heard someone outside on the landing and knew my fun had to stop, so I slipped out and turned off the light behind me.

I slipped up another flight of stairs to the attic room and there I saw two women. They were almost naked and were kneeling opposite each other on a bed, kissing and holding each other. I stood in the doorway and watched them. It was like peering through a transparent wall – they had no idea that I was there; they were off in a world of their own.

One woman leaned over the other. "Kiss me, Alba," she said in a flat, calm voice.

Alba replied, "Ask me nicely." Even though she spoke softly, her mouth was open and clear enough for me to lip-read.

"Kiss me," the woman repeated, without changing the tempo of her demand.

Alba smiled. "Ah Jane," she sighed, "I'm not going to do it until you ask me nicely." The words seemed rehearsed; it was as though they were playing a secret game with each other.

Alba and Jane looked like twins. Both were tall and very thin, the kind of women that hand-wringing politicians would denounce as encouraging girls to develop eating disorders or drug habits. I would gladly have stopped eating and jacked-up between my toes if I thought it would help me look as good as these two. Their tits were very small, like bumps on their chests, breasts that could barely fill a bra cup, real sexy starving-artist tits. They had their arms around each other, long limbs, skinny, the skin of which was criss-crossed with a thousand lacerations. Beginning at the shoulder and ending at the wrist were scars in every stage of healing, like sleeves made of spiderwebs.

Alba lay back on the bed and Jane pushed up her full skirt. Alba was wearing vintage panties, white, silky and full with Chinese rosebuds embroidered on them. I felt as though I was in a dream as I watched her open her legs. Jane reached into her back pocket and unfolded an old-fashioned cut-throat razor, the kind of thing you'd see in a Western, or in the hands of a murderous Victorian. She sliced off Alba's underwear, hacking through it with great concentration because the blade was blunt. Alba shifted and lifted her arse so that Jane could pull out the pants and toss them over to my side of the room, they landed at my feet. They must have known I was there. I picked up the knickers and held them like they were made of something magical.

Alba looked beautiful, passive, her thick pubic hair glossy in the light. I wondered how she would feel if I buried my face in her – like moss, or like the top of a warm dog's head?

Whilst Alba lay without expression, Jane pulled up a piece of leather that was dangling from her belt. It was a strop. She took the razor and flicked it first this way and then that over the strop's rough grain, pausing once in a while to hold the blade up to the light or test the edge with her thumb. It took several goes to get it as sharp as it needed to be.

Alba closed her eyes and Jane sat between her legs. She ran her fingers through the pussy hair and held up her hand to her nose before one last stroke. Jane pushed Alba's thighs open further so that I could see the tendons straining where they joined the rest of her body. She held the blade against Alba's cunt and told her not to move. Alba lay as still as a corpse.

Jane drew the blade across and, with a tearing sound, carved off a handful of hair. Within three more cuts she had removed the whole bush; all that was left was uneven stubble.

Jane sharpened the blade again then leaned in closer to Alba, steadying her arm. She scraped the razor across Alba's prominent pubic mound in small methodical movements, wiping the hair away on her jeans. She worked systematically, left to right, top to bottom. The room was still but for the gentle rasping of the dry blade on skin. She passed the razor over Alba's taut tendons to catch some stray hair. Alba held her breath, as did I, when Jane shaved the loop at the top of her vulva, and the hair along the outer folds of her cunt.

I stood on my toes to catch a glimpse over Jane's shoulder at Alba's shaved pussy, naked and gleaming. Her inner labia poked out, wet, pink and rude, and she had goose-pimples all over her legs.

Jane folded up the razor blade into its tortoiseshell case and crouched over Alba, her face close, just smelling. She must have smelled so good because soon Jane needed a taste to accompany it. Alba smiled down on her lover as she licked and gobbled at her snatch, undulating her hips, holding Jane's head with her thighs. She laughed and giggled when it tickled, and was serious when it did not.

I actually said "Oof!" like a cartoon character as someone shoved me aside in the doorway and thundered into the room.

"Who the fuck are you?" and "Get out!" merged into one big

scream from the mouth of a dyke fuming in front of me.

I was about to run from her as fast as I could, but then I noticed that she was not talking to me.

Jane looked up like a rabbit caught in headlights. "Are you Inky?"

Inky did not answer; she just pulled the women off the bed and started to bundle them past me, down the stairs and out of the door.

Alba tried to explain, "Molex said we could come; she said it would be fine."

"I invited her, not you, you little shits," raged Inky. "Now fucking go!" Whilst they were leaving, no one saw me slip back into the living room, away from my earlier crime scene. I knew Alba and Jane would get the blame, but it didn't matter.

Like a joke from a terrible sitcom, I backed into a woman who thought my clumsiness was a come-on.

"You're gorgeous," she said when I returned with a replacement drink, "have you been here long?"

"No, I just arrived," which was metaphorically if not literally true, given the still relatively recent loss of my muff-diving cherry.

"Come home with me," she lisped with sad puppy eyes. Her boozy breath stank.

"Hey Lisa, leave her alone." Someone held my hand and pulled me away; I felt like I was being rescued. I shrugged "sorry" at my admirer, as though I couldn't help but be whisked away, but inside I was glad.

"She's such a mess; she's always hitting on the new ones," laughed the owner of the voice of the person who had come to help me, but I barely noticed what she was saying.

It was the Player, the woman I had seen flirting at Girlina's all that time ago.

Wow! She was talking to me.

I kept cool and charmed her with a clever line, which made her laugh.

I checked to see if she was loaded, but she looked together; in fact, she looked good with her bleached hair, liquid eyes, and sharp clothes. She told me she was Louise and when I used her name it felt exhilarating, like she was letting me in.

She said she'd heard about me, about how I'd shagged Molex. Jesus, I thought, was that ever a career fuck.

"So you know her then?" I chatted.

"Me? No! We've played online a few times. She's a trip, but I've never met her." Louise continued, "I'd love to, though, she's hot. What's her real name? Juanita or something?"

"Bonnie," I corrected.

"Ah yes, that's right. And doesn't she do poetry or something weird?"

"Yeah. She's good."

Louise tried her hardest to make it sound like a casual enquiry but I knew that the answer to the next question was what she really wanted to know: "Are you close friends?"

Me being a dumb-arse, well, I completely misunderstood her. Did fucking someone mean that you knew them? Where I came from it didn't, but who knew what the etiquette was in this peculiar strata of society. I answered non-commitedly, "Yeah, kind of..." but of course Louise took this to mean that we were soul sisters or something equally lame.

She pulled at the neck of my T-shirt with her cold hands, like she was looking for something. I resisted and she yanked up my top whilst I fought with her to hoik it down again, I didn't want any of these skinny dykes tutting over my spare tyres.

"That tickles, stop it," I lied whilst wrestling with my clothes. I was afraid some of my swag from earlier would fall out and I'd be rumbled.

"Did she brand you?" said Louise.

"No, what are you taking about?"

"She didn't brand you?"

"No, we had a shag."

"I thought she branded everyone she fucked."

"You heard wrong. Maybe I should have suggested we do a little

Farmer Jack and his squealing little pigs scene if I'd wanted to get branded."

Louise looked puzzled for a moment then changed the subject.

"Do you want a line?"

"Yeah."

We found a quiet spot and my new pal chopped it out on a CD cover – 'Party Mix 300' or something duh-brained like that. The powder tingled in my nose and ran down the back of my throat like a sour poison river.

Louise held me as though she was making sure I wouldn't fly away and we snogged like two romantic leads in a schmaltzy Hollywood film. Twenty minutes later we were gnashing our teeth, dancing like crazed chickens, chewing the insides of our mouths, and talking six kinds of shit as the pharmaceuticals kicked in.

By the time we left that party to go off and fuck on drugs all night I saw myself as someone with a respectable history, someone good. I realised that I might be a player too, that these dykes might really want me. I felt as though anything could happen as long as I made the right choices, and I knew I would.

In my imaginary movie, I was having a grand adventure in the big city, swinging round lamp posts and doing natty dance moves with my brolly. And then the camera panned out, up and away and left me standing, a tiny speck on the big earth singing my heart out like Ethel Merman at the end of a big musical number.

I hung out with Louise a lot, both of us basking in the glow of each other's presumed fabulousness. I got to know some of her friends – more on them later – and I stepped up my shoplifting sprees so that I could be suitably attired when in their company.

Having learnt from my mistakes with Nicky, I was careful about inviting Louise over, but then there was little need to; she was clearly disinterested in finding out too much about me. She lived in her own super-snazz flat in Covent Garden and she liked having me as a house-guest, so there was no reason for me to worry.

We partied hearty, alright.

Here's how it went: We'd spend hours getting ready, calling each other up to talk about nothing, and making constantly changing arrangements for meeting up later on in the evenings. Louise would have already worked out, but I could never get into that scene much to her annoyance. The time we spent dressing and primping was laughable because the look we were all chasing so desperately was this kind of street industrial chic thing, very rough and ready, but that's the absurdity of fashion for you. Maybe earlier in the day we'd have gone to get our hair seen to because it was very important to have the right 'do, and we all went to the same place to get it seen to.

During the pre-evening hang-out, we'd eat pizza and smoke Marlboros, flashing our Buitts about, comparing them and generally showing off. I should explain that we were insanely susceptible to the most preposterous crazes; it used to be skateboards, and before that – thankfully before my time – it was bloody awful Celtic-inspired tattoos.

Louise bucked the trend, of course – she had a corporate logo inked discreetly on her side. I'm too embarrassed to say what it was; it makes me cringe even now, but everybody else thought it was the coolest thing.

Anyway, during my tenure as an A-Dyke the thing to have was a Buitt lighter. These mothers were not cheap, naturally, and they were imported from some place in Wisconsin, having been featured in a fashion campaign by some label or another which is the reason they were a famous brand, and the source of our desire for them. The gimmick was that they were all numbered, and they had a special gizmo inside them which meant that they would never run out. Someone made a record with a sample of the company's tag line "Do it with a Buitt" and we used to dance our arses off to it.

Hanging out was a daily occupation, nobody seemed to work, although everyone had plenty of money and all lived beyond their means. Just about all the group had parents who doted on them and who were only too happy to pay off their bills, the only means of maintaining a relationship with their bratty, ungrateful progeny. My new-found friends would disappear home to Surrey and Somerset every few weeks to load up with more handouts, lucky buggers.

Louise and her friends were like a herd. For a while I stopped using the first person pronoun and started using the "Royal We".

At some point in the evening the hanging out had to stop. Someone would give the signal and we'd all head out to Bar Barella or Girlina's with lots of mobile chatter and plans and arrangements. The night held so much promise but nobody ever wanted to be the first at a place, our outings were all about making an entrance and being seen.

We would take over a place, bumping into mortals, spilling their drinks without an apology and guzzling our own Diet Coke and vodka or champagne cocktails, dancing around and stepping out to the toilet together for a line chopped out on the cistern.

Each dyke was a sister to the other, but I never remember spending much time alone with anyone except Louise, and even then it was simply to have sex. I was intoxicated by the never-ending discussions we all shared about how great it was being a dyke. In our world every straight woman was really a wannabe lesbian and we were the chosen ones. We never really noticed anyone who was outside our group, there were certainly no men. Louise was unusual in the group for knowing a few gay guys, but that was it. Occasionally we'd go to one of the clubs where her gay friends DJed and let them fuss over us for looking so cute. Mostly though we busied ourselves catching up with news about who fucked who and who had split up. We talked a lot about dildos, which was weird in retrospect, I can't believe they were that important.

Oh my God, but the sex was good. Louise had a fine body, with rich skin. She looked like a touchstone when she lay on clean sheets, the debris of the earlier part of the night strewn on the floor around us, the bed like an island. I liked to imagine that I was a ghost when I was fucking her, shooting up inside her cunt and inhabiting her body from the inside.

Louise would stretch out like a cat and let me stroke her as though she were doing me a favour – which she was, of course. I couldn't comprehend that she would want me grunting and sweating over her, like beauty and the beast; in my eyes she was like a perfect doll. There were no weird surprises on her body, no lumps or discoloured veins, or scars that could be described as anything but cute; she looked like a model in a magazine, all smooth and fresh. I never told her that this is what I thought – I didn't want to fuck it up, and I wouldn't have been able to bear the truth of how she really saw me.

When I stroked her hair the wrong way, it formed rococo curlicues at her nape, which I liked to trace with my finger. Her face was even and girlish, her cunt neat from the outside, her arsehole tight. From top to tail she smelled like talcum powder. Louise had small tits, which were high and hard, everything about her looked awake, nothing drooped or sagged.

She had a surprise in store for me when I fisted her.

We were lying on her bed smoking and watching trash on the telly. Louise loved re-runs of quiz shows and I humoured her. I tried to read, but it was impossible with her interruptions.

The quiz master boomed: "In which continent would you expect to find Patagonia?"

"What is a Prairie Oyster – animal, vegetable or mineral?"

"The space shuttle Challenger exploded, but in what year?"

I dropped my novel down the side of the bed, rolled over to face her and stroked Louise's warm belly. I liked running my fingers down her sides; she had sweet spots which made her squirm when they were tickled in the right way. If she had been a dog, I could have got her shaking and twitching her back leg for hours.

It wasn't long before Louise became distracted from her entertainment and I knew she was ready for me. Her expression was a mixture of resignation and desire, her eyes made a silent deal with me, her pupils were dilated and her lids were heavy. Blood rushed to her lips; they looked red and lush.

She opened her legs and I held her hot cunt through her pants; it was moist and swollen. I pulled off her underwear, lay on top of her and kissed her deeply. Her eyes were closed in surrender. My breasts pressed against hers. I had one hand behind her head, holding her mouth to mine, and the other creeping its way down until I found the wet spot between her legs.

I sunk two fingers inside and felt her whole body sigh and relax. I held them in there, still, and let her begin her slow grind against them; it felt as though she was testing them out because we both knew she could clearly take more. I gave her three fingers to fuck, them four. I started pumping them in and out, and she responded by arching her back and twisting her head away.

"Oh baby, that's good," she sighed into the pillow, "could you give me a little more?"

I kept my fingers inside her whilst I scrabbled around for the lube under the bed with my other hand in an unseen feat of incredible balance and dexterity. Then I poured some of the goo on to my fucking fingers. It was cold at first, but it soon warmed up. She was slippery and wet around my hand as I fucked her silky snatch. It was like mixing up warm melted chocolate with your fingers. There were different textures inside, smooth vag walls contrasting with rough areas where she loved to be rubbed. The feeling of muscle and heat up close, all throbbing and alive, was like being inside a beating heart.

I felt her sucking me in so I eased in my thumb and held my fist in her cunt opening before slamming it right to the back of her cunt. She roared with pleasure so I didn't stop, I just pumped and fucked her like a machine.

Even though I'd had sex with Louise plenty of times, I'd never noticed the size of her cunt before. Maybe I'd been too wasted to notice, or maybe we just had trashy sex that sped past before there was time for me to, ahem, take in my surroundings. She had fucked me more than I her, maybe that was it, or perhaps today was special in that I would give her something back.

The more I fucked, the bigger her cunt felt. It was as though I was making more space for myself, like I was blasting away at the surface of something plastic and malleable. The edges fell away until it was like a cathedral. My fist was usually tight, hard, massive and unmissable when it was inside a woman; this time it felt small.

"How can you be so tiny on the outside, and so fucking big inside?" My concentration was going, but I was determined not to be intimidated by Louise's unexpectedly huge cunt. I was not going to lose my hard-on, and I wasn't going to let her lose me in her body. I wanted her to know I was there and never to forget it.

I flipped her over on to her hands and knees and crouched between her legs. Her cunt felt like an ever-expanding universe, now bigger than ever. I continued to fuck as I coated my other hand with lube and slid it along my wrist, as though I was attempting to form a set of praying hands.

Bitch, I'm going to make you pray in a minute, I thought. This was going to be my holy communion.

Louise knew something different was happening and she slowed down her fucking the better to accommodate this new set of circumstances. I licked her delicate arsehole to reassure her not to be afraid.

Without saying a word, I made my hands like a point or a wedge which I squeezed into her slowly. Her cunt lips were stretched shiny, dark and tight around me as I pushed my knuckles, the widest part of this fuck-shape, past her gates. Her pussy mouth closed in around my wrists, holding me prisoner.

Inside I clasped my hands together, as though I was begging for mercy.

Louise groaned with a deepness that was shocking. I swayed my clasped hands from side to side.

"Stop, stop, stop!" She was panicking. "Go slow!"

"It's okay, baby; just ease yourself around it; I'm not going to hurt you."

"Ohhh Goddd," she moaned, "It feels so fucking big." She was flexing her back and hips, testing out how far she could go. She rocked forwards then backwards, seating herself on my hands buried deep in her cunt. "Move it a little," she said, "fuck me."

My wrists were aching; she could have broken my arms if she had moved suddenly. Fucking with both hands required a lot of strength; there was nothing to brace myself against; I just had to dive in and do it. Louise was timid at first, but she was soon reciprocating, shaking her head and collapsing her arms when she lost the strength to support herself, then rising up again and fucking me as hard as I fucked her.

I pulled my hands apart, formed two separate fists and fucked her with each one. There was no space inside where it was not hot and burning. Louise was drying out as my pumping fists ate up all her pussy juice like fuel.

I pulled out one hand to get more goo.

"Fuck my arse, fuck my arse," she panted desperately. "I want to be full," she couldn't catch her breath, "I want to come."

I wet her arsehole with my dripping hand and poked my index finger in and out of it, my own cunt oozing as I saw it disappear. I inserted two fingers, then more. Louise rolled her arse, teasing me in. She sat back on me until she had swallowed up a second fist, comically unaware of my shock and amazement.

I could feel my wrist and hand through the thin wall separating the two chambers, one clean, one dirty. Little fragments of hard gritty shit floated around, like an asteroid belt orbiting a planet. Each hand felt as though it belonged to a stranger.

I couldn't do anything and, thankfully, I didn't have to.

Louise metamorphosed from a woman in control to a slobbering beast. Her head twisted round and her tongue lolled in her mouth. The sweat rolled off her back as she bore down on me with all of her strength. Her muscles stood out from under her skin. She was laughing and then moaning with weird crying sounds that had nothing to do with being sad. She twisted and moved on me as though she was filled with elation, then sunk down and rested her weight on her left shoulder. She needed space to reach down to fuck her clit.

I wanted to laugh – after all this, it was still the clit that would finally get her off.

She worked it for a couple of minutes, but I could see that she was tiring.

"I can't get it, I can't," she panted as she jerked herself off. She was crying proper tears now. I relaxed my hands and they slid out of her like newly born baby seals. Louise rolled on to her back as I knelt and watched her hands working between her legs. Her eyes were shut tight and she had lines of concentration on her forehead.

I saw everything as she made herself come, her cunt a mess of goo and lube, slippery and shiny, and her heels digging into the bedsheets all rumpled with secrets.

After I had washed my hands I came back to bed and stroked her cheek with my finger. Louise looked embarrassed.

"Don't you dare tell anyone," she threatened, "I mean it."

I was confused, as far as I was concerned it had been a great fuck and I wanted to tell the world about it. "Don't worry," I reassured her, "I won't."

"You'd be proud of me."

"Why?" asked Alex, disengaging from the straw poking out of his milkshake.

I leaned across the sticky café table and said: "It's only been a short while since you fisted me for the first time and yesterday I got both my fists inside Louise, one in her cunt and one up her arse!"

Alex laughed, "Blimey!" and mock-congratulated me.

I continued, "She may look small from the outside, but she's got the biggest fucking bucket-cunt ever – it's great!"

Louise came back from the bogs and I changed the subject quickly. She fiddled with her Buitt as Alex tried to coax smalltalk out of her. He gave up when she started messaging her friends.

"Have you seen Molex lately?" I asked, hoping that that would make Louise more sociable.

"Not for ages. I heard she was on tour with her new book. But you know, I think she might be back in London this weekend because one of her friends is launching a club – like rock 'n' roll, but for homos."

"Wow, sounds good," I said, elbowing Louise, "shall we go there this weekend?"

"Where is it on?" she asked.

"It's in the basement of the Revolver, over in Marshall Street."

"Didn't that use to be Sisterette?"

"Yeah, but that ended when they got busted for dealing, or something," he explained.

"What's this one called?" I wanted to know.

"'Murder Death Kill', I think."

"Charming," said Louise flatly.

"I'm into it," I told Alex as he picked up his stuff to go, "Can I call you?"

"Sure," he said, pecking me and then Louise on the cheek, "Nice to have met you, Louise. See you laters, potaters!"

As soon as he was out of the door I turned and said, "So what do you think of him?"

"Did you fuck him?" asked Louise, by way of an answer.

"Yeah."

"You used to like men, right?"

"Yes, and I still do."

She pulled a face. "Well," she concurred, "at least he's a dyke."

I replied, "He was man enough for me."

She moved on: "I've heard he likes weird shit."

"Like what?"

"Like cutting people up. I hope he didn't do that to you."

"No, he didn't, but I wouldn't mind if he did. Anyway, it's no weirder than the things you like."

"Like what?"

I waved my two fists at her.

"I told you to shut up about that," she sulked – and the conversation ended.

I had to use all my powers of persuasion to get Louise to agree to go to Murder Death Kill.

"It's mixed," she whined, "that means there'll be no cute women there."

"I thought you liked gay men."

Louise ignored me and added, "And what if there are straight people there? Yu-uk!"

"Don't be pathetic."

"The music will be shit," she wailed, "we hate those places. Let's go to Bar Barella."

"We always go there; let's try something different."

"How about Girlina's?"

"Duh!"

"Or we could slum it out in Hackney, if that's what you want."

"Listen," I reasoned, "I'll go on my own and catch up with you later."

"You can't do that!" She was aghast.

"Why not?"

She made some excuse about how my friends would miss me, but I wasn't sold. Instead I dangled the chance to hang out with Molex as a carrot on a stick.

Even more torturous was the whole nightmare of getting everybody else to go, because there was "no fucking way" that Louise was going to go to a place like that without reinforcements. "If it's shit," she warned, "and it will be shit, no one will ever trust you again."

"Jesus, it's only a club."

Boom boom boom, the bass made the walls vibrate as we queued up outside the Revolver. Yak yak yak, the complaints about queuing went in one of my ears and out the other. The pouting increased when it started to rain. Louise's friends were actually hiding in case any passers-by recognised them. By the time we got to the head of the line, some sneered at the cheap entrance price and conveniently looked away when I asked for an unemployment concession.

Once inside, I ran to the dancefloor to shake it to one of my favourite songs. I could see Louise standing there looking lost, her pained expression mirrored on each of her friends. She crept over to me. "Where's Molex, then?"

"I dunno, look for a woman with grey hair. Maybe she isn't even here yet."

I carried on dancing until I needed a piss, which is where I found my gang huddled together in the dingy lavs taking turns to get a noseful from one of the cubicles. They were chewing sugar-free gum, talking the usual shit and looked like well-dressed refugees.

Louise introduced me to a woman who was hanging out with them, cadging free lines.

"Hey Ramona!" she said, "this is my best friend; come and say hello."

Louise's best friend was Jackie, the dyke who had inadvertently introduced me to Girlina's and had ignored me ever since.

"Hi Ramona," said Jackie, giving me a warm and familiar hug, "how are you? I haven't seen you for ages."

Louise laughed, "Oh! Do you both know each other?"

I shrugged at Lou. "I think she's mistaking me for someone else."
Then I shook Jackie's hand formally, patted her on the back and said,
"It's great to meet you," before moving on.

I went back to dance. I am long past the stage where I worry
whether or not I look good when I dance; I've had no complaints
about it so far so I tend to brush my self-consciousness aside and go
with it. I can dance to just about anything, but I especially love dancing to loud rock 'n' roll, big guitars, a heavy beat.

I empty my mind and just think about myself moving along with
all the other bodies around me. I like a busy dancefloor, but not one so
packed that you're always bumping into everyone around you. I feel
free when I dance. I love to watch other people moving and shaking it
all together. People dance the way they have sex – some move conser-
vatively, some are predictable, some of the wildest look the most modest. I like to let my backbone slip and feel the music working its way
through me from my head to my feet. Sometimes I just can't help it; I
just have to move my hips to that thing. I love it when you hear a
phrase and amplify it so it takes on its own meaning in relation to the
night, "Just give it to me, give it to me, give it to me, now!" And then
you're dancing with somebody else who has moved into your orbit and
you don't need to talk to them because the music says it all.

Louise and the coven left Murder Death Kill without me. I saw
them filing out and Louise shrugging over at me before she too left,
arm in arm with Jackie. They were coked up; it was too bad.

I saw Molex's familiar grey head under a spotlight. She was smiling
and nodding at someone; she looked hip with her tight face and deep
laugh lines. She looked great, actually.

Molex looked over to where I was and she smiled at me. I zipped
over to her part of the room and kissed her cheek.

"I'm so glad to see you," I shouted into her ear.

"Thanks," she replied graciously. "You look good when you dance,
I've been watching you."

"I'm flattered. Hey, you just missed some of my friends; they wanted to meet you – you're one of their heroines."

"Really? Well, that's kind."

I touched her arm, "I haven't been online for a while; I'd like to have another adventure with you." Molex smiled. I continued, "I've been hearing about you from everyone – you're famous! And your friend Iris showed me a good time."

"Ah, you met that naughty Iris; she did say something about that. Are you healed up? She can be quite vicious."

"I'm fine," I laughed, staying close to her. I decided to be blunt. "Can I see you again?"

Molex turned to me and held my hot face in her cool hands. "It's gone," she said, smiling kindly.

I was stunned. I didn't know what she meant and I was too frightened to ask.

She saw my shock and tried to soften it. "Go on," she continued, "go and have a good time tonight – go and dance, there are plenty here who want to dance with you; I can see them."

I started to reply, "I don't want them, I want you!" but Molex had pushed me back towards the dancefloor and I was swallowed up by the crowd.

I found a guy dancing close to me who was interested, he said, in the taste of my pussy. I kissed him with one eye on the corner where Molex stood talking to one of her friends. We went back to his place; I got down on my knees and sucked his dick. He told me he was going to fuck me until I was dry. He pushed some fingers into me to test me out; he inserted them and I knew he had never had his body invaded like that. When I was wet enough for him he got over me and put his dick inside me. I felt it slide in. I held him as he did the fucking movement with his hips. I wanted him to be Molex fucking me with her dick; it was her back I wanted to scratch. I trashed the condom, washed away the residual come from between my legs and was out of there before the last night bus had gone.

I didn't want Molex to think of me as desperate, but I knew that I was. I couldn't bear to think that I might have thrown her away, and I didn't even know what I had done. But if Molex had wanted to make me more and not less interested in her, she couldn't have gone about it in a more effective way. Her ghost hung over me, permanently haunting my life. I knew where she was in that club, like a nuclear device latching on to its co-ordinates. I made mental notes on everybody she talked to, trying to think of ways that I could get close to her. I felt as though lasers were piercing me every time she looked my way. I moved for her the whole night before I left and felt sickened at the idea that she had taken my dancing freedom away from me.

I couldn't sleep that night after I got home from that guy's. My mind replayed the same scenes over and over again.

In one fantasy, Molex would be walking through my door. She'd see me on my couch, she'd walk up to me and, stroking my long hair, she'd ask me to take a deep plunge with her, whatever that means.

Our clothes would evaporate and we'd hang together in mid-air, like acrobats on wires or insects suspended in amber. We'd be kissing and spinning round; we'd always be together. We'd feel and know each other's hearts beating, the smell of each other's hair and skin.

In another image, Molex would be in a long dress floating up above me as though she was going to heaven. I would reach up and touch her slit and feel electrified with desire for her.

Or I'd be on my back on my bed with Molex cooing, "You look so good; you look so fine." She'd be holding me in her arms but also fucking me and stroking me and kissing me, her breasts hanging over me. She'd be able to do a hundred things at once but still look human. I would be doing the same to her.

I tired myself out jerking off so that I could at last sleep. My clit was bored of the attention by the time I was done and my soul ached with the idea of this woman.

It wasn't enough for me to know where she lived, who her friends were and how she liked to fuck. I wanted more of her. I got up the next day and went to the library to try and find her online, but it was like looking for a leaf on a tree through the wrong end of a telescope. Alex was out when I called for him, so nothing there. Refusing to be discouraged, I mooched around the West End and shoplifted the full set of Molex's poetry books to look for clues – my imagination hit overdrive, but I found nothing. After that I was hungry and tired, so I went over to see Louise for some cold pizza and cigarettes.

The first thing she said was: "What happened to you?"

"Nothing, why?"

"We waited for you at Bar Barella."

"Oh. Shit. I'm sorry."

"So?" She wasn't going to let it go.

"I got caught up with Molex."

"Oh, did she turn up?"

"Well yeah, I think she was there all along. I don't know how you could have missed her; maybe she was hiding from you," I joked, realising immediately that it might have been true.

"Did you go back with her?" That was a loaded question. If I had gone back, Lou might be pissed off that I hadn't called and invited her, or maybe she'd be upset that I had fucked someone else. But if I told the truth and said that I hadn't fucked Molex, Louise might think I was lying about knowing her, and she'd probably want to know what I had really been up to last night.

"Would it matter if I had?" I replied evasively.

"No, not with her."

I was emboldened with false self-righteousness. "But with someone else it would have?"

"Maybe."

"Like who?"

"I don't know." Louise pretended to be disinterested.

"Like Becky?" Lou's oldest friend from school, also on the fringes of the A-Dyke crowd.

"Forget Becky," she snorted.

We shared an uncomfortable silence, then Louise asked: "Where were you? I missed you."

I decided that honesty was the best policy. "I hung around for a bit, then I fucked some guy and then I went home."

Louise got up and walked out of the room, slamming the door behind her. I didn't think I had been that offensive. I sat for a moment then followed her. I didn't want any bad feeling between us or, rather, I didn't want to be kicked out of the A-Dykes just yet.

She was in the bathroom washing her face with cold water. I put my arm around her waist and she jerked away, saying "Leave me alone."

"No," I replied.

"Get away from me!"

"I'm sorry if I've hurt you; I didn't realise it would be such a big deal."

"It's not a big deal," she sulked.

"Well, what's going on?"

"Just fuck off."

"Stop being so upset, it was just a shag."

"I don't care about you shagging anyone else."

"Don't you?"

She turned to face me and let the tears roll.

"What's going on?" I wanted to know.

"How could you?"

"I don't understand you; he was just some guy..." I trailed off.

"Yes," interrupted Louise. "Exactly!"

"What?"

"'Just some guy'," she mimicked me sarcastically.

Suddenly I understood. "It's the dick, isn't it?"

"Don't be stupid."

"You're upset because I fucked some guy," I snapped angrily. "What's the matter?" I spat, "do you think you're going to catch some fucking bisexual disease off me? And then your friends won't like you and you won't be cool? Is that it?"

It was Louise's turn to placate me now. "I'm sorry," she said, "I'm being stupid – it's okay, let's leave it."

I decided to open myself up a little.

"Lou, will you beat me sometime, please?" I asked it quietly, hoping that that would make her less appalled.

"What?"

"Can you beat me?" I repeated. "I'd like it if you slapped me around a bit. Maybe you could beat me with my belt."

"Beat you?" she said, distastefully.

"Yeah."

She thought about it for half a second and then replied, "No."

"Why not?"

"I don't want to hurt you."

"But I'd like you to," I tried to reason.

There was no point in explaining. Louise simply answered, "You're fucked up," and that was the end of it.

I cooled down. "Let's be nice now."

I ran a bath for us both and we had a couple of lines as a reward for not freaking out too much. I became embarrassingly grandiose. "I am one of the chosen few," I blahed, "it's people I fancy, not gender." Luckily Louise's bullshit detector was turned off by the time I postulated that "everyone is really bisexual."

She looked pretty all covered with bubbles, her hair wet and sticking to her. She let me soap her tits, so I held the slippery little buggers up and let them flop down out of my hands. We slid and squirmed around in the oversized tub, and then my fingers flipped and wriggled under the surface and inside her big dirty snatch.

Later that night, sitting in a booth at Bar Barella, wired for the night, my pants got wet at the memory of it.

"So, do you swallow?" Orla interrupted my reverie.

"What?"

"Do you spit or do you swallow?"

Orla tried to look nonchalant, practising moves with her Buitt. She avoided my gaze, but her leg tapped nervously under the table, which said it all.

"I swallow, of course, Orla – don't you?"

No one knew what to say until Louise laughed out loud and everybody copied her. As they laughed, I imagined myself wrapped up with a big fat label. I knew I wasn't the only cocksucking dyke round that table, but I was the only one to say that I liked it and that I'd do it again. I hoped my honesty would be rewarded, but it wasn't.

"How can you?" sneered Becky.

"It's disgusting!" agreed Orla.

Someone only had to say "prick cheese" to get them falling about all over again.

"I heard that you like it when men treat you rough," said Orla, smugly.

"Where did you hear that from? I never even heard it myself."

"A little dykey-bird told me!" she chuckled, adding, "You're a freak!"

Oh man, I thought, Molex would not be this uncool.

The badgering went on and on. I even caught Louise doing an impersonation of me sucking a dick for everyone's amusement. She looked up at me guiltily.

I tried to be generous with them, but they were acting like a bunch of spoilt brats. As the night progressed, we all got more and more wired until someone was dumb enough to say what they all had been thinking. "Ramona's a straight girl."

I tried laughing it off, but they knew they'd hit a nerve; in fact, it was pretty blatant that my friends were getting on my tits in a big way.

I came all this way for this? I thought – I fucking earned my dykehood, thankyouverymuch.

The tired bar manager threw us out and we all ended up back at Louise's.

Orla and Becky asked the cabdriver if he fancied me because I was the only straight one among them and they told him I'd do anything. He was scared of them; he didn't understand.

"He wants you," Orla leered at me.

I made tea and we smoked and snorted the last of our lines, just cheap whizz tonight because everyone was due for a trip back home for more money.

Orla wouldn't leave it. She'd found the joke of the night – me – and she wasn't going to let it drop.

"Hey Ramona," she said, pretending to be friendly whilst barely concealing her malice, "show us you're a dyke."

Becky, her patsy for the night, piped up, "Yeah, prove it; let's have a look at you."

"I bet you don't even know how to fuck a woman," chipped in Louise, the dirty bitch.

"Funny, you don't say that when you're getting fisted." She shut up.

Orla was on a roll: "I bet you really go for women who look like men," she sneered. "I bet you couldn't fuck a real woman." This was nasty.

"I don't see any real women in this room," I sniped back, "just stupid little cunts."

They were having fun winding me up, but I felt like a bear in a pit. The pressure was building and the joke was losing its humour because these women were fast turning into a *Lord of the Flies*-style rabble. I was not going to let them win.

"Come here, Orla, and put your money where your mouth is." I decided to put a stop to her. "How much are you worth?" I asked innocently.

"I'm priceless," she beamed.

"How much is a fuck with you worth?"

"Darling, you should be paying me," she said in a fake posh accent.

"Okay, as a random figure, I'll pay you £500."

"What?"

"I'll pay you £500 if I can't make you come." I didn't have the money, but I didn't care.

"You're fucked in the head."

"Yes, I am," I said it to shut her up. "If I make you come you'll have to give me the money." I knew that amount was nothing to her. I also knew that she wouldn't be able to back out with an audience.

"Do it here, in front of everyone, then," Becky said, "so there's no cheating."

Orla was trying to keep her cool.

I looked over at Louise to see if there was going to be any trouble with her, but she was chatting happily on her mobile.

"Okay," I said, "let's do it here."

I told Orla to get undressed.

"No, you go first."

"Fuck you, you coward," I said as I peeled off my top and stepped out of my jeans.

Louise put her phone down mid-sentence, looked at me and said: "You have got to be joking."

I shrugged an apology at her.

Orla stood stiffly in her bra and pants.

"Come here," I beckoned, and she took a small step forward. Five pairs of eyes were watching us but only I could see the tiny blobs of nervous sweat on her top lip.

"What are you going to do?" she asked.

"What's the matter, are you scared?"

"No."

"Well, come here then."

She walked into me like a ghost melting through a wall. I closed my arms around her and came down on her open mouth as though I was going to eat her alive.

"Fuck!" squealed Becky and another woman, simultaneously delighted.

I did not waste any time. Orla's clitoris was hardening in my hand. She was wet and excited. I knew it was going to be easy and I wasn't afraid of what anybody thought of me. She was silent now.

"What's the matter, Orla, do you want to find out how I treat my men?"

She had no idea how to reply to this, and neither did the rest of my audience apart from Becky, who squeaked out loud and inappropriately, "Oh my shitting fuck, what's she going to do now?"

She was met with a collective "Sh!"

I ignored this and called over to Louise, "Hey babe, will you fetch me my dick?"

"Your dick?"

"Yeah, hurry, will you?"

"But Ramona," she smiled, "you have lots of dicks." Louise had been very generous on the dick-buying front. She bought me a new one just about every week. There were so many that they tumbled off the bedside shelf where I kept them.

"Well honey," I continued.

"What, sweetie?" she replied.

"Why dontcha bring them all!"

She ran out and then returned a short while later with rubber, silicone and plastic dildos spilling out over her arms. In polite company I might have felt slightly shy about my abundance of cock, but here I didn't care. There were black ones, weirdly coloured ones, fat ones, long ones, double-enders, and a couple of tiddlers. Some were shiny and new; others had seen better days.

Orla was starting to lose her frames of reference, I noticed gleefully. The word "pandaemonium" floated around in my head, like a target to aim for.

Louise dumped the dicks and my harness on a table nearby and I picked out the most realistic-looking one. It was big and floppy, with fake veins all over it and a snake-eye at the end.

My harness was custom-made for me – stiff leather and lots of buckles that enabled me to strap it on in various permutations. It was a handful, even for me.

"Hey sister," I called over to Louise, "could you come and help me with this?" Instead of just Louise, everyone came over and helped me into that thing, like they all wanted to handle me. I was surprised they were so keen.

Orla looked forgotten standing alone in the middle of the room. As the others sat down again, I waved a little packet at her.

"In this wrapper I have a plain unlubricated condom." She looked at me blankly. "I want you to roll it on to my dick with your mouth."

"Fuck off," she snapped, "I'm not putting that dirty cock in my mouth."

Smack. I clapped my hands in front of her face and Orla reeled back as though I had actually hit her. The sound was loud and shocking. I warned, "The next time you slander me and my cock, that smack will be the sound of my hand on your face." She shut up. "Get down there and do it." She did and it was obvious she was hungry for it.

The group of women watched with big saucer-eyes as Orla put the condom on her tongue and held it in against her lips in a way that made her mouth look like that of a blow-up doll. She knelt down so that her face was cock level.

I held the back of her head with my left hand and had my dick in my right.

I held her face close to mine and looked into her eyes, speaking quietly so that what followed was just between us. "I've got a little something to say to you, sweetheart," I said. "You seem to have his funny idea that because I like a little bit of real live cock in my diet, I let men dick me around. Now, you're very much mistaken about this," I smiled meanly, "I think you need a bit of an education, so I'm going to show you how I treat my men."

Gingerly, she held the head of my cock with her hand and brought her mouth down over it. Orla had her other hand down her pants and was fingering her clit. The ladies craned their necks to get a better view as she worked her tongue around and swallowed as much of my cock as she could get into her throat. I helped her a little, pushing up my hips the better for her to get a grip on it. She was breathing heavily through her nose, concentrating hard on doing it right.

She looked really pretty.

My nipples were sticking out and my cunt was tingling. With it still in her mouth, I jerked off my foul rubber dick as though it was a real cock.

"Hey girl, you'd better like it when I shoot my load into your filthy whore mouth."

Her eyes said yes.

"You keep it in there; you keep that condom on; I don't want you dirtying up my beautiful cock."

As I jerked off my dick, I was pushing Orla back further and further until she was teetering on the very backs of her heels, with me standing right over her. Her knees were open and she was digging at herself. She tried to talk but it came out muffled, "Mmumph, eugh."

"Say it in English," I spat.

I pulled out my cock and in the split second before I slammed it back into her mouth she peeped "Fuck me," as fast as a humming-bird's wings.

"You want a fuck?" I hammed it up. "You want big daddy-man cock to fuck you?" She nodded, knowing that I was going to fuck her over. "What kind of a lesbian are you?" Orla looked down at the floor, her turn to overact now.

"You want a fuck, I'll fuck you," I said generously as I pulled off her pants, climbed between her legs and got on top of her, missionary style.

She was playing with herself, dipping her fingers into her wet hole, making it big and wide for me, opening herself up.

I held the tip of my dick up against her cunt hole. She wriggled up against it, trying to get it inside her, but it was out of reach and I knew it. "You'll have to try harder than that."

"Please fuck me," she said. It sounded convincing. "Please." She said it again; she was almost wheezing, "Please."

Our audience was breathing with one unified breath and watching with one collective eye. It was bizarre how the group dynamics had changed. Everyone had switched sides. I was not the freak any more, Orla was.

I slid closer towards her and I swear I felt the heat rising from her cunt on the end of my dick. I started sliding it in; she held herself open; she was so ready and still.

I released the buckles on my harness and the dick popped out and fell into her.

I got right in Orla's face and said, "Fuck yourself with it," before pulling back minus cock to watch what she would do. She grabbed it and pushed it inside her, rubbing her clit and coming in no time at all. It was not enough of a show for me. I snatched a butt-plug from the table, wet it in my mouth, rolled her over on to her front and eased it up her arse.

"Hey kids, dig in!" I announced, as though I was a wholesome dad in charge of a pre-teen barbeque.

No one needed any encouragement; it was like a feeding frenzy. Louise and Becky stuck the dicks down their pants and out through the zips of their jeans. They looked like a cross between good-looking rich young dykes and those dirty old men who expose themselves on the top deck of the bus. Louise's phone rang and she answered only to say, "Fuck off, I'm about to get a blow job," to the puzzled caller. The others followed. One stuck a double-ended cock up inside her cunt and let the other end hang out; she looked a treat.

It was weird, those women looked to me for encouragement until I felt like Charles Manson directing his fucked up little Family. I handed out the condoms and we all stood in a circle around Orla. She did us one by one, getting shouts of encouragement from the group. Her hair was all over the place, crazy-messy, her body started to flop, and by cock number three, her eyes had glazed.

We all chipped in with dirty talk: "Come and eat me, Orla," "Oh, look at that greedy girl," "She loves having cock in her mouth," "She loves it up her arse too," "She just wants to gobble it up," "Fuck my cock."

Someone said, "Fuck my penis," only it came out as "peeenis," which caught on, and soon everyone was chanting "Peeenis, peeenis, peeenis," whilst Orla, poor cow, tried to service us all.

The women were getting into it; the scene was no longer a joke, not that it had ever been for Orla or me. Some pulled at themselves like johns waiting to gang-bang a hooker, keeping themselves hard so that they would be able to perform when the time came. Others had fingers blatantly poking and rubbing at themselves, or down someone else's pants. It was turning into a regular A-Dyke orgy.

Louise went to get something nice for us to snort. She wanted to add an edge to things, as though it needed it.

Orla was on her back with her legs in the air, and Becky was fucking her like a dog at a bitch. Orla was very tired, judging by the way she lay there passively and let the women shake her down, but she would not say no. We took turns lining our nostrils with powder and then getting to work on her. Someone took a line off her breasts and then everybody wanted to go, cheered on with more "Peeenis" encouragement. By the time I was at the head of the queue, Orla had Louise's cock down her throat, someone else was straddling her and fucking her tits and yours truly was jamming my big ugly monster-dick inside her cunt hole.

"We made our own fun back in the days before television," I sniggered.

The grand that Orla insisted on giving me more than sorted me out, and for the next couple of weeks I lived like a king. She even gave me her favourite Buitt and showed me some moves with it.

Suzanne's face lit up with pleasure when she saw the bouquet I'd brought her and I was glad because it meant that our last argument was forgotten. Instead of our usual cups of tea we drank a couple of bottles of champagne and scoffed fancy chocs at her kitchen table, although Suz refused the gram of coke I'd brought her.

"No thanks, babe, give it to someone else, eh?"

Her face fell when I chopped out a dirty fat line and had it myself. I saw her expression and put the rest away guiltily.

"Sorry," I burped the word out loud and we both cracked up.

"You look like you've been doing a lot of that," said Suzanne once we'd stopped giggling.

"Not as much as some people I know."

"Why do you do it?"

"I get fucked up because I like to get fucked up."

"Be careful, Ramona."

"I will," I said, adding "Mum," afterwards. She ignored me.

"How can you afford this anyway? I thought you were getting dole hassle. Have those lovely Employment Service people paid you an extra dividend?"

"Do you really want to know?"

"Don't shit me, I worry about you."

I told her everything. She was not impressed. "What's the matter?"

I asked, "Don't you think it's funny?"

"I don't understand you; why do you want to hang out with these twats?" I couldn't answer. She went on, "I thought Nicky was an idiot, but this lot sound like a nightmare."

It took me a moment before I remembered who Nicky was. "Don't lecture me; they're my friends," I whined.

"Some friends. Friends don't fuck you around like that."

"They're dykes," I said, as though that explained everything. "You just don't get it because you're straight."

"Don't patronise me," she said sternly.

We sat in silence. I looked at the ceiling, then the door, then the walls, then the floor, and then at the three large tears blobbing their way down Suzanne's face. They startled me.

"I love you Ramona," it came out all wobbly and high. That startled me more. She continued: "You're my best friend. You're so fucking lovely and you don't even know it."

What could I say? I looked at her dumbly.

"You're wasting your time with these shitting fucks and I don't want to lose you," she went on, "I miss you when you don't call, I'm scared you're going to slip away and I hate it when you treat me like a cunt. I won't tolerate it forever."

I burned hot.

"You're so special to me, please don't fuck it up."

We sat together, saying nothing for a few moments, until I blurted "I've got to go." I didn't turn to hug her as I walked out of the door; I didn't want her to see me crying.

My face was a blotchy river of snot by the time I got to my house. I had to wipe my nose on my sleeve like a child as I bent to pick up a note that had been left on my doormat. I went inside and washed my face and tried to forget about Suzanne, an impossible task, so instead I opened the envelope.

Inside was a paper slip from 'Girls Like You', a lesbian dating agency that I'd seen advertised in the gaypers. "Jesus fuck, that's all I need right now," I muttered, before noticing the writing on the other side of it.

It said: "Ramona, you're the sexiest lesbian in London. Let's get together." There was a phone number and it was signed, "Maxine x x x."

Becky knew Maxine, and it was probably through her that she'd found out where I lived. I'd seen her around. My first impressions were that she was a generic A-Dyke, distinguished from the rest of them by her age, she was maybe in her mid-thirties, a good decade ahead of the others. The second thing that struck me about her was that she had a vibe of desperation about her: for attention, for approval, for love. I took her for a rube and, frankly, I was surprised that she'd even clocked me.

Wow, I thought, now I'm a trophy fuck.

Maxine owned Girls Like You, along with a string of other niche-marketed lesbian businesses. She was sexy in a boring way but she was totally fucking loaded and that was what made my heart beat faster and my eyes go ker-ching like a cartoon cash register.

I called the number, got through to her secretary, and arranged a date.

Maxine lived in a chi-chi Islington neighbourhood. Two doors down: a Cabinet minister; over the other side of the road: a prominent stage actress, OBE; three streets away: a row of crack houses.

A maid – yes, she had a maid – answered the door and led me into a sitting room for which there were only two words: Minimalist Chic. The big square settee and shiny white surfaces I recognised from seeing them featured in a couple of lesbian mags. Wow, famous furniture.

Maxine glided in smoking a joint. She wore a baseball cap backwards, which looked stupid, and she was over-friendly, which I hated. I wanted to keep it businesslike.

We had some wine and a couple of lines.

"Come and eat," she said, showing me to a dining room.

Whilst Minnie, the woman who had answered the door, served us food, Maxine gabbed about her employee's "gorgeous" children and "awful" husband as though Minnie was not there. I tried to give Minnie a look of apology, but she stared straight through me.

Maxine punctuated each course with another line. She was so busy gabbing that she barely touched her food, but I managed to scoff; it seemed rude not to.

Even without the coke, Maxine was nervous, twitchy and excited, and it was kind of flattering to think that I had this effect on someone. She was also idiotic, boastful and shallow. She preened herself in the dining room mirror. If someone had taken a snapshot of her, Maxine would have looked dynamic and go-getting, the secret of her success, I guess. But in real life her energy was staged and phoney. The lady talked shit.

I zoned out, imagining fucking her on a bed made of cash, with furniture built with bullion, amongst flowers perfumed with wealth. It was the idea of money that made me wet.

Maxine talked non-stop. I imagined that she did this a lot.

"I've never met anyone like you before," she rabbited.

"Oh."

"You're so exciting and different."

"Thanks." Great. What could I say?

"Shall we have another toot?" she asked.

"Yeah."

As we brought our heads together over the mirror, Maxine finally got to the point.

"I've heard a lot about you," she said.

"Oh yeah, like what?" I was truly monosyllabic.

"I've heard that you like toys."

"They're okay."

I don't really have a thing for toys at all. I can take them or leave them.

Clever me, I realised that she was talking about her own preferences, giving me information I could use to get her to like me. The smell of her cash was intoxicating, so I played along.

"I bet you've got quite a toy chest," I smirked.

"That I have."

"Can I have a look?"

"You're eager." I could see that this excited her.

"Just curious."

She left her plate of food and I managed to cram in and swallow another mouthful before following her up the stairs to her room.

Her bedroom was big and flashy, all white and sleek. Maxine sat me on the edge of her magnificent bed and wafted off to the bathroom, saying behind her, "I won't be a moment."

I didn't poke around in case she caught me at it, even though every cell in my body was screaming at me to do so. I'd have to save that pleasure for another time. I checked my teeth for stray bits of food. Over on Maxine's bedside table were two hardbacks: *The Art of Sensual Love-Craft* – groan – and *The Third Little Book of Emotional Intelligence* – puke.

I felt queasy and clenched from the drugs and half-digested food. My legs were shaking, but I wasn't nervous.

"Shut your eyes," said Maxine from behind the bathroom door.

I shut them and, two seconds later, turned to kiss the cool hand that was stroking my face.

When Maxine told me to open my eyes, I struggled to look convincingly impressed. She was wearing a black rubber bikini with cutouts for her nipples to poke through. I guessed that Minnie had polished her up, because the rubber was very shiny. Maxine was a funny combination of skinny and curvy, she obviously worked out, but there was no disguising her full wobbling arse.

She licked her finger and ran it around one of her nipples, making it hard. It was a cheap gesture. I liked it. Then she teetered over to a cupboard and bent over.

I gasped with shock and surprise, but managed to muffle it before she noticed. Her bikini bottoms were crotchless and her cunt was hanging out all pink and ready. The sight was unspeakably vulgar! It was like seeing your grandad snog a teenager under the mistletoe at Xmas. It was shocking, more so because I knew that the display was calculated for me. I'm almost ashamed to say that I liked it in a sleazy way.

Maxine hauled out a large leather box.

"You wanna play with me?" She lisped in a little girl voice.

I nodded, unable to speak. I think she thought that I was because she came over to sit with me as though she was comforting me.

"Oh, poor baby," she cooed. "Don't worry, I'll look after you," she added, sticking her tongue in my ear.

"I've got lots of toys," said Maxine, "would you like to try something?"

"I'd like to see you playing with them.

"Ooh, so you'd like a show!" her eyes sparkled. "I can be a real showgirl," she said, adding, "for the right woman." That meant me.

"Show me how you use those," I said, pointing to some love eggs that sat on the top of the pile.

Maxine pulled a chair in front of the bed and sat down in it daintily.

"Ask me to open my legs," she said.

"Open your legs."

She did and I got another look at her unbelievable crotchless outfit.

"Ask me to finger myself," she said.

"Finger yourself."

She licked her middle finger, the "fuck you" finger you give at someone you hate, and inserted it neatly in her hole. She never once broke eye contact with me. I felt as though I had nowhere to hide.

"Ask me to fuck myself a little,' she said.

"Fuck yourself a little."

Maxine pushed a second finger inside and slid it out again. I could see that she was very wet. Her cunt was shaved and her lips were glazed with juice.

She picked up a string of love eggs, red plastic balls with weights inside, and massaged the end of one against her slit, coating it in moisture. Then she popped it inside. The cord with the second and third ball was hanging outside, like a fucked-up tammy string, but soon she had pushed those in too.

"Ask me to rub my clit," she said.

"Rub your clit."

Maxine threw back her head and teased her clit. She looked like a woman in a stroke magazine. The weights in the love eggs rattled inside her whenever she moved; it sounded as though she was creaking. I was mesmerised.

"Oh, I want to come, I want to come," she gasped.

I said nothing.

"Tell me I can't come, not yet," she said.

I echoed: "You can't come Maxine, not yet."

"But I want to!" she wailed.

I wasn't ready for that, not yet. It was too far too soon. "Show me something different."

She pulled out the eggs with a pop-pop-pop and slung them aside. I felt sorry for Minnie, who would inevitably have to clean them later on.

Maxine looked hot and bothered, momentarily confused, but she was soon on the case again.

"How about some buzzing fun?" she asked, without expecting a reply from me. She went to the box and pulled out a candy-coloured vibrator with a wire and control box attached to the end. The vibrator looked like one of those crazy sweetie dispensers that you can buy in Woolies, all clear plastic and tiny acid-coloured beads inside. It had a couple of moulded plastic branches poking out from the bottom. "This is the clit tickler," said Maxine, "it'll take a woman higher than she's ever been before." She sounded like an advert. The whole thing looked cheap.

"I want to see you fuck yourself with it," I said.

"Oh, I'll fuck myself, alright," she said, retaking her place on the chair in front of me. She pulled up one leg over the arm of the chair and switched on the vibrator. It made a tiny buzzing sound, like a mosquito.

There was a part of me that couldn't believe I was encouraging this woman. The imaginary angel of my conscience sitting on my shoulder squealed at me to stop teasing the poor cow and to get out of there. Meanwhile, the devil on the other side was thoroughly enjoying seeing Maxine get so wonderfully humiliated. In another universe Maxine was a hot babe, thankfully I had enough imagination to edit out all of her extremely annoying characteristics and get off on this prime piece of rump steak crawling around for me so desperately. It would certainly provide me with a good anecdote one day. In the meantime, my cunt was oozing sex goo.

Maxine dragged the vibrator down her neck and between her breasts. She ran it around first one nipple and then the next. She wet the end of the vibrator in her mouth and then teased it inside her cunt, the buzzing becoming muffled and then returning as it disappeared in and out of her. She shifted in her seat a little and positioned the clit tickler on her "love button", as she called it, turning the power on full.

She waited and I waited for something to happen – some miniature explosions perhaps, the earth shaking underneath us, at least a minor-grade orgasm. The thing hummed quietly, then more quietly, then stopped altogether. Maxine whipped it out of her and threw it on the floor, not far from where the love eggs lay. "Fucking batteries," she swore petulantly.

This might turn into a major fucking drag and I knew I had to do something, so I crawled over and dug a larger smooth vibrator out of the toy box. "Why don't you try this?" I said, trying to save the scene.

Maxine perked up with, "I thought you'd never ask." She continued: "I need to get in the mood a bit more; why don't you tell me your fantasy?"

It wouldn't be too difficult to work out what she wanted, the woman lacked imagination, but I wondered how far I could push her.

"You're in a room," I started, "with this big, beautiful witchy femme."

"Are you kidding?" Maxine interrupted, "I don't want some stinky fat bitch sweating all over me."

Clearly I couldn't be too imaginative. "Sorry, I'll start again. You're in a room with this young boyish dyke – she works out a lot and she's got an incredible six-pack."

"Mmm," said Maxine, she had closed her eyes to concentrate and was playing with herself.

"She's got the hots for you; she really wants to do you, but you're too cool for her." Maxine smiled at this. "She's a boxer; she's really fit. She looks and acts like a lad but she's not; she's a woman. She wants to eat you out and you think that's just dandy; it's what she deserves. Tell her to get down in front of you, why don't you, Maxine?"

"Get down there, you dirty boy," she giggled, holding the vibrator against her clit.

"She's down there now, looking up at you with big eyes; she wants to do you so much; she knows that you're the best."

"I'm the best," she murmured.

"She's got her tongue out, it's very long and rough and strong. You're standing over her and she's got her head back, ready to receive your slit, sorry, I mean your pussy. She's so excited that her own pussy lips are big and wet; she knows that you'd never fuck her but she'll probably come from the mere privilege of going down on you."

"She's begging for me," said Maxine. She was fucking herself with the vibrator with one hand and holding open her cunt lips with the other, the better for this imaginary boy-girl to eat her out, I suspected.

"Yes, she is," I continued, "and she's licking at you with big strong licks. She's loving it, you taste so good, she's greedy for you." I tingled with bad-girl pleasure at the audacity of my outrageous lies. No amount of fantasising about her bank statements was going to make Maxine appealing to me. She was a dumb bitch, full stop.

"Come and eat me out, Ramona," said Maxine, her eyes still closed. Although I wanted to get off, I ignored her demand and continued winding her up, enjoying my power.

"You look amazing and sexy, there's no one in the world who wouldn't want to fuck you, you're the hottest women in the universe, completely irresistible, and..."

Eureka, I'd struck oil. Maxine had the most preposterous orgasm I've ever seen. She shrieked and hooted like Little Richard or Jerry Lee Lewis hollering on an early rock 'n' roll 45. She head-banged. She held her breath and then let it go in little grunts and puffs. She stamped her feet in the ground and then was still, the silence complete but for the thud of the vibrator landing with a bump on the floor.

I waited for her to make the next move. She opened her eyes and focussed on me, like Linda Blair in *The Exorcist*.

"Baby wants more," she lisped.

The angel on my shoulder pleaded with me to leave it all well alone, but the imaginary devil with the dirty wet cunt shoved her out of the way and urged me: "Do it!"

I charged at Maxine like a runaway train, knocking her over on to the floor. I rummaged around under my clothes and pulled them up and down enough to expose my cunt. Maxine wanted to touch, but I wouldn't let her. Instead I pushed her down so that she lay on her back. She looked surprised but, thankfully, went along with it. Maybe she thought she was being hip. Her legs got caught up beneath her; it couldn't have been very comfortable but I didn't care.

Everything happened so quickly, like a real dirty job that you secretly and furtively enjoy. I sat on her face and humped with all my might. I looked up at the ceiling as I tried to recall every sexy image that I had ever seen rather than see Maxine pinned underneath me. I could feel her trying to lick and react, maybe she was trying to make out that she had a stake in my forthcoming orgasm. Luckily I was too heavy and strong, and I moved too forcefully for her delicate mouth to have any real effect. This show was all mine.

I squatted and rode and rubbed my cunt up and down her face until the friction was right, the angle was good, the moment came and the pleasure zapped through me. I felt like the filthiest slag in the world, and I liked it.

I slid off Maxine, stood up awkwardly and rearranged my clothes.

Immediately, although breathlessly, she started yabbering away: "That was amazing! Oh my god!" She looked over at me and I knew she wanted some of what I'd just had.

Oh shit. She was getting up. Oh fucking fuck. She was closing in on me. She had a tube of edible banana-flavoured lube in her hand. Oh bugger. She pouted. "How about we play with some of this?"

"Shall we have another line?" It was the only thing I could think of to get that manic look out of her eye.

"Yeah! Great idea!" she agreed. "Minnie," Maxine yelled down the stairs, "Bring us the charlie!"

I would rather have died than let Minnie see me, so I made an excuse to go to the bathroom.

I locked the door and looked at my face in the mirror opposite. I was feeling pleased with myself although I was still dizzy from my recent orgasm. I was playing for time whilst I decided what to do to get out of having to have any more sex with Maxine. I peeked in her bathroom cupboard in case there were some tasty pharmaceuticals, but I found only some moisturiser and a container of Tiger Balm.

I came out and found Maxine on the bed with both of her holes stuffed. She was buzzing on two different frequencies. She looked unbelieveable, and not in a good way. Around her on the bed she had a load more toys lined up, some made of that beige-pink plastic that's supposed to be flesh-coloured, others with bits of elastic and wires attached to them.

"Do you think I should use the big one or the small one in my arse?" She asked. "The big one is battery operated, but the small one is more powerful."

I smirked, trying to remember everything so that I would be able to relay the story later and add more to her humiliation.

Maxine had a small mirror balanced on her chest and was straining to get the powder up her nose. I thought I could sneak out without her noticing, but I was wrong.

"Where are you going, honey?"

"I don't feel very well; I need to go," I lied, wide-eyed.

"What?"

"I said I've had a lovely time, but I don't –"

"I heard you," she snapped. She sat up, and one of the vibrators popped out of her cunt, though she managed to catch the mirror and prevent any of the coke from being wasted. "Fucking typical stupid dyke." She started to rant. "I get you here, I feed you, let you share my drugs, I put on a sexy show for you, I let you get off on me and now you can't get it up. It's the same old story every fucking time."

"I'm sorry, Maxine. It's been great; you were fabulous, but I have to go." It was hard not to laugh at her.

"Yeah, you go, you go now." She was losing it. "Get the fuck out, you fucking loser! Get out now!"

I ran and cackled until my lungs nearly popped and I couldn't run any more.

Louise was having one of her sexy episodes when I called. She answered the door in a pair of high-heeled mules and not much else.

"Come in, babe," she said, "I won't be long."

Every once in a while, when she was alone and had nothing better to do, Louise liked to get out of it and spend a couple of hours jerking off. She said it helped her feel less stressed, although her life seemed completely stress-free to me, so it was difficult to imagine what it was that made her so uptight.

There was a joint in the ashtray, which I finished off, after which I helped myself to some more of Louise's stash. It was all part of the experience. I looked around at her flat; there were specks of some drug on the glass coffee table and gelatine pill capsules that had been emptied of their riches. A half-full vodka bottle had its top screwed back wrongly. Under the table, in danger of being kicked over, was a ridiculous bong made of rainbow-coloured glass in the shape of a sexy naked hippie lady. Blue smoke hung in the air and clothes were left dumped where they were originally removed. Louise turned up the music; it was something nameless and dancey. The blinds were open, someone else might have shut them for modesty's sake, but she got off on the idea that a neighbour might be watching her whilst washing up the soup bowls.

Louised danced around me. She smelt like spring flowers, which is unbelievable considering the air of grubbiness she exuded. Her eyes were bloodshot and her hair was all over the place.

"Wanna watch me, baby?" she winked.

"Okay."

"Say please."

"Please."

"You know what I mean."

"Please can I watch you jerk off, you sexy whore!"

"Anything for you, my sweet."

Everyone has at least one surefire thing that gets them off and most people keep their kinks to themselves. Louise was different – she had a thing for doing it in front of a mirror, she really liked to watch herself and she was shameless about her narcissism.

"I'm cute," she reasoned, "why shouldn't I do it?" I never could think of an answer.

Louise had a very big mirror in her bedroom. When no one was about, I liked to mime and dance to my favourite songs in front of it, but Lou enjoyed different pleasures.

Today she stood square in front of it, legs apart, hands on hips, as though she was a drill sergeant inspecting her troupe. The squareness gave way to a slinky little dance move, like vogueing, where she raised her arms and wrapped them gracefully around herself in that comedy way which makes it look from behind as though someone is fondling you. She turned to check out the effect. "Funny girl," she said to herself.

Louise bent over and put her hands on her knees. She looked over her shoulder and looked at her pussy, hanging there between her legs, available. Then she turned and walked up to the mirror. She rested her foot up high; she would have done the splits if she had been supple enough. She twisted sideways and rested her forehead on the glass, balancing delicately with one foot on floor, one in the air.

"Mm," she hummed, "pussy girl." She continued with her private song, "I love the taste of pussy/ I love the smell of pussy/ I want my little pussy/ I got my little pussy." It was like a mantra and she repeated it over and over again.

Whilst she sang, Louise put two fingers either side of her clit and rubbed a little. Then she rubbed a bit more, grinding her hips to meet her fingers.

Her position was unsustainable, so she stood back on two legs and turned her back to the mirror, then flopped down and looked through her legs. The reflection of her own cunt was there right in her face. It was irresistible. She wormed a finger inside herself, pushed it right in the wet part. Louise fucked herself with three fingers; I was surprised that that was enough, but she knew exactly where to touch herself, the speed and pressure that was needed and she worked her pussy with sharp little flicks.

As I watched, my own fingers curled inside and worked away at my clit. I was so caught up in what Louise was doing that it almost seemed as though we were the same person.

She was getting worked up. Her breath condensed then evaporated off the mirror. She licked her reflection as though she was kissing herself. Louise dragged herself across the mirror, her tits stuck to it. She stood to face the glass and humped herself; it was like she was trying to break on through to the other side, to pop out of the glass and find herself in Wonderland. I don't know when she came. It was modest; it had to be, compared to the build up; it was like clearing your throat and then it had gone.

I pulled my fingers out of my pants because I didn't want her to see that I had been jerking off to her. I don't know why, maybe it felt too intrusive.

Louise came and flopped next to me. We smoked a couple of fags, or at least I did, she just let hers burn down until there was nothing but a flaking column of ash where paper and tobacco once existed. The ashtray on the table was full of the ghosts of cigarettes, all burned down without being smoked.

We watched television with the sound off. Some woodworking programme – yes, really! We made a bizarre sight.

Louise fished around and found another capsule which she twisted open and emptied on a smooth glass tile. She set it out into two lines.

"Want some?" she offered.

"Yeah, okay," I replied and took a hit. "What is this?" I asked.

"New German tranquillisers that Bobby gave me last night at Girlina's."

"Who's Bobby?"

"You know her; everyone does."

"No, I don't."

"She's fantastic."

"Who is she?"

"She's gorgeous."

"Louise." Something had caught my eye, a sobering sight.

"What?'

"I think you should go to the bathroom."

"What's the matter?"

"Um." I didn't know how to tell her without freaking her out.

"What?"

"Your nose is bleeding."

"So?" This was not the response I had anticipated.

"Well," I tried to be tactful, "there're clots. Quite a few of them. Big ones."

"Oh, not again," she replied, as though I had told her the punchline to a corny joke. "Fuck this," she added, and wiped away the blood with the back of her hand as best she could. She lit another fag and zoned out. The guy on the telly was staining a piece of pine.

I watched TV and dozed on sofa for a couple of hours, then I went home. Louise paid for a cab, I was in no state to walk or catch a bus.

"Fuck fuck fuck fuck fuck fuck fuck." My legs gave way and my temples throbbed.

The letter was generated by a computer; it was written in capitals and you could see where my name and details had been inserted.

"DEAR REF: NB362586Z

THE EMPLOYMENT SERVICE HAS PAID YOU A TOTAL OF £2567.39 JOBFINDER'S BENEFIT IN THE LAST 11 MONTHS.

BECAUSE YOU DID NOT ATTEND THE MANDATORY JOBQUEST™ JOB FOR LIFE WORKSHOP, YOUR BENEFIT HAS NOW BEEN CANCELLED.

NO APPEALS CAN BE MADE ON THIS DECISION. PLEASE CONTACT YOUR EMPLOYMENT SERVICE REPRESENTATIVE FOR MORE INFORMATION."

At the bottom of the page there were some italics: "*The East London Employment Franchise has helped 18766 jobfinders back to work in the past 23 months. Why don't you drop by to find out how we can help you?*"

That fucking stupid waste-of-time course. I knew there were going to be repercussions from that cunt who threw me out.

No dole meant no money. I had no savings, no rich relatives, nothing except for rent to pay in two days.

I threw up and then I marched to the Benefit offices.

"I did go on that course," I shouted at the Jobcentre guy, "you can't cut off my money like this."

He went away to confer with his supervisor. I could see them looking over at me and then looking at the letter.

"I'm sorry, there's nothing I can do. You can make another claim for the money in six months' time, but our records state very clearly that non-compliance will result in the cancellation of your Benefit."

Crying didn't help; they merely ignored me. They didn't even bring in the heavies to drag me away kicking and screaming. Some of the other claimants laughed at me. In the end I just left.

I called Suzanne. She was out.

I called Louise. She said: "I can't help you, babe, I'm skint myself. Why don't you get a job?"

"Oh yes, I'm very employable," I snapped back.

"Look, don't panic. I'll ask around and I'm sure something will come up." She added: "Put yourself out there."

I went home to bed dreaming of lottery wins, glamorous and highly paid media jobs, and generous benefactors."

Orla rang. "I heard that you're looking for work," she said. "My friend may be able to help you."

Orla's friend Milla was more of a distant shag. Putting it bluntly, Milla was a pimp but, in Milla's own words, she was "Director and Founder of an exciting new addition to the lesbian community".

Angelz was not the original lesbian escort agency; it was one of a handful of imitators who popped up when they saw that there was good money to be made out of whoring to non-scene dykes, or to men who wanted to give their wives a spicy little birthday surprise.

These days I would probably be a lot more squeamish about the prospect of becoming a hooker, with or without the "we're doing it for the community" spiel. But back then I was desperate for cash and I thought that being paid for having sex would be a bearable way of acquiring rent money, plus maybe a little bit more.

I met up with Milla at the Funhouse, her nickname for the Angelz headquarters. The Funhouse was a 1960s office block that had been converted into luxury apartments. Milla had two flats which were connected by a door. Six rooms were tastefully decorated with beds, mirrors and low wattage lightbulbs, the seventh was a sitting room and changing area and the eighth was her private office. The whole place smelled of air freshener.

Milla wore a lot of black. She had an expensive-looking watch and a light tan.

"Why do you want to be an Angel?" she asked.

"I'd like to give something back to the community."

She smiled and told me to stop the shit.

"I like sex and I need money," I answered truthfully.

"Okay, do you have any specialisations?"

"I'm good at fisting, I like to bottom, but the main thing is that I'm open minded, so anything goes really."

"How about men?"

"How about them?"

"I'll be blunt," she said, "would you fuck them?"

"Yes."

"Are you happy about dressing up? Some of our clients specifically ask for feminine women."

"Yes, that's fine."

"Would you wear a wig? Can you be butch? Can you switch?"

"Yes to all of these."

"What is your stage name?"

"Ramona is fine; I prefer to keep it real."

"Do you have or have you ever had herpes, hepatitis, or any sexually transmitted disease?"

"No."

"Have you ever tested for HIV?

"Yes."

"Are you positive?"

"No."

"Are you a recreational drug user?"

"No." She knew I was lying about that one.

"That was all off the record,' she said. "What I should say officially, and this is what you must say to anyone who asks is: you are hired through me as an escort, but you are free to make your own arrangements if the client is interested in alternative services."

Milla said that she had to go and pick up her kids from school. She told me, "Your shift starts tomorrow at four and ends at two. We supply gloves and lube, and there are a few outfits knocking around. I'll ask Lea to look after you."

Lea welcomed me with a hug the next day and I was grateful for her kindness. She wasted no time in showing me around. "Basically, you wait in the living room for dates. They can last anything from an hour to an evening, although sadly that's rare because you can make some good money when that happens. Do you know about safe sex?" I nodded. "We always use gloves and barriers. No fluid exchange, that includes kissing. Try and keep yourself healthy too; this job wears you down."

Lea gave me some tips on how to get rid of people quickly, saying, "All the girls will back you up if you say an hour has gone and it's only been 40 minutes." She told me to take the money first every time, and to talk through what was going to happen beforehand.

Yeah, whatever, I thought.

"We tell them that there's a sliding scale too, so that they think they're not being ripped off," she added.

"What about ones that just want to talk?" I asked, naively.

"Everybody wants to do something." She continued: "there's a panic button by the light switch, don't be afraid to use it if you want help, and don't do anything you don't want to do. It's just not worth it."

Lea mentioned one last thing: "Milk the fact that you're a new girl because the novelty won't last long."

"How come you're here?" I asked Lea.

"Don't ask," she said, "it'll break your heart."

I sat around for three days before I got a "date". No one was interested in me, despite my newness I was not girly enough for most of the punters. I read a couple of novels, gabbed with the others, painted my nails and bleached my hair. The "no drugs" rule seemed a little harsh and made the shift drag.

Lea said, "Last month one of the girls got sacked for smoking dope out by the fire exit, so we don't chance it. Milla never tests anyone, though. All she wants is for us to turn up on time, so you can do what you like when you're not here."

Two hours into my fourth shift, a woman wheeled out of the lift and rang the Funhouse bell. Marie had a lot of things going for her, but I should mention the boring bits first so that you understand the scene a bit better. She had two stumps where most people have legs and her spine was very crooked; she seemed always to be twisting round to look behind her. Marie was also one of Lea's regulars.

Today Lea asked her, "Do you mind if Ramona joins in?" It was more of an order than a question. "It won't cost you any more."

"Okay," she replied, looking me over.

"Ramona's a new girl," said Lea, nudging Marie's arm, "shall we be gentle with her?"

"Heh heh!" came the dirty laugh response.

Marie wheeled herself into one of the bedrooms and lifted herself on to the bed. We helped her undress and propped her up with pillows. She behaved as though she was used to being naked and handled. She lifted herself up when it was appropriate, and made herself floppy and compliant. She was heavier than I imagined, kind of podgy and doughy. It was weird seeing her pubic and armpit hair; I expected her to be more like a kid. Marie's back was beautiful where her bones curved; she looked like a fossil that had been worn smooth by the elements.

"You're a good-looking woman," I said, the words just popped out of my mouth. Lea stared in disbelief. Later I would say that I meant it, that it was true, but in the meantime Marie thanked me with a saucy wink. I guess she often got such compliments.

"Marie doesn't say much but she loves to fuck," announced Lea. "Have you ever had a threesome?" she asked. I shrugged because I thought she was talking to me.

Marie shook her head.

"Well, perhaps you could fuck us both today," Lea continued, "does that sound good?" Yes, it did.

"Do you want to be fucked?" I asked Marie.

"No thanks."

"Or eaten out? Or teased?"

"No," she replied, "I just want to fuck."

Lea interrupted, "Shall we start? How do you want us to start, Marie? Shall I play with Ramona's tits?"

"Yeah!" came the enthusiastic response.

We undressed each other in a sexy way. That is, we did a lot of display type manoeuvres, like a magician's glamorous helper removing knives from a trick box. Then all three of us put on gloves.

Lea and I sat close to Marie and stroked each other's tits. Lea had a great pair, big and round. I felt Marie's hand on my leg; she was feeling me up, tickling my pubes with her fingers, but she never took her eyes off Lea and I as we tried to get in the mood.

Marie stroked the outside of my slit; it was all tucked up, dry, waiting for someone to break the seal, open it out, let it bloom. She had a delicate touch; it was mesmerising. I straddled her and Lea sat behind me. I let Marie get a good look at me whilst Lea continued to work on my tits, her hands rubbed up and down my belly, and then crept between my legs to hold my cunt open.

Marie lubed up her hand and pushed her thumb into me. Then she pulled it out and marked my belly with an invisible wet cross, like a kiss. I inched closer to her.

"You're the good-looking one now," said Marie, and I reciprocated with a cross between her breasts.

She was inside me again and I rocked on her hand. She was good, I felt her fingers pushing high, fucking my cervix, filling me up, but I was too nervous to come, it was all too new for me to let go.

Lea understood and changed the pace. She said: "Ramona's so greedy – let me have a go."

I got behind Marie and held her between my legs, I wanted to get closer to her spine.

"Can I touch it?" I asked, afraid that it would be painful for her.

"Yes," she said, "scratch me please, I like that."

Lea looked really hot – she was kind of undulating on Marie's hand, going, "Oh baby, that's good, fuck me harder, fuck me more." Marie's breath was heavy and concentrated. Lea said that she was going to come, but she could have been faking.

"Fuck me some more," I whispered to Marie.

"I can't," she replied.

"You've got two hands, haven't you?"

Lea knelt whilst I crouched over our client. Marie's hands were wet with our pussy juice. She fucked us with the same actions – it was a peculiar sensation watching someone else being fucked and knowing that they were feeling the same thing as you. We held hands across Marie, who looked blissful beneath us. Her arms were strong and supple as she pumped her fists into us. It was a lovely moment.

Lea mouthed "Come now," at me, like a secret signal, and we both started in with the familiar grunts and sighs, and part of mine was real, and none of it really mattered because Marie was there beneath us looking like a studly motherfucker, totally satisfied with herself.

I don't know who Marie spoke to, but I started to get more dates after that afternoon. Lea soon found that she didn't need to hold my hand; I was more than capable of taking care of business myself. Most of my tricks wanted me to do them. They'd get me to tell them how sexy they were and how much I wanted to fuck them. I was a right slick shit, and I got even better at lying. My work was no big deal to me, the sex was not challenging and I liked getting paid in cash at the end of a shift. When I wasn't working, I hung out at home and got stoned.

Two weeks into the job and I did my first couple. Milla lined them up for me, saying, "None of the others will do it with a man around." I didn't care, in fact I charged him extra for the pleasure of letting me fuck his frumpy wife.

He wanted us to "be lesbians" for him, although neither of us knew what he meant by that. I couldn't believe he'd ever met any real dykes, and I wondered how he knew what "being a lesbian" meant.

The wife looked at me, waiting for my lead. I was tempted to double-bluff her to see what she thought lesbians did, but I decided against it because we only had a short hour and I didn't want to get into anything too bizarre.

I started with a "Come and sit on my face honey, I'll sort you out," and ended up fucking her arse rigourously with a strap-on.

By the time they were out the door, she had already booked two more sessions with me – without the loser husband.

Emboldened with new dyke confidence, she also invited me to a swingers' party, but I had to turn her down; there was only so much tragic sex I could have without being paid.

Suzanne told me that she couldn't cope with seeing me. She said that I was turning into a monster. When I thought I was looking good, Suzanne told me that I was rapidly transforming into a skinny sack of shit – she didn't mince her words – and that I was looking like a skanky crack whore. Where I said that I was having the time of my life, she replied that me and my friends gave her the creeps. When I said that becoming a dyke had been the best thing that I'd ever done, she reminded me of the time that I sat with an old guy who had been run over until the ambulance came, and at least five occasions when I had made her laugh so much she had peed her pants.

"People change," I said, "you can't live in the past and expect everything to stand still for you."

Suzanne replied, "It's what you're changing into that I'm not happy about."

I didn't tell Suzanne about my new job; I didn't think she'd be able to handle it. She knew something was going on, and she knew even better not to ask about it.

She told me, "You're losing me, Ramona, and I think you don't even care." I made a mental note not to call on her for a while, to let her slip away from me quietly, and that maybe she wouldn't even notice that I had gone.

I thought I would be fine without Suzanne and that I had plenty of friends, but that was before Maxine opened her trap and they all started dropping me.

Orla was first to spill the beans. She rushed up to me with, "Is it true?"

"Hi Orla, nice to see you too," I sneered back.

"I knew it," she said.

I had to shut her up. "I don't understand you," I said slowly, "please speak more clearly."

"Maxine's been talking about you; she's told everyone what you did."

"What did I do?" I answered smugly.

"She said you fucked her over."

"She's a liar. Her maid served me food and then Maxine got off. She's just pissed off that I didn't want to fuck her."

Orla's eyes were big. "You didn't want to fuck Maxine?"

"Nope."

"But she's loaded."

"I know."

Orla shut up for a moment, then she said, "I'm just going to get some fags; I'll see you later."

"Laters," I echoed.

I had the lurgie.

I would approach people and they would shrink away, afraid of becoming infected by whatever it was that I carried.

At first I thought the lurgie was a joke. I expected my gang to come back and resume the discussion about where we were going to go that night, who was shagging who, who looked good, who was out of town at their parents. But it never happened.

I stopped getting calls.

I went out, nevertheless, but was met more often than not with indifference. Nobody flirted or chatted with me; I was the one fighting to get attention. People looked shifty, embarrassed to be seen with me. I knew that look, I wasn't stupid.

Jackie – remember her? – was hanging around with that crowd too, and she resumed her practice of ignoring me whenever I was in danger of showing her some recognition or friendliness.

I heard that Orla was having a party and assumed that I was invited, although nobody offered me the customary lift, no one rang to see if I had set off yet, to find out what I was wearing or to ask if I had any drugs. I knew something was going on, but the full impact eluded me, like a half-remembered smell.

A-Dykes never went anywhere by themselves, but there I was, ringing Orla's doorbell, waiting to be let into her home, standing on her doormat like every other time I had been there.

There was sound inside, I know that. There was music. I could see shadows under the door, feet approaching the entrance, tip-toeing up to the spy hole. I heard someone hold their breath, as though that would disguise the presence behind the door. From the corner of my eye, I saw a blind twitch from the corner of my eye, and someone knock the windowpane clumsily with their elbow as they tried to hide from me. I heard someone go "Shhh!" I did not hear or see somebody at that party, maybe even Louise, mouth "It's Ramona! Don't let her in!" but I certainly imagined it.

And they would have seen me turning round and walking away, back to my house where I held a party of my own, with myself as the only guest.

No one believed my side of the story, of course. Ramona stole Maxine's stash; Ramona couldn't get it up; Ramona is a fucking bitch, don't go near her. I heard it all from one source or another. It was quite a smack in the face how little anyone listened to me. I wasn't the golden girl any more.

I overheard Becky badmouthing me. I caught the tail end of, "Everyone knows Ramona's a thieving cow, I bet she'd be the first to rip off Maxine."

"We only had one date, and that was a waste of time. I didn't get a chance to rip her off." Everyone ignored me when I interrupted.

Only Becky answered: "That's not what Maxine's saying. She told me that you've been trying to turn her friends against her."

If only I had, I thought, and cursed at all the bitching opportunities I had left unexploited.

"She said you're ruining her businesses by hanging around and stalking her."

Becky said that Orla said that Maxine said that everybody said that I was a bitch.

"You've fucked up," she said.

"Fuck off, you little runt," I answered, and that was that.

I saw Maxine at Girlina's, buying everyone champagne cocktails. It was a new "everyone". It was funny how the scene had such a high turnover of faces.

Maxine had her arm around Louise. Lou looked like shit, she could barely focus or stand, but Maxine didn't care; she'd shove her tongue down her throat at any opportunity. I secretly hoped that she'd hit Louise's gag reflex and end up with a face full of junkie-dyke vomit.

Louise went to sit down for a rest.

"Hey Lou," I said, "how's it going?"

Her head swung around like a puppet with a string for a neck.

"Are you there?" I snapped my fingers in front of her eyes.

"Hi Ramona!" she smiled, and I warmed. She punched my arm gently and affectionately. "Shall we have a line?"

"Okay baby," I replied.

I helped her up and supported her to the bogs. She had the gear, but she couldn't get it together to chop it out. Her hands were all over the place, shaking and grabbing at things that weren't really there in order to support herself. I took over, scared she was going to knock it over and waste it all. She had no trouble hoovering it up, though.

Louise needed help sitting down afterwards, so I propped her against a wall and tucked up her legs so that she would be comfy. She waved me goodbye as I re-entered the main room.

I crept up behind my nemesis and made her jump. "What's the matter with you?" I demanded, "What are you trying to do?"

"Who are you?" Maxine laughed.

"You know who I am." I added, "Why have you been bitching about me to my friends?"

"Your friends?" She looked around me. "I don't see any friends."

"Very fucking funny, you pathetic bitch," I spat. "You are nothing."

"No," said Maxine, "you are nothing."

"Just wait until next year, sister," I sneered, "or even next month, you tired old fuck." I said the words slowly and watched her flinch.

We stared each other out until some lumbering butch came to break us up. "What's the matter, baby?" she said to Maxine, "Is she hassling you?"

"Yes," she pouted and pointed at me, "this is that woman who's been stalking me."

The lunkhead turned to me, wanting a fight.

"Dream on Maxine," I shouted over to her, but she had already turned away.

I was gone.

I guess you want to know what happened to Louise. Me too. All I know is that she changed her locks and moved house. I tried to find her, but I didn't even know her surname. Even now I would still like to see her. I called, but got her answering service every time. It was creepy the way that she just disappeared. I threw away her Buitt. It was really very disturbing.

What do you do when you suddenly find yourself without friends? It's true that I wasn't completely alone, although the rhythm had changed somewhat between me and Suzanne, me and Alex. I doubted Molex would ever want to see me again, or at least I knew it would be too much for me to see her, knowing that she didn't want me any more.

I stayed far away from Bar Barella, Girlina's, the Nås Bar and Hackney in general; I didn't want to know the gossip about me.

I went where nobody knew me, and I liked it like that.

I worked.

I drank.

I slept.

I spent my money on snortables.

I grew my hair.

I bought skin creams for the dark rings under my eyes.

Sometimes I fucked my clients for free.

I felt numb, like I was waiting in the cold for something to happen.

I thought I was doing just fine until some drunk guy in the street said, "Hello, are you a lesbian?" and before I knew it I had him up against the wall by his throat and was hissing in his face.

The poor guy just wanted to know. Maybe he'd never met a lez before, maybe he was gay himself. The fear in his face stayed with me for a long time. I was thoroughly ashamed of myself.

My birthday came and went, I stayed in and watched TV by myself and stared at the lone card Suzanne had sent me.

I knew I was the stupidest, ugliest, meanest, most pathetic and lonely fuck-up in the world.

I tried to buy myself some friendship, I didn't want Suzanne to see me like this, I didn't want to admit that she had been right all along.

Whenever we heard about a new bust or a raid, or read about some poor woman getting beaten up, or worse, many of my colleagues at Angelz would thank their lucky stars that they weren't working on the streets. The streets were where only the most desperate women would go to find work, and we escorts at Angelz liked to think that we were far above that sort of thing. Sometimes we'd see them when we were out to buy some fags and we'd pity them and wish they had the sense to get out of there. The streets were the dumping ground for hookers nobody else would touch, so it seemed right that the streets were where I should go to find someone.

I had a night off so I went to Paddington, a part of London where I was certain that nobody knew me or my business. I walked a circuit around a block near the railway station and saw three hookers waiting for some action. The first looked alright, a bit like Suzanne's mum but younger and more fashionable.

"Are you looking for business, love?" I asked, despite my own line of business it felt outrageous to say such a thing – women just don't.

"Pervert!" she seethed back at me, adding "Dyke!" for good measure.

The second looked prepubescent from behind and considerably older from in front, no way did I want to touch her.

In true Goldilocks fashion, I settled for the last. She was a big tall skinny woman in tight pants and a fur jacket, real, not fake. She had big wiggy hair and a jelly-mould silicone tit job.

"How much?"

"Whatever you can afford," she replied.

We worked out a price and I gave her the money.

There was a door behind her, next to the chippy. She rang the bell three times and pushed it open when a buzzer rang. We went up some dimly lit stairs and into a small room with a bed, one of several on that landing.

"You have to wash." She pointed at a sink in the corner of the room.

I thought that it should have been me asking for her to wash. She threw me a look and I washed without complaint.

"Okay," she was businesslike, "what do you want?

"I want you to call me 'boss' and to beg me to fuck you."

"Fuck off," she said, "you're fucked."

"I can pay extra," I said.

"I don't do head-games."

"I need a friend." I thought that might explain it.

"You won't find one here." She looked at me. "What do you want, you want to get fucked?"

"Yeah, I guess."

She immediately turned mumsy. "Let's get your clothes off." I took off my trousers and underwear, but kept the rest on.

She said, "I don't get many dykes," as I crawled on to the bed and lay down.

"I bet," was all I could think of to say in return.

"Would you pass me a condom and that lube please?" I did.

I watched her pull down her pants and pull out a big stiff dick. It looked fake at first, but it turned out to be the real thing. She pulled at it to make it harder and then rolled a condom down it.

"Oh shit!" It came out before I had time to think.

"Fuck! Shit! Not another one!" She stamped her foot. "Don't tell me you didn't know! Don't fuck me around!"

I shrugged.

"You're fucking wasting my time," she barked, "you can't have your money back."

"I don't care, I'm sorry." I was so embarrassed, how could I not have known? I apologised. "One day we'll laugh about this," I offered.

"Ha. Ha. Ha," came the robotic reply. She calmed a little. "Do you want a fuck or not? You paid for it; you can have it if you want."

I felt bad. "Okay," I said, "let's have a go."

"Fuck you man, I've lost it, I've got to get it hard again," she said, yanking off the condom and throwing it on to the floor.

She shut her eyes and breathed in deeply, touching herself on her forehead, her heart and then her dick. She cradled her balls in one hand and jerked at herself with the other. She was muttering something but I couldn't tell what it was.

She caught me watching.

"Is this what you want, baby?" she asked me aggressively, "is this what you like? A bit of both, yes?"

She was scaring me, but I liked it.

"You want to touch me with your dirty dyke hands? I know where they've been."

I smiled, not knowing whether or not she was making a joke. "I'm paying you," I said, "remember that."

She ignored me and started ranting, "I know you girly girls; I know what you want. I know that you want to open your legs for some fine cock like this," she said, stroking her dick all the while.

"I've always loved cocks, I'm not ashamed," I said. Hers looked particularly tasty.

"Now you tell me that you want the privilege of fucking my fine cock." Oh Christ, she wanted me to beg her – fuck that.

"I would like to fuck you."

She put on a latex glove and smothered it with lube. "I need to see if you're ready."

I was ready. I was tingling with desire for this woman, despite the huff that she was in. She was big and broad; I got wet at the idea of her holding me down whilst she fucked me.

"Open your legs for me," she said. My legs were already open, I whined. "Open them wider." I did so. "That's not enough, I want them spread wide open for me." I spread open my legs as much as I could, the tendons and muscles in my thighs and calves felt electrified from the stretch.

She crawled over me on her knees and one hand, the other hand was holding her dick, stroking it to stay hard. Then she inserted one lubed finger into me. I was wet and slick, swollen.

She lined up her dick at the mouth of my vagina and said, "I'm going to fuck you now." My cheeks were flushed as she kind of collapsed into me. That first thrust, that first feeling of being full – well, it made me groan with pleasure.

I had forgotten how good a real cock feels, hot and human. Her face was next to mine, but she did not kiss me; this was all about the fuck, the weight of her pulling out and then ramming herself into me again. A dyke and a tranny, this was not like any missionary position I had ever seen in a sex education book.

"Hold me down," I asked.

She grabbed my smaller hands in one big grip and held them above my head. I wanted to remember it all, the veins of her cock through the condom against the walls of my cunt, her belly on mine, her tits pressing into me, her breath, the friction. My legs were trembling; she was fucking me fast and heaving the breath out of me with her weight.

"I wanna come, let me come." It came out urgently.

She held her hand against my clit. She must have been able to feel her cock sliding in and out of me, and that thought turned me on. I was pinned down and filled with pleasure. I needed to catch my breath and come, but I was out of puff and my orgasm was as elusive as a butterfly.

"Oh God, I want to come," I gasped, "oh fuck, oh fuck."

She whispered, "Dirty, slit fucker, pussy gobbler, gash hole," in my ear, "I hope you like what you paid for." Her words sounded like the filthiest, sexiest things I had ever heard and they pushed my orgasm into my reach, and I grabbed it, and I shook like a lily underneath that woman, pinned to the bed by her cock. She banged me twice more and then pulled out and jumped off the bed to wash her genitals in the sink. I lay stunned, trying to make sense of the sudden absence.

She clapped her hands in my face. "Okay lady, time to go." I put on my clothes and shoes.

"Come on," she pulled me off the bed and hustled me out of the door, "it's time to go."

I was out on the street and she was back on her corner again in no time, both of us feeling lonelier than ever.

Life carried on as before.

As I walked home from work after a late shift one evening, I got the feeling that I was being followed. At first I brushed off my uneasiness as drug paranoia, in recent times I'd had to fight the feeling that strangers were laughing at me from behind trees and pillarboxes on more than one comedown, and I just assumed that this was more of the same.

The feeling persisted, so I stopped and scanned the road behind me. Shit, I thought, wondering if tonight was going to be the night I got queerbashed. I heard giggling.

"What is that?" I said out into the night.

The giggling was familiar.

I threw my head back and yelled "IRIS!" with all my girl-might and with all the gusto left in my lungs.

A small dark shape jumped out from behind a bus shelter and pelted towards me. I didn't move out of the way. Iris, yes it was her, locked her hands round my neck and swung herself around me like a naughty monkey.

"Ramona! Hiya baby!"

"You're a bad one!" I laughed with relief. "You had me going."

"I know!" she replied, boasting, "the cleverness of me!"

Her joyousness was infectious and I said "It's great to see you." Usually people don't mean it, but tonight I was genuine.

Iris looked coy, she said, "I've got a little surprise for you."

I shut my eyes and held out my hands wide in anticipation.

"Not that," she elbowed me, "it's a place."

"Is it far?"

"No," she said, "just up the road."

It felt so good to be remembered by someone, even if their grip on reality was tenuous. I slipped my hand into hers and she held on tightly. It was very late and the streets were very empty. It was so romantic that I fizzed with excitement and I wanted to kiss and hug and tickle Iris with gratitude.

We walked for five minutes until we came to the municipal baths. The building was tiled in Victorian red terracotta. There were old entrances for men and women, which had now been consolidated into one. A figure of a woman was imprinted above an arch; she wore a shield that read "Progress with the People".

"They're closed," I said.

"I know."

"Where are we going?" Suddenly I lost my trust in Iris and started to think of my own safety.

"Come with me," she said and we walked to the back of the building, which was drab plain brick in contrast to the flamboyance of its façade.

Iris stood above a basement grating and an open window. I knew what she was thinking. "Iris!" I stage-whispered, "you can't go in there!" It was too late; she was strong enough to lift the grating and small enough to crawl through the window.

She unhooked a latch and opened a larger window for me. If I was hesitant, I showed nothing and instead I hoisted myself through the gap and into the warmth.

The room was painted an institutional yellow and, like the rest of the building, was lit with emergency lights. In the centre of the space was a large drum with pipes coming out of it and big riveted sheets of metal. I saw a handful of gauges with quivering needles ready to encroach on the red.

I followed Iris through a couple of doors, up some steps and along a corridor. We were silent as mice.

I pushed open a final door and we were there standing at the side of the pool.

A still pool is a thing of beauty that the rich only ever get to appreciate. Proles have to make do with splashing kids and lane nazis churning up and down as though they are the ones who own the water.

The pool surface looked like dark blue glass in the dim light. It was rich with potential, so ready for action that the slightest movement would show in its face. I was afraid to breathe.

"Surprise!" she whispered.

Iris saw my trepidation.

"It's okay," she reassured me, "there's no one about. I checked the timetables. It's deserted at night and their alarm system is on the blink too."

I could not take in the loveliness of her gesture, but she didn't care.

"Shall we take a dip?" she asked saucily.

It took less than two seconds to take off my clothes. We slid into the pool together, cold water creeping up my belly and making my nipples stand out.

We tried to make small unobtrusive movements so that the water would stay flat and still with us, but we could not stop the ripples spreading out around our bodies.

The moon shone through a skylight, reflected off the surface and created a solid-looking bar of light beneath the water.

We held hands and waded out to the deep end, like Virginia Woolfs with pockets full of stones, only instead of sinking we took off into the water, floating and gliding as though we were flying. We were luminous, radiant. I dived to the bottom and opened my eyes, half expecting to see sunken treasure and oysters yielding pearls. Instead I saw my skin against the tiles, covered with thousands of tiny air bubbles that were trapped against the downy hair of my arms and legs.

Iris and I twisted around each other like exotic fish. Her hair streamed out behind her in a slick trail.

"This is like the best dream ever." I smiled shyly at my corniness. Iris took my head in her hands and drew me towards her. I twisted until I was floating on my back, then let her pull me gently through the water, her gentle hands around my throat. Liquid ran between my breasts and over my limbs. Every tightness within me became loose, every knot was undone. It was so peaceful. She made me feel loved. My quiet tears dripped away into the pool unnoticed.

Iris kissed me and I kissed her back. Iris held my breasts, my belly, my arse and I did those things to her. She slipped her hands between my legs and I felt myself disappearing; I could not look or feel or accept that someone would want to touch me like this. Whilst it was true that I fucked and occasionally got fucked by my clients at work, in real life my pussy had been locked away for some time.

"Come on." She motioned me closer and I knew what she wanted.

"You have to be gentle this time." I looked away, embarrassed by my neediness.

"Yes," she answered solemnly, and I believed her.

Iris bit my neck gently then pulled me under water to kiss me. Bubbles rose around us as we shared the same breath. I hadn't felt so frightened and ready for a woman since that day on the beach with Nicky.

As we surfaced I said simply, "Come on Iris, come in to me now." She slithered inside and made the inner and outer wetness fuse together.

Our bodies were simultaneously weighed down and made weightless by the water. She fucked me against the poolside so that I could lever myself against her hand and arm. The surface barely moved. Iris held my clit firmly against my pubic bone as she fucked me. I felt alive again and the relief was like being bathed in warm rain. Iris' hands were both comforting and thrilling; she fucked beautifully. I felt full and sexy and wanted and vibrant, like black and white turning into colour.

"Woo hoo," hollered Iris, "I'm going to make you mine, sister!"

"Woo hoo!" I echoed.

Our voices were big in the silence.

I raised my hands up above my head as elegantly as a ballet dancer. "Woo hoo!" I sang, "Woooo hoooo!" I brought them crashing down in the water, thrashing and splashing and coming like a marlin on a line, hot electricity going through me, air and blood and throb rushing around under my skin. "Woo hoo!"

I wanted to slink beneath the surface and breathe in the water, but Iris hoisted me up on to the edge of the pool. As I recovered, we sat dangling our legs, talking about nothing.

"Have you seen Molex lately?" I had to ask.

"Maybe," she replied.

"What do you mean maybe?"

"Maybe is maybe."

"Why doesn't she want to play with me any more?" I wasn't sure that I wanted to hear the answer.

"Why are you asking me?"

"Because you're her friend," I said. "Listen, if you see her, tell her I miss her."

"You hardly know her."

"I know her," I snapped.

"Ramona, look at me." I turned to look at Iris, but could barely hold her gaze.

"I'm trying to help you. Let her go, eh?"

We dressed in silence and crept out the same way as we had come in. One of my socks fell into the pool and was probably found floating in the shallow end by the puzzled lifeguard on the early shift the next morning.

Iris hugged me hard and then ran away down the road, leaving me there alone, my hair dripping.

I don't know if you've ever been lonely, but I was in the capital city of loneliness; I was experiencing the king boss of lonely. I was so lonely that my idiot A-Dyke pals did not want to know me, let alone anyone who actually, genuinely, really, honestly liked me.

I went back to the old places to try and find someone who knew me, who could see me.

I wanted to see Chrissie. I went to the bar in Hackney where she befriended me when I was a piece of raw chicken dyke. I waited for her by her stool. I had one drink, and then another. As the bar filled up, someone came and sat in Chrissie's place and I imagined how pissed-off my friend would be if she saw this major infraction of the rules. I had another drink. The woman left, and there was no sign of Chrissie.

I asked the barmaid, "Where is the woman who usually sits here?"

"I don't know," she said, "I'm new." She went to grab her colleague.

I repeated, "Where is the woman who usually sits here?"

"You mean Chrissie?" the colleague replied.

"Yeah."

"Didn't you know?" she said.

"What?"

"She got ill, she went home to her folks."

"What kind of ill?"

"I don't know."

"Where are they?"

"I don't know," she answered, as if it was stupid to assume that she would know. Chrissie had only sat in this place ordering drinks and chatting to strangers every day of her life, why should anyone know about her?

Loneliness chipped away at me.

There was a number in my book that I had not called for a long time.

"Hi Johnny."

"Who is this?"

"It's Ramona."

"Hey –" it was more like "Heeeeey!" "– Ramona! It's great to hear from you! How are you? What are you up to?"

"Oh," I said, flummoxed by the flood of questions, "this and that. Same as usual, really." I couldn't say "I'm dying of loneliness and you're the last person I could think of to call."

Johnny said, "Hey babe, do you want to come over?"

I felt like someone crawling through a desert who spots a mirage that turns out to be real. His invitation took me by surprise.

"Pardon?"

"Come on over; it would be great to see you." His enthusiasm was wonderful.

"I'd love that," I stammered.

By eight o'clock that night I had been and gone. Johnny's girl-friend answered the door with a tear-stained face.

"He can't see you," she said, "I'm sorry."

I stood there dumbly, not knowing what to say.

"For God's sake," I could hear Johnny in the background, "at least let her come in for a cup of tea."

The girlfriend left the door open and walked away. Johnny called me in. He gave me a funny little pat on the arm and then we stood awkwardly in his kitchen.

"This is silly," I said, "I should go."

"It's okay," he replied, "please stay."

"She's really upset. You need to sort this out."

Johnny bit his lip. He looked desperate and I couldn't believe that I had finally met a person for whom I felt pity.

"It's the sacrifices you make for the ones you love," he kind of sang, as though he had learnt the words by rote but didn't quite believe them enough to repeat without irony.

Bye bye, Johnny.

Instead of going home, I jumped a tube train heading to the West End. I was going to swallow my pride and call in at Hell. Nightclubs are no places for apologies, but I was sorry for having ignored the doorman that night when I was out with Nicky; it really haunted me. I wanted to go back and make it all better and make out that I'd never forgotten my Hellfriends.

But no one was going to welcome me back there, and it wasn't because they felt sore with me for deserting them. Hell, the dirtiest place in town, the rocking-est, sleaziest dump, had been refurbished as a theme pub, and there was a queue of city boys and their girlfriends waiting to get in.

I thought Hell would be there forever. I had no idea that things would change so quickly.

I was so alone that I began to think of shop staff as my friends. I was invisible to the world, dancing to records in my home; I was never noticed as I chopped myself a juicy fat line and turned on the television. I was so lonely that I stopped noticing that I was lonely and it became my normal state. I was lonely enough to think that work was life.

The lonelier I got, the seedier my tricks became.

It wasn't enough just to eat me out. One of my dates told me, "I crave the smell of pussy, I must have it, I need to breathe it, to feel it pulsing through me." Jesus, the drama was just too much! Not only that, but she wanted to go down on me whilst fucking herself up the arse with a manky old dildo. As if that wasn't enough, she wanted me to tell her how much I wanted her, how beautiful she was, how sexy, how turned on I was by the sight of her hand fiddling about with her arsehole. Of course I did.

It was strange how many of my tricks wanted me to tell them that they were beautiful. Sometimes it felt as though I were performing a public service, telling these women that they were beautiful so that they could feel confident enough to go out into the world and take their place between the legs of someone equally insecure. I liked it though, even with the horrors that turned up to ask for me; I liked giving my clients a little bit of something good, lame though that sounds.

Iris' swimming pool seduction had reawakened something in me too, I realised one night as I was jerking off to something trashy.

"I want someone else's hand instead of my own." The words formed like a visual trail in my mind and then disappeared like smoke.

The most obvious analogy I can think of is that my cunt felt like a rusty old machine in need of some oil. The sex I was having at work was enough to put me off genital pleasure for a long time. I masturbated infrequently, disinterestedly and awkwardly. My snatch seemed to belong to somebody else. My fantasies dried up and became predictable. I was too afraid to go out and meet new people. I felt cut off and adrift.

I needed some human contact, something real, so I went out to find some for the first time in what seemed like forever.

I read in the paper that Chicklets was the new girl club that was sweeping the scene clean. Everyone went there and, if I was going to pull, it seemed like the logical place to go.

I was nervous about being seen out on the town or, more truthful, scared about who might see me. The whole A-Dyke thing didn't seem so far away and I was sure that Chicklets would attract them like flies around a cow's arse.

I needn't have worried, because when I turned up and took up my place at the bar there was no one I knew there. Whilst the clubs provide the same terrifying egos, overflowing toilets, overpriced beer, fights and flirtations year after year, it's the punters who change. Chicklets was populated mainly by women whose average age looked to be around seventeen, all fresh-faced, ready, keen. In comparison, I felt about a hundred years old.

Half an hour after entering that place I was ready to call it a night, because clearly none of these babes were going to give me a second glance. It was only then that I noticed one woman who looked a little closer to my demographic and, luckily for me, she was checking me out.

I wasted no time. "Do you want a drink?" I asked.

The woman seemed to light up at my question, which was flattering to me; I didn't think anybody in that place would ever welcome my attention.

She smiled benignly when I placed her beer in front of her. She looked alright, a bit dorky, but she had good clothes, a hairdo that looked like it got dyked-up at the weekends and flattened down again for work, and she was friendly and willing, which is all that really mattered to me at that point.

"*You're* thirsty!" I exclaimed when she drained her glass in one big gulp. I drank my drink in one swallow too, no point in being left out.

"Do you want another one?" I asked. "Maybe a short?"

She nodded.

I set up a round of tequilas, which we both drank in one go, leaving me with a welcome fire in my belly.

"You don't say much," I commented.

She smiled back at me, which was kind of cute.

I asked: "Do you come here often?" I knew I was becoming a cliché, but I didn't care. She smiled and shrugged in return, as though she knew what the game was.

"What's your name?" I ventured.

"Lisa."

I replied: "I'm –"

"Ramona," she interrupted, giggling to herself.

I was surprised. "Oh," I said, "do I know you?"

She shook her head. I shrugged.

We had another round of tequilas; she bought them this time. As soon as we put down our glasses, her face was in mine and she was snogging the life out of me. I know this sounds like the biggest boast in the world, an exaggerated story I'm telling to make myself look like the most irresistible woman ever, but it's true. Lisa literally leapt on me; it was as though she had been holding herself back, like she had wanted to get a mouthful of me for a very long time. She held my head as she kissed me forcefully and she moved close to me and pressed her breasts against mine. Of course I was thrilled, that one gesture made me feel like the horniest bitch in the room. People tutted and gasped as they pushed past us to get to the bar – we were making a scene, we were showing those kids a thing or two about hot dyke action!

I pulled away to get some air but Lisa kept hold of me. She kept kissing, so I melted back into it.

"Come with me," she said, leading me away to the toilets. The imaginary choir in my head was singing "Hurrah! Ramona's going to get a fuck! Hallelujah!"

To a soundtrack of jeers and complaints, we barged to the head of the queue and forced our way into one of the cubicles. As soon as we were in there I braced myself against the door, blocking anyone else's access, there was nothing anyone could do about it.

Lisa's access was not blocked. Her fingers were immediately up inside me. It was so sudden, but it was fabulous and I loved the idea that someone could desire me so strongly. I held her close to me and ground against her hand. Her arm, her muscles pumping, her fingers fucking me – all were relentless. She was strong – the force of her thrusts made me jerk against the cubicle door and it made the toilet shake; it made *me* shake too.

She put her fingers against my clit and that was enough to get me off. My knees buckled but she supported me as I came with big gaspy groans. I heard some sarcastic applause from outside the toilet.

Lisa looked like one proud fucker, despite being out of breath and sporting comedy mussed-up hair. I went to rearrange my clothes and get out of there, but she made a move to show that she wasn't finished.

Shit, I thought, I have to sort her out too.

I put my hand up Lisa's shirt to feel her tits, but she pulled me away and, smiling, pushed her fingers into my cunt again.

"You stud," I smirked, and eased back on to her hand. She was a little rough but I didn't mind, the contrast between the hardness of her knuckles and the tenderness of my recently orgasmed cunt was intense and delicious as she worked me over. Her fingers probed inside for my G-spot. She pummelled it, releasing all the tension in my body and making me come again.

I was out of breath, my cunt was on fire, my legs unsteady. I needed to sit down.

Lisa's fingers remained inside. I tried to hop off her hand, but she stayed with me, still.

There was a strange atmosphere.

"Wow," I said, trying to diffuse the scene. I thought that Lisa was just shagged out, like me.

"Wow," she mouthed back at me. Her fingers twitched and she was forming her hand into a ball, which she then pushed up to fuck me again. She was fisting me, pushing it in and building up some speed again. I wanted to go with it – I was afraid of saying no, I don't know why. But it was too intense for me; I was too tired. And it was too hard, because I wanted gentleness. I collapsed back against the door. I'd had enough and I didn't want any more, but Lisa continued fucking.

"Lisa..." I said. She took no notice. "Lisa, no!" My voice came out much more loudly than I anticipated. I grabbed her wrist and pulled her fist out of me. It made a funny sucking sound, like a broken vacuum seal. Then, more gently, I added, "I've had enough, okay?"

Lisa looked crestfallen. I said it again for extra emphasis, "I'm sorry, that was great, but I've had enough now." She looked so sad. "Do you want me to fuck you?" I asked gently, not wanting to, but feeling obliged. I hoped she'd say no and, to my relief, she shook her head.

Lisa's voice cracked as she said, "Come home with me."

"No, thanks," I answered, trying to be tactful, "it was great, but I've had enough for now."

She perked up and said, "It was great?"

"Er, yeah," I lied, just a little white lie.

Lisa gushed, "Thanks! I can't believe it!"

Her response was really peculiar, but funny. "Are you shitting me?" I asked, bemused.

"You really thought it was great?" she asked. I didn't want to have this conversation. I had to get out of there, because I was starting to get very claustrophobic.

"Lisa, look, I'm going to go now," I said, "I'm going. Bye. See you."

She beamed in return. "Ramona, I'll see you! I'll definitely see you!"

My smile turned fake as I got out of there as fast as I could. "Fuck off, you loony cow," I laughed as I ran down the road.

And then I met Tina.

Tina worked part time at the newsagent where I bought my porn and sweets. She was 23, chubby and fresh. She wore T-shirts with names of bands on them through which I could see her small tits, which rested on her tummy when she sat down after serving a customer.

"You must have quite a collection," she remarked one day. I was buying a copy of *Slutty Housewives* and I didn't care who knew it.

"Not as much as one guy I know." I smiled politely, remembering Johnny.

"Can I be cheeky?" she asked.

"Sure," I said, "not that I could stop you."

"Are you busy on Friday night?"

I pictured myself snoring alone on my settee, my most likely Friday night activity. It was an unbearably lonely image. I was afraid of finding and fucking someone new. After all that I had been through I didn't want anyone to know me on that level, but I was so charmed by Tina, and heartened by the idea of a shag with someone cute, that I accepted her invitation. The promise of a real date seemed too good a lifeline to ignore.

On Thursday, I started bleeding. I stopped by the shop to postpone the date. "I feel ill," I said, "I'm on my period."

"Oh, poor baby!" said Tina, coming over to put her arms around me. "I'll look after you," she said. Those words felt like magic balm, turning my cunt to liquid. The date remained.

Tina lived in the flat above the shop. She opened the door to me and welcomed me into the living room, where her mum and dad sat watching snooker on the television.

She said: "This is my friend Ramona – we're going to sit in my room."

"Hi Ramona," said Tina's dad, "See you later!"

Tina made us a plate of toast: we sat on her bedroom floor and munched it with jam. I spilled crumbs down my top.

Around the walls were photographs of Tina hugging friends, laughing and gurning into the camera.

"Who are they?" I asked.

"Just my mates from college."

"What are you doing?"

"Business studies," she said. "Dad wants me to take over the shop when he retires."

I pointed out one of the recurring faces, "Is she your girlfriend?"

"No, she has a boyfriend."

"But you love her?"

"Yes," she said, "I do."

Tina changed the subject. "What do you do?"

"Don't ask." I smiled.

"No, really, what do you do?"

"Don't ask! I mean it."

There was a moment's silence whilst she sized me up, then Tina said, "I know what you do."

I couldn't reply. I was exposed. I felt naked and vulnerable.

"I should go." I struggled to stand up.

"No, please don't." Tina held on to the bottom of my jeans. "I'm sorry," she said, "I don't care about what you do. Let's just have a nice time; I think you're cool."

My panic evaporated and we finished off the toast in silence.

"Do you want to watch some telly?" Tina asked.

"Yeah, okay."

She switched on her portable and adjusted the aerial. We watched a talkshow hosted by a comedian. His guests were a model and a TV chef, both of whom were promoting new books. We took the piss out of them.

Tina's mum knocked on the door gently, which made me jump with fright.

"Can I come in?" she asked. "I've made you some tea and biccies." She plonked down the tray on the floor. I nodded a thank you. "Your father and I will be off to bed soon," she said to Tina, "so keep the noise down, okay?" Then she left, unobtrusively.

I can't begin to imagine how Tina's mum processed the sight of me sharing a cushion with their precious daughter. Even Suzanne, my best friend, had described me as a haggard-looking drug-addict bulldagger (I'm sure she would have added prostitute if she had known). Whatever Tina's mum thought, she said nothing. I wondered if this sort of thing happened all the time.

Tina looked at me and laughed. "I want to kiss you," she said and she did before I had the chance to agree.

She was a great kisser, and we snogged for ages as though we were 1950s American teens necking at the drive-in. I kept my eyes closed, enjoying feeling chaste for once. Tina had her hands on my tits over my clothes; she pounced on me, pushing me down to the floor beneath her, where she continued to squeeze and paw me like a hungry devil.

"How are your cramps?" she asked.

"They're okay," I said, "I feel okay."

"Do you want to fuck?"

"Pardon?" I spluttered.

She repeated, "Do you want to have sex with me?"

"What about the blood?"

"I don't care if you don't."

She could see that I didn't care as she pulled down my trousers and ripped off my pants.

Tina's mum knocked on the door and we froze. Tina put her hand across my mouth.

"Don't worry, girls," said Tina's mum from the other side of the door, "I won't disturb you. We're just off to bed now, night-night!"

"Goodnight!" we chorused.

"Nice to meet you, Ramona," said Tina's dad, "see you soon."

"Bye!" My voice came out weak and high, like a mouse's squeak.

We heard them shuffle down the hallway to their room, but stayed gripped with silence for at least two whole minutes after that.

Tina massaged my thighs, unaffected by how close we had been to discovery.

"What are you like?" I said incredulously.

She answered with a single word: "Dirty."

We got down to it. Tina looked great muscling over me; her hair hung in my face and she smelled of lemons. She pulled up my T-shirt and kissed my shoulders and collarbone. I was nervous, much more so than she, so I lay still and tried to concentrate on the pleasure. Tina tickled my pubic hair with the tips of her fingers.

"I'm going to pull it out," she said.

"Eh?" I was off to dreamland; I didn't understand her.

"I said that I'm going to pull it out. I'll be gentle."

She wrapped her fingers round the tammy string and gave it a tug. It felt as though she was pulling out a tooth.

"Ew!" Tina dangled the tampon in my face and I batted it away.

"I'll save it for later when I'm a bit peckish," she joked, wrapping it in a tissue and tossing it in the bin.

Reality jarred. I was disappointed; I thought the moment had been lost.

I grabbed Tina by her ankle and hauled her back towards me across the carpet. "You filthy girl," I scolded, "I might have to punish you for that infraction of the rules."

"Ooh, miss!" she squealed, though quietly so as not to disturb her parents.

I had her on her back and was tickling and poking and prodding her, watching her wriggle and squirm with pleasure. Then my digs and jabs became a bit more smooth and gentle and it wasn't long until she was helping me pull off her clothes so that I could suck on her soft breasts.

Blood and sex goo blobbed down my legs.

"You're so fucking wet!" she exclaimed.

"Whatcha gonna do about it?" I sang in reply.

"This is what I'm going to do." She held up her fingers to her face in a V-sign and poked her tongue through the gap; the gesture was obscene on her.

"Oh my God," was the only thing I could say – her boldness was breathtaking.

Tina did not hang around. She soon had her fingers inside and was pumping at me whilst I stretched and flexed to meet her.

The fucking was oddly grainy with the added blood, not smooth like lube or cunt sauce. I'm no earth mother, but it felt kind of elemental, like molten lava or placenta, to which my mild cramps added an extra layer of texture.

Tina fisted me and as she pulled out I could see the mark my blood made high up on her forearm. I wanted it to reach her shoulder; I wanted her to be right inside me; I was going to suck her in.

Tina's fist was small and determined. The more I tried to envelop her, the more she fucked. She leaned in to fuck me with the whole of her body adding heft and weight to her arm, which was squeezing up against my clit. Her tits were crushed against my hole and my blood got smeared all over them as she tried to get ever closer to me, ever deeper.

I came but I didn't care; it was no big deal. I was happy to be there with this cute girl covered in my blood. Tina felt me tense then relax.

"Was that good?" she asked.

"Mmm." I was blissed out.

She still had her fist in me, and I could sense her watching me through my closed eyelids. She closed in on my face and I felt her breath on my cheek. I was expecting a friendly peck, but she stuck out her tongue and licked me like a puppy. "I don't know why I did that," she said, "I just wanted to."

"It was lovely, do it if you feel like it."

She licked me more, and I licked her back, her skin was salty with sweat.

Tina pulled out her fist from my cunt, and I made a popping sound for a joke.

"Jesus," she said flatly. I looked up to see her squatting between my legs. She had blood all down her front, on her thighs, and up her arms. The more she tried to wipe it away, the more she spread it about.

"Fuck!" She laughed. "I look like a serial killer."

I reached down and rubbed both my hands against my pussy until they were red. Then I sat up and ran two fingers down each of Tina's cheeks, leaving blood stripes, like warpaint.

I said, "I've blooded you."

"What's that?"

"When dumb rich toff kids go foxhunting for the first time, they get their faces blooded with gore from the kill."

"How foul," said Tina, slapping my belly. She wiped goo and blood down me in a curvy line.

"Now I've blooded you too," she said, adding, "I want to see you again."

"No," I answered straight out.

"Why not?"

"Because you're too young."

"I'm not," she said, "I'm twenty-three."

"You're too young for me," I substantiated my previous remark.

"I wasn't too young for you just then."

"Fuck you!" She was a fucking smartarse.

Tina grinned; she knew she was right. "I won't be heavy," she said, "I just want a bit of fun."

"Okay," I capitulated, "but give it a couple of weeks, alright?" I hoped her post-fuck haze would have worn off by then.

"Okay." She smiled and kissed me on the cheek. "Shall I run us a bath? Do you want to stay over? Shall I make some more toast?"

"Yes, yes and yes."

I managed to avoid Tina for a couple of weeks. I started buying my supplies from another shop that was slightly further away. I walked a different route to work, and I kept my curtains closed, not that I'd told her where I lived, but you never could tell what anyone would do. I took on extra shifts at work to avoid being home, and I worked even more unsociable hours to avoid the chance of seeing Tina in the street. I did not stop once to consider why I was behaving like this – I just did it.

The inevitable happened. Late for work, I was forced to go past Tina's shop. She must have been eagle-eyed, because no sooner had I nipped past the doorway than she poked out her head and yelled "Ramona!" after me. My heart was racing and my mouth was dry. I carried on walking, hoping that I could pretend not to have heard her.

Tina came running after me, simultaneously apologising to her customers, calling for her dad and saying that she would be back in two seconds.

"Are you okay?" was the first thing she said, once she had caught up.

"What do you mean?"

"I haven't seen you since we shagged."

"So? We agreed to leave it a while."

"But it's been ages; you haven't even stopped by to say hello, or buy your mags," she said, "did I upset you?"

"No, don't be silly." I wasn't going to let her in.

"Well, what's up then?"

"I don't know – you tell me." I sounded petulant, but she didn't care or notice.

"I want to see you again," she said, "I like you."

I didn't know what to say.

She went on, "I wondered if maybe you'd like to come out with me, do something nice."

I stared at her.

"Would you like to come to the pictures with me? We could go and see something dumb and lightweight."

"I don't know."

"Sure you do," she said, nudging me and grinning. "Come on, it'll be good. We can go and get a pizza."

I thought of the rancid pizza boxes piled up in my flat and felt sick.

"No," I said, "I don't like pizza."

"Okay, well, just a film then."

"Okay." I don't know why I agreed; it came out small. I stood stiffly as Tina gave me a hug and a kiss.

"Shall we dress up?" she asked, "make it a bit special?"

I didn't answer.

Tina continued: "I have a dress at home that never gets an outing. It's so girly. I could wear that. Have you got any frocks? That would be fun, wouldn't it? We could get glammed up and stuff our chops on popcorn."

"Okay." It was the only word I knew.

"Do you want to come and call for me on Saturday? That is, if you're not working. I finish at six."

"Okay," I turned away from her and started hurrying, "I'm late, I have to go."

"Alright, Ramona," she laughed and called down the road after me, "hey, and don't be a stranger!"

I couldn't shake the panic all day; I couldn't concentrate. I had one punter that afternoon and managed to get rid of her within twenty minutes – a record for me. Milla said that I looked ill; she told me to go home.

I didn't know why Tina wanted me, because it didn't make sense. I wasn't like her – I was a skank. Maybe she just wanted a girlfriend, perhaps she was going to get me and cling to me like Nicky had done. Maybe she was playing me around for a joke, or to get back at her parents in some way.

I was afraid. I didn't want to go through with it; couldn't face letting anyone else in to see me only to shit on me. I could call it off, but then I'd have to see her and she'd probably be able to talk me out of it. I could tell her that I had to work, but she already knew that I was free that day. I could just not turn up, A-Dyke style, but then she'd hassle me afterwards, and I didn't want to hurt her.

I couldn't sleep Friday night, so I took an extra sleeping pill. Someone at work had given me a stash of them after she had squeezed a prescription for some stronger stuff out of her doctor. I called in sick for my Saturday morning shift, and then I stared at my ceiling, gripped by anxiety.

I had to do something to shake myself out of it, so I pulled some of my old dresses out from the back of my wardrobe. They looked crumpled and forgotten, as did the ultra-femme bras and pants that I dug out from under my more utilitarian underwear. I laid out these clothes on my bed, they were like ghost outlines. I stood and looked at them for a long time, then I had a cup of tea and some yummy powder to help me think.

The drugs gave me a headache, so I went to lie down amongst my frocks and ended up sleeping for five hours.

I awoke and dressed in time to call for Tina. My pride and joy, a 1950s shift that used to cling to my flesh, now hung off me when I put it on. My tits were empty in my bra; they did not spill out and strain the darts as they used to. Somewhere along the line I had forgotten how to walk in heels, so I put on a pair of trainers instead. I could still manage to carry a handbag though, into which I put some emergency drugs and a toothbrush. I glanced at my tired eyes in the mirror on my way out. I looked – what's the right word for this? – I looked beaten.

"Wow," said Tina, "you look fantastic, look at that frock, it's fifties, right? Oh my God, and look at your shoes; that's hilarious!"

Tina was wearing a tight black dress which was unbuttoned and revealed a push-up bra and big round cleavage. She wore fishnets – "stockings, not tights!" – and very hot black high heels. She was a commotion of curves. She did a twirl for me and jumped up and down with excitement as I swallowed and tried to form an adequate compliment.

When we were far down the road from her shop and her parents Tina took out a cigarette and asked me to light it for her. She held the filter to her lipsticked mouth and my hands shook.

"Do you like my outfit?" she asked.

"Yeah!"

"I thought I'd vamp it up a little," she winked at me.

The cinema was not far from our neighbourhood, so we walked and smoked. Some guys bibbed their car horns at us and Tina waved back at them like a Hollywood starlet.

"Come on," she said, "wave with me, don't let me be a hussy by myself." So I waved, bashfully at first, and then a little bit more boldly.

Tina wanted to treat me to the film. We picked a thriller, and I loaded up with junk food, nipping into the bathroom for a quick toot before the trailers began.

If I was jumpy about seeing Tina, I was even more nervous by the end of the film. She was a beast, grabbing me and making me jump at any opportunity. Some of our audience chuckled when I screamed out loud at an inappropriate moment, whilst others tutted and told us to "Shh!" We both shook with silent giggles at the film's very solemn and pretentious ending. As we burst out of the auditorium laughing our heads off, I felt happy and released from my worries.

We walked back arm in arm, doing impressions of our favourite bits in the film, and laughing at inconsequential comments. I was hoping that Tina would invite me in, and kept waiting for the moment when she would do so. We were almost at her front door and the invitation had not been made. I was starting to panic again.

"Well, thanks for coming; I had a great time," said Tina. I thought she was stringing me along with an opening line, like a pastiche of a teen date.

"Is your chaperone waiting up for you?" I asked, thinking that I was running with the joke.

"Um, no," replied Tina, uncertainly.

I knew I was going to have to say it. "Well, can I come in with you?"

"You're welcome to come in for some tea," she said, "But I don't want to sleep with you tonight."

My ears were ringing and I felt dizzy. Why was she rejecting me? I must have looked crushed because Tina hugged me and said, "It's been great tonight, but I know there was something going on the last time we had a shag."

I stood and stared at her.

"Let's just keep it light and have a good time, give each other a bit of space. You know where I am if you want to see me," she said, adding, "I really fancy you, but I don't want to hurt you." She gave me a kiss and asked, "Do you want some tea?"

"No, no," I replied, "I'll leave it for tonight, I'd better go." I walked off as fast as I could and hardly noticed that I was crying until I had collapsed on my bed, my dress billowing out from under me like a deflated balloon.

"Oh my God," I sang to myself over and again, rocking and holding my head, "Oh my God, oh my God." Tears and snot oozed down my face. Tina, I thought, was going to fuck me and then dump me; she was going to be nice and build up my hopes and then scarper. I chattered to myself quietly, like a real nut.

"I've been so lonely, I can't go through this again. I don't wanna say goodbye. Not again."

Then my thoughts changed direction, I started to wonder why she didn't want to fuck me tonight. "She wants to control me," I supposed, "she's fucking with my head. Why would she be so mean? What have I done?"

I realised that Tina could fuck me over at any time and I resolved not to be a victim but to do something about it. I dried my tears and went right back out to break down her door and demand the truth from her.

By the time I saw that the shop was closed and the shutters were down I had lost my motivation – the big confrontation would have to wait until tomorrow. Meanwhile, I decided, at least I'd have some time to think about it, and establish a plan. I called by my dealer to stock up on supplies; it was going to be a long night.

The next day, Tina's dad told me that she wasn't working today, but to go straight on up. I found her in the kitchen helping her mum cook.

"Hi Ramona," she waved, "an unexpected visit, this is nice!" She came over to hug me. "Would you like to stay for some food? We're doing some chicken."

I wasted no time. "Come with me," I said, "I want to see you; I'm not playing games."

"Okay." Tina put on her shoes and I pretty much dragged her out of the door.

"Dad," she called down into the shop, "I'm just going over to Ramona's. I'll see you later, not sure what time. Eat without me, okay?"

"Be good!" He chuckled.

The first thing Tina said when she got to my place was, "Do you live here alone?" The room was gloomy and smoky.

"Yes," I replied.

"I thought you had a girlfriend," she said, "I thought that was why you were avoiding me." I was ashamed of the state of things. "You're a messy one, aren't you?" she said, moving a stack of dirty underwear off a chair so that she could sit down. "My mum would have a fit."

"Do you want a drink?" I offered.

"Yes, please."

"I've got vodka, about half a glass worth of Diet Coke, some ginseng pop – sorry, no milk."

"I'll just have a glass of water."

I couldn't find a glass, but washed some ancient coffee out of a mug for her. She sipped politely and watched as I arranged a couple of lines on a picture frame. "Do you want some charlie?"

"No thanks, I'm fine."

I nearly called her a stuck-up cow, but I censored myself in time, there was no use in getting her defences up this early.

"Who is that in the picture?" she asked.

"It's my mum."

"She looks beautiful; you look alike."

"Thanks, that's what everyone used to say." I needed to get to the point. "Do you want a fuck?"

"Oh!" she sounded flabbergasted; I was glad to have caught her off guard. "Um, okay," she said.

"You don't have to if you don't want to," I sulked.

"No, I was just a bit surprised, that's all."

She wiped the residue of powder off from under my nose and brushed it on the arm of the chair. It was the same place where Nicky had sat all that time ago. I kissed Tina hard, to show her how much I wanted her. She was reticent in her response, but still soft and warm, inviting too.

We floundered on to the bed and lay together. My hands roved over her, feeling her chubby arms and hips under her clothes, and kissing and biting her neck. She was tense and still. She did not touch me in return. There was something weird about it.

"Let's stop," she said suddenly, "this isn't working out."

I jumped off her, instantly enraged. "Oh, so it's different when I call the shots. You can't handle it."

"What are you talking about?" Tina looked genuinely confused.

"I'm not going to let you control me," I fumed.

"I'm not trying to. What's the matter with you?"

"Nothing's the matter with me, it's you. What do you want from me?"

"I don't want anything, I just want us to be nice together; we've had some good times and I want that to continue."

"What do you want?" I was getting hysterical, "Do you want my drugs?" She shook her head, but I threw the empty wrap at her and it fluttered to the floor.

"Do you want my money?"

"No, Ramona!" Tina ducked and cringed as I chucked a handful of coins at her feet.

"What is it? Do you want to learn how to be a dyke whore? Because that's what I am; I can certainly show you that." I was screaming at the top of my lungs.

Tina looked frightened and angry. She grabbed her things and ran for the door. "I'm not your enemy," she shouted over my roar, "I'm going now; you're scaring me. We can talk when you're not in such a state."

"I never want to talk to you again," I sneered, "leave now, just go!"

As the door slammed behind her, I thought about Tina running home, about the smell of chicken in that warm kitchen, of her mum and dad hugging their beloved daughter and drying her tears, and I was filled with jealousy and grief.

"Please don't leave," I cried to no one, "please."

I needed to knock myself out so I took a double dose of sleepers and nodded on the settee for a few hours. Then I needed to pep myself up a little, so I had a couple more lines. Then I was feeling too whizzy, so I ate more sleepers. Then I don't remember what happened.

Then it was time for work.

"You look fucked," said Lea, slapping my face to try and bring me round. She made me some strong coffee whilst I dozed in the corner. "Let's get you washed," she said, and got a couple of other Angelz to help her scrub me down and rinse my hair. Milla kept some spare clothes at the Funhouse in case of "mishaps", whatever they might be, so Lea raided the cupboard and found me something clean and fresh to wear.

I wasn't the first to turn up to work a mess – the usual protocol was for everybody else to cover; we all knew that the fuck-up could so easily be any of us. Today it was risky, because Milla was on the prowl.

Lea told me, "You should get out of here or Milla's going to throw you out."

"I can't miss another day of work," I mumbled, "she'll sack me anyway."

Lea told me that I already had a client waiting, someone new who had asked for me specifically. She said that I would be better off working in one of the rooms where I'd be hidden from Milla than hanging around in the communal areas. She was right.

Usually there's a comment in the log book about what the client wants, but this time there was none. I didn't recognise who it was, but that didn't mean much because our punters rarely used their real names. Maybe I should have been more wary – after all, no one ever asked for me specially these days; I was definitely common or garden trash as far as Angelz was concerned. It was unusual that someone had picked me out from the rest of the girls; I should have been suspicious.

So who was my mystery client? Who wanted me? It was Lisa, the strangely intense woman who fucked me at Chicklets.

I was surprised, in as much as I would be to find myself having to fuck anybody I knew professionally, but mostly I was flattered. I guess she liked me, and that counted a lot in the context of how I was feeling at that time.

"I hope you don't mind," said Lisa, as though she was anticipating the answer to a question.

"No," I smiled and shook my head, "it's fine." In truth I was surprised that it hadn't happened before, fucking dykes I knew for money, it being a small world and all that.

"I wanted to see you again," Lisa said, "I haven't been able to stop thinking about you."

"Don't worry." I didn't want to dwell on her excuses; she was here and that was all there was. I was feeling desperate and fragile after the fight with Tina. I didn't want to think about any of that, so I slipped into work mode and moved straight on to my professional patter. "I hope our receptionist explained the establishment rules to you."

She nodded.

"Do you have any questions before we begin?"

Lisa shook her head.

"What is it you're interested in?"

"You," she replied.

I laughed off her answer and continued, "What I mean is, what would you like us to do today?"

She looked like a startled rabbit. "Well," she peeped, "anything, really."

"Is there something specific that you particularly enjoy?"

"Oh," she blustered, "I like it all." Lisa was endearingly awkward; when she spoke to me, I noticed her hand shooting up to twizzle the hairs on the back of her neck. I sniggered inwardly at the thrill this "dirty talk" with me must have been giving her, whilst trying to get her to open up a little.

"How about things you don't want us to do?" I ventured.

She replied, "I don't mind, I'm not fussy." It was clear that she wasn't going to help me.

"Is there something you'd like to try that you've never had a chance to do?"

"Whatever suits you best."

This was going nowhere. "Lisa," I said sternly, "this time is yours, okay? You're paying for it. It means that you can do whatever you want."

She looked at me blankly, as though she was stunned by the possibilities.

I continued: "We can fuck if you want to fuck, or maybe you'd like a bit of SM, some role-playing – would you like that?"

Lisa gulped and nodded.

"Just say what you want, I won't laugh. We can do anything."

"Anything?"

Now it was my turn to nod.

"I don't know how to say this," she stammered.

"Just get it out."

"I'd like to…"

"Yes…" I prompted.

"I'd just like to…" She took a deep breath and spluttered, "Look, I just want to worship you a bit, that's all."

I was all geared up for her to say that she wanted to shit on me or do something gross, so I was relieved by her answer. Easy money, I thought.

"That can be arranged," I told her coolly, ignoring her blushes. "Do you want to tell me how you want to worship me? Or do you want me to just tell you how I like it?"

"That one," she said, "the second one, just tell me."

"Okay." I paused to think and then said, "I'd like you to undress so that I can have a good look at you."

Lisa took off her clothes and folded them neatly into a pile. She had what people call a good body. She looked strong, as though she spent a lot of time at the gym. She was tall too, even naked she was imposing. Her hair had grown a little since I last saw her, but she still looked both queer and straight.

Lisa looked uncertain as she waited for my next instruction. Just for fun, I made a sudden movement towards her, which made her jump out of her skin.

"Make me feel like a princess," I said.

Lisa took my hand and led me to the bed. I stopped and would not go on. "Aren't you forgetting something?" I said.

Lisa's expression betrayed her -- she was caught out.

"You don't know what it is, do you?"

She shook her head. "No."

I said simply, "I want you on your knees."

She was down like a shot, still holding my hand, looking up to me for approval, which I nodded.

By the time she had made me comfortable on the bed – shuffling around me, tending to me, placing me in the most relaxing position – her knees were raw, but she didn't seem to care.

"Kiss my feet," I commanded. Even though I was still wearing all of my clothes, Lisa made no hesitation in licking and nibbling me enthusiastically, smooching and caressing my feet, my ankles, my calves, even my shoelaces.

Her eyes looked into mine the whole time. I smiled down on her, my temporary servant.

I didn't know whether to laugh or cry when I thought that my life had come to this. A funny woman paying to worship me, the most friendless and fucked-up dyke in town.

I made Lisa crawl around a little for my amusement, performing silly and pointless jobs, although really it was for her pleasure I was doing it. She seemed to enjoy the scene more as I became increasingly coquettish and demanding. Although she was silent and intent for most of the time we spent that afternoon, she never took her eyes off me.

"I want a massage," I pouted, reasoning to myself that I should milk as many rewards for my hard work as I could.

Lisa helped ease me out of my top and got down to business on my back. Her hands were fabulous as she mauled and prodded and smoothed away the knots of tension in my muscles.

I was exhausted, sick and tired of the pain and bullshit in my life. I let my mind drift and I thought about other hands that had soothed and flattered me, about how they had stroked and explored my body, how I had let fingers creep inside me and open me up.

To my astonishment, I was getting wet.

I opened my legs a little and ground my hips into the bed. Lisa read the signal without my having to explain a thing. The heels of her hands worked down my back, lower and lower until she was massaging my arse cheeks inside my undies. She slipped her cool hand between my bum crack and felt the outer lips of my cunt with her fingertips. I raised my arse so that she could feel my clit, and rubbed myself lazily against the edge of her hand. I could sense her breath on the small of my back.

"Just hold it still," I said as I ground against her, "I want to come." She did as I said and soon a familiar hot gooey warmth flowed through me. "Good girl," I sighed dozily.

Lisa resumed my backrub and I must have nodded off because the next thing I knew, she was shaking me gently and saying, "I think our session might be over now. There's someone knocking at the door; I think they want to use this room."

"Oh shit!" I leapt up. Lea was hammering at the door, saying that she had Marie with her and she wanted us to clear up and get out.

"Sorry! Sorry!" I called back, pulling on my clothes. "Yes, of course." I groaned when I thought of how she and the others would tease me later on, it was very unusual for a job with a client to run overtime.

Lisa was still on her knees, still naked. "Put your clothes on," I ordered, feeling somewhat guilty that there hadn't been time to get her off.

She stood still. "What's the matter?" I asked.

"Will you come with me?" she replied.

"What?"

"Come with me, back to mine." She looked vulnerable, pleading.

"No," I answered, straight out. I remembered how intense she had been with me at Chicklets.

"Please?"

"No," I repeated, substantiating it with, "it's against the rules."

Lisa said, "It would be a work thing – we could finish this thing off properly. I can pay you more, if that's what you want. No one would have to know."

I stopped to think as Lea continued to bang on the door. I reconsidered – going back with Lisa would get me out of Milla's way for the rest of the day. Lea could stick it in the log book as a last-minute outcall. Plus, I'd get more money. Plus, it would be an easy job. What did I have to lose? Nothing. Who would miss me? No one.

"Okay," I said, "get your things on and let's go."

Lisa lived in one of the new fake loft conversions in Bow, overlooking the flyover. It wasn't so far from where I lived, which appealed to me because I reckoned I could be out of her house and on my way home, via the off-licence, in an hour or so.

Her place was clean and light. It looked like one of those homes you see in magazines, the "after" picture.

There was a funny change in Lisa too as she led me into her flat – she was somehow less meek, more in control as she showed me to her living room. She reminded me more of the woman who had fucked me at Chicklets and less like the crawling, cringing slave she had been an hour or so before.

"Would you like a drink?" she asked. "I've got some tequila, your favourite," she added slyly.

"Why not?" I let my hands fly up in the air, all devil-may-care.

She put the bottle and some glasses on a table near to where I sat. We drank a couple of shots each. Lisa pulled herself close to me and stroked my head. "You're hot," she said.

"I'm glad you think so." In truth, I thought it was amazing that anybody could think that about me. After all that had happened with Tina, and Suzanne, Molex even, and all the people who I cared about had gone, it was more than reassuring to think that somebody desired me.

Lisa said, "I know you're on duty but I've got some snort, if you fancy a go."

"Bring it to me," I laughed with a munificent gesture. This was going to be fun.

I put some music on whilst Lisa chopped us out a couple of lines. I didn't ask what it was; it looked like coke; I didn't care; I just wanted to lift off and get fucked.

We drank more tequila and filled our noses with more shit. "This is good!" I gibbered.

"It's just a little something to get us in the mood," she grinned in return.

I got up to look around at Lisa's stuff a little more. I knew she was watching me, so I did a few moves to show off a little, and to let her know I knew she was looking.

She came up and danced behind me. She didn't touch me – there must have been an inch of daylight between us – but she clung like a shadow and it felt as though she was all over me.

"I've got some porn," Lisa said, "do you wanna watch a dirty film?"

I turned around, kissed her deeply, then pulled away before she could start anything more. "Yeah," I squealed, "let's do it!"

We kept the music playing on repeat and watched the tape with the sound down.

Like a lot of porn, the film had a negligible plot and consisted mostly of scene after scene of guys fucking. Lisa, it seemed, had a thing for men doing each other up the arse, and she was far from put off by the tape's stupid name (*Hot 'n' Heavy 14*), or the generic nature of the images. Her eyes were big as she sat glued to the screen, and she stroked my head distractedly.

I chopped and snorted another line; I never could say no to free drugs.

The guys in this section of the film were in the backroom of a leather club. The dialogue was in German or Dutch or something, not that it mattered. There was a long camera shot of a group scene. One of the men was sucking off his boyfriend whilst a stranger looked on and jerked off. It was kind of obvious that the stranger wanted a piece of the action; he cocked his head at the guy being sucked and was motioned over. The stranger undid his leathers and manipulated himself into hardness. He slapped the sucker's arse a few times, making the guy jump, spat on his hands to lube himself up, and then got down to some fucking.

The camera closed in until there was nothing else in the frame but cocks fucking holes: the boyfriend's dick in the sucker's mouth, the stranger fucking his arse. Mouth and arse began to look the same, both dribbled saliva, both clung to the cock shaft as it plunged in and out.

Lisa groaned with relief at the money shot. The stranger pulled out his dick, ripped off his rubber and spunked all over the sucker's smooth arse cheeks. Almost simultaneously, the boyfriend came in his lover's face. The camera lingered over the sucker's face – he appeared ecstatic there on his hands and knees in the middle of the room as he licked away the juice from around his mouth.

Lisa was stroking my thigh and pulling at one of her nipples.

"Wanna fuck?" she said, still watching the screen. She was squirming back and forth on the couch, grinding away.

The next scene took place in another backroom, in another club. Two leather men were already fucking, their hands were all over each other. They wore a lot of black leather, chains, harnesses, the whole uniform. The fucker pushing his lover against the edge of a table, the lover supporting himself, then half collapsing against the force of the thrusting. He struggled a little, obviously for show, until the fucker, who was much bigger and stronger than him, pushed his head against the table and held him down whilst he finished him off. You could see the guy smiling as he was being fucked.

Lisa's hand was in her pants. I pushed her back, so that she was lying before me.

The scene was not over. As the men rearranged themselves, a woman entered the room, a real woman. She looked quite young, maybe twenty or so. She also looked too hot to be appearing in some tenth-rate sex tape, so perhaps she was doing it for fun, or because she had to.

Lisa held her breath, she knew what was coming next and she didn't want to let anything interfere with her pleasure.

The woman was wearing pink PVC hotpants and a white halter top; her outfit was very slutty. She had platform sandals, and a tacky plastic handbag. She walked into the scene as though she was taking a carefree stroll in a park on a sunny day. She stopped to look at the men. She stared at them and they stared back at her. She held up three fingers at them, like a Scout's Honour sign, then she wedged them between her legs and flexed her hips slowly.

They knew what she was after.

The bigger guy picked her up. She was facing him and she placed her arms around his neck like a bizarre pastiche of a romantic embrace. He locked his arms around her back, not to imprison her but to support her. She levered her long skinny legs against the table until she was balanced. The other gut got between. His cock was hard and ready. He pulled aside her hotpants and lubed up her arsehole with her cunt juice. A close-up of his dick showed a drop of pre-come shining in the cheap studio lights before he rolled on the condom. Another close-up showed her tight arsehole twitching slightly as he entered her. We saw everything. She stretched open for him as he began to fuck her. We saw her easing herself on to him, supported by the man's lover.

What with the drugs, the tequila, the music, the film and the funny atmosphere in Lisa's flat, nothing felt real, neither me nor the girl on the tape.

Lisa's eyes were glazing over; she was watching the screen and talking to me, but she wasn't really there.

I blew on her belly and on her thighs. I stroked her legs. I held up her left foot and sucked on her big toe.

"Ooh, that tickles," she said, deadpan.

"Do you like it?" I asked, mechanically.

"Oh yes," she replied, dreamlike, as if reciting a script.

I rubbed my hands up her inner thighs, pressing firmly. I could feel her body unwinding for me.

She let me open her legs. Stray curly hairs peeped out from the edges of her panties. I trailed a finger over the gentle ridges of her cunt through the fabric of her underwear. She was perfectly still.

"Is this okay?"

"Oh yes."

"Would you like me to put my fingers inside you?"

"Yes, please."

I pulled aside Lisa's gusset and pushed my finger inside her as slowly and as stealthily as I could. She sighed.

"Shall I fuck you a little?" The words seemed too coarse.

"Yes, please."

I drew my finger out and pushed it back in smoothly. Lisa made small grunting sounds, as though she was clearing her throat.

Then I fucked her. Lisa's backbone flexed and she rolled her head around as I pushed my fingers in and pulled them out. I lay down on top of her, still working away at her cunt, and made her suck the fingers of my free hand. My face was so close to hers that I could feel her damp breath on my cheek. Her eyes were tightly closed; she was in another world.

"Do you want to come?" I asked.

She nodded, her gesture hindered slightly by my fingers in her face.

I pulled out and she stared at me suddenly, affronted that I could abandon her so abruptly. Before she had time to say anything, I stuck them back in again and fucked her hard. I felt my way inside her slippery wet body until she arched her back and made those noises, tightened then reddened, until I knew what I had done to her.

Lisa wasted no time. No sooner had she come then she was up and at me, wanting to sort me out, as I had apparently done for her.

I wasn't bothered if she didn't. My cunt was wet and buzzy from fucking her and watching the porn; that was enough for me. I suddenly felt so tired, drug tired, booze tired. What I really wanted was to sleep rather than to fuck. Lisa was persistent.

"No," I slurred, flopping back. "Let's do it later."

"But I want you," she whined.

"Later."

Lisa pouted. "If you're not going to change your mind, let's at least have another hit," she offered.

As I said, I never could refuse free drugs.

"I've got something to mellow you out," said Lisa, opening up her stash box. She picked out four brightly coloured gelatine capsules from a smaller box inside. "I believe these are your favourite," she muttered as she emptied out the powder from the pills on to her mirror. I had never seen these things before. Lisa arranged a couple of lines for me and I did them. It took the last of my energy to hold my head over the mirror long enough to get that shit up my nose. Lisa watched me as I sank back.

"Aren't you going to have some?" I asked.

"Nah," she breezed, "it's not my thing."

The woman in the film was still getting fucked by her two leather boys, only now a group of their friends had turned up to join in.

I nodded and dozed, thinking vague thoughts about how glad I was to have met Lisa, how she was kind of odd, but not as crazy as I thought she was when I first met her. I congratulated myself for landing on my feet, having found someone who wanted to look after me, after all I had been through.

The room became hazy and I lost consciousness.

I must have been really tired, because Lisa told me that I had been asleep for two whole days by the time that I came round in my host's large and comfortable bed.

I felt dehydrated, groggy and weak, but I didn't mind because, it seemed, Lisa had a thing for looking after me. Over the next day or so I wasn't about to complain about the soup she cooked me, the back-rubs she gave, the baths she ran and all the snacks and drinks she brought to where I lay. She soothed and flattered me. I was particularly pleased by her generosity where her stash box was concerned – she let me take what I wanted, and replenished the supply when it ran low. Lisa even paid me extra money for the fuck we'd had. She made me feel like a queen.

I knew she'd want something in return sooner or later, and I knew it would probably be sexual in nature. I didn't mind; it seemed a small price for the life that she was giving me.

That time came later in the night.

Lisa had been feeding me chocolate, brandy and valium. We sat together, watching the East London skyline twinkle in the night outside her window. I would almost say that it was a romantic moment.

Lisa said, "You're amazing."

"You hardly know me," I spluttered.

She said mysteriously, "Don't be so sure of that."

"Have you been stalking me?" I joked.

"Maybe," she replied cautiously. She smiled, but I couldn't tell

237

whether or not she was serious. She stroked my hair and nibbled my earlobe.

"I'd like to eat you up!" declared Lisa, changing the subject.

"Oh, so you're a cannibal now," I mocked, "a cannibal serial killer stalker."

"Yum yum!" she pretended to gobble my face, "delicious flesh!" she teased.

"What part of me would you eat first?"

"Your cunt, of course."

"What about my tits? There's plenty of flesh there. Or my belly," I offered, shaking it at her.

Lisa said: "I'd eat your cunt first, then your tits, and then I'd drain your blood out and drink that. In fact, I think I'd prefer to drink you anyway."

I took a gulp of brandy.

"Would you drink my tears?"

"Yes," she replied without hesitation. "I want every part of you."

"Would you drink my saliva?"

"Yes," she said grandly, "I'd love it."

"Would you drink my piss?"

"Yes," she replied, and her voice dropped to a whisper.

Bingo.

"Do you want to drink my piss?" I said straight out.

Lisa didn't say anything, but she trembled as she met my gaze. She understood that I knew what she wanted.

A stranger peeking through Lisa's giant windows two seconds later would have thought they were watching a pair of women scuffling awkwardly with each other. They would have been wrong.

I grabbed the top of Lisa's head as though I was lifting a melon out of a fruit basket. She was caught off-guard and her legs slid from beneath her as she struggled to regain her balance. Lisa's arms flailed to steady herself as I shoved her on to the floor. She was on her knees facing my crotch. I was wearing what had become my only outfit at my host's place: a loose T-shirt, nothing else, no underwear. She had an eyeful. I could see she was smiling.

"Eat me, Lisa," I told her.

I still had my hand on her head. She tried to shake it off, but we both knew that the game was for me to pretend to force her to go down on me, and for her to pretend to resist.

She was really strong, but I was in a better position to dominate her. I pulled her face into my cunt. I had to stand awkwardly to open my legs enough for her mouth to reach everything, but I enjoyed that feeling of teetering over someone whilst maintaining my power. It was as though I was standing on the edge of a cliff and letting somebody else decide whether I should fall forwards to my doom, or backwards to safety.

Lisa gorged on me. Her eyes were closed; she looked blissful. The room was silent but for the sounds of her licking and sucking at my juicy parts. It felt good propped there on her face, so sweet, so much pleasure surging around my hot wet cunt. I cackled inwardly as I thought of the mouthful I was going to pour into her.

I said, "I'm going to piss on you, I'm going to piss in your mouth, I want you to swallow."

Lisa groaned with pleasure.

I needed to let myself go so I tried to empty my mind; to let the sex pleasure flow freely and to allow all the tension in my body to evaporate. I concentrated on Lisa's tongue working my clit, the lazy softness oozing around inside me, and then I was coming, as though I had accidentally happened upon it and allowed it to take me over.

Lisa's eyes were tranquil as she looked up at me. Her mouth was still devouring my snatch and my hand was still on her head, but re- laxed now. I could see her own fingers jammed between her legs, jerk- ing herself off vigorously.

I released a fierce jet of hot piss; it shot out of me without any warning. I had no idea my bladder could hold so much – my piss went on and on like some fucked-up fountain.

Lisa tried drink and eat me simultaneously, but it was too overwhelming for her; she couldn't keep up. My piss gushed down her chin and formed little puddles around her.

Eventually she threw back her head, opened her throat as though she wanted to inhale me, and then let my pee flow down into her stomach and into her heart.

I squeezed out the last drop. Lisa gulped and then collapsed sideways on the hard floor, gasping for breath with dull eyes, filled to the brim with me.

I patted her head paternally and sunk back into the sofa.

I needed a line of something.

Lisa spoke in a monotone. "I want more," she said. I turned on the television and ignored her. She picked herself up and stood in front of the screen.

She repeated, "I want more."

I craned my neck to see round her, but it was no good. "Lisa, you're in the way."

"Piss on me again," she said.

"Don't be silly."

Her voice cracked: "Piss on me, Ramona!"

"I can't," I grumbled, "I'm dry and out of piss."

She ran to the kitchen where I heard her fill a large jug with water. "Drink this," she urged when she returned.

"Lisa, give it a rest," said exasperated. "Let's chill."

She put the jug down sharply, spilling some of its contents. Then she cupped her hand to my ear as though she was telling me a secret.

"You know I'd let you..." she started. "I'd let you..." I batted her away. "I'd let you shit on me if you wanted to," she blurted.

It was too much. "Lisa, fuck off, okay?" I snapped back. "You're really pushing it. Give it a rest."

She was startled by my reaction. "Yes," she said, "Okay."

After that outburst we sat together in sulky silence for a very long time. Lisa busied herself clearing up where we had fucked and I had pissed earlier on, and then she cooked us a meal – pasta, I think: "Your favourite," she said.

People ask me why I stayed at Lisa's place for so long when I knew that she was losing her grip. Whilst my answers may seem flaky to some, they are the truth.

Lisa obviously had enough money to support me, and the time I spent with her was, for the most part, extremely comfortable. If I'm honest, I have to say that I didn't notice that something was wrong for quite a while. In truth, I was dazzled by her flattery and the way that she wanted to look after me.

I actually welcomed the opportunity to leave my own life behind me for a little while. If I could avoid facing her obsessiveness, I thought Lisa's care would somehow heal me from the loneliness and heartbreak I had been through. After fucking up with Tina, my recent past could burn up and rot as far as I was concerned.

Lisa's behaviour might have looked extreme to an outsider, but to me it was just more of the same kind of thing I had been dealing with for a while. Compared to Maxine or Louise, or even Nicky, Lisa's craziness was not that bizarre.

I barely noticed or cared at the time, but Lisa kept me fairly well sedated, not that I would have said no to any of the drugs she offered me. The grogginess never lifted entirely. I always felt out of it; I had no standard of normality with which to compare myself except Lisa and consequently my own grasp of reality was quite shaky.

I should have been suspicious.

After about four or five days at her place, I was beginning to go stir-crazy. Lazing around, being waited on, barely lifting a finger except to fuck was one thing, but I wanted to breathe some fresh air and stretch my legs. The sun was shining outside, so I decided to go and buy a newspaper and some fags.

I had to get dressed but I suddenly realised that I had not worn any proper clothes for days except Lisa's T-shirts in which I'd been slobbing around. My own had disappeared.

Lisa looked completely freaked out when I asked for my jeans and boots.

"They're in the wash," she stammered.

"My boots are in the wash?" I asked incredulously.

"Yes," she said.

I didn't know what was going on. Her reaction seemed extreme, so I tried to diffuse the situation. "Oh," I said, "I'll just grab them and put them on. I don't mind if they're dirty."

"No!" exclaimed Lisa in a panic. I looked at her bemusedly. She ushered me over to the sofa and made me sit down. "Aw honey," her voice softened, "just stay here and get comfy." She tried to calm me down, but her suddenly soothing tones were more for her benefit than mine. "You don't have to go anywhere. Look, I'll go out and get us both some treats."

I was unsure, there was something peculiar about her behaviour, but I went along with it. There seemed no point in upsetting her.

She left. I did not hear the sound of her locking me into the flat. Instead, I hunted around for my clothes. I searched through Lisa's drawers in case she had put them away; I looked under the bed, in all the cupboards, even inside the washing machine. I could not find them anywhere. I was beginning to feel panicky when Lisa returned with champagne, an armful of glossy magazines and a baggie of coke.

We spent the rest of the day drinking, whizzing and fucking. I tried not to worry. Finally, we went to bed at three in the morning. By five I still could not sleep. I was beginning to suspect that I was in trouble.

"Where are my clothes?" I said it out loud, suddenly, in a clear voice designed to wake Lisa and catch her unawares.

"Go to sleep, baby," she murmured sleepily.

I held my breath and counted to ten. Then I repeated in a voice that was in danger of turning into a shout: "Where are my clothes?"

Lisa turned over and muttered: "I sent them to be dry cleaned; they were filthy." Soon she was snoring gently again.

When I was sure she was safely asleep I crept out of the bed. I needed to talk to someone, anyone, just to feel safe. I picked up the phone in the front room, dialled the Angelz number and put the receiver to my ear. There was no dial-tone; the phone was a dud.

If I had been starring in a Hitchcock film, there would probably have been a soundtrack of loud, screeching, chilling violins to illustrate my shock. My heart was pounding high in my chest; I was becoming overtaken by fear. Something was very wrong. I'm being paranoid, I told myself, calm down.

I had to escape. But how? Lisa rarely left the place. There would come an opportunity for me, I thought. Even if the worst happened – whatever that might be – I could shout as loudly as I could to attract attention from a neighbour. I also believed that somebody would notice I was missing and come and get me. I remembered Lisa's address in the log book. But nobody had come, nobody missed me. I learned later that Milla had noticed I was drugged up and decided to sack me anyway. Lisa was just one last job as far as she was concerned, and she was glad when I didn't turn up the next day.

My mind was racing.

"What are you doing?" Lisa was right behind me, her voice clear and sharp. I nearly died of fright.

"I couldn't sleep."

"Poor baby," she consoled, "shall we have a little toot to knock us out?" By "we" she meant me.

"Okay," I agreed. What else could I do?

She gave me some more of the funny powdered tranquilliser that she'd been dosing me up with. It soon did the trick, and melted away my anxiety until I was floating around again in a muggy mental haze, until I finally dropped off the ledge into sleep.

I didn't wake up until late afternoon the next day, I still felt spaced out, but I knew I had to leave Lisa's place. I hunted through her clothes for something that might fit me. The only thing I found was a weird skirt-thing tucked away at the back of a wardrobe, never worn, and a pair of flip-flops.

"What are you doing?" It was the second time that Lisa had caught me unawares.

"I'd like to go," I said, "Don't worry, I'll make sure you get your clothes back." I felt foolish in my outfit.

"Don't be silly," she replied, trying to coax me. "Stay awhile," she said, "let's have some fun."

"I'm not being silly, I want to go." I added, "I'm leaving."

Lisa said: "You can't go."

"Why not?"

"You just can't."

That was not enough of a reason for me. "Get out of my way, Lisa," I shoved past her, "you're fucking mental."

Lisa moved quickly to block my exit. She looked terrifying. All the softness in her eyes had gone, she looked ready to rumble. The realisation that I was in big trouble hit me, like waking up with a massive hangover after a week of drunken pleasure.

I pulled at her shoulder and tried to force her out of my path. Bigger and stronger than me, Lisa shoved me back. She stood squarely in front of me as I regained my composure. We stared each other down.

In the moments before what happened next I had a brief sensation of pure clarity. Everything pulled into focus: the mess of my recent life, my sexual awakening with women, all those I had loved and lost, my self-destruction, Lisa, even all the angles and curves in her house, lit up by the afternoon sun that shone through her window. My pupils dilated and contracted; all the synapses in my brain started humming with electrical movement. Then I saw stars.

From nowhere, Lisa's right fist shot out and landed in the middle of my face. The movement was sudden and devastating. She broke my nose. Then she punched me again. I fell and twisted my wrist on the floor as I tried to soften the blow. I pulled over a chair, which landed on me. My feet slipped around, a flip-flop fell off. I spat out a spray of blood. I felt around in my mouth for loose teeth. She had split my lip. Lisa kicked me in my ribs and belly whilst I was on the floor. I was too shocked to feel any pain, but I was afraid that I would lose consciousness if she kicked my head. I thought she might kill me and I knew that I didn't want to die.

I grabbed her foot and twisted it hard. She lost her balance and thundered to the ground. As soon as she was down I leapt up to sit on her. Actually, leapt isn't quite the right word; I was so dazed that my movements were sluggish and dreamlike. I brought my fists down on Lisa's face but my blows were clumsy, weak, not how I would imagine them to be in a fight for my life.

Lisa fought back. She snatched the chair by its legs and battered me with it awkwardly. Neither of us said a word the whole time. Blood poured out of my face and splashed everywhere. She dropped the chair and scratched at my face. I flapped my arms to make her stop and she heaved me off her with a powerful shove.

I stood up and ran for the door but Lisa bulldozed me to the floor again. Our fight was sloppy and pathetic, not like some slick choreographed shit you'd see in a film. My punches and kicks were more like fumbles and gropes. Lisa headbutted me, but I think it caused her more damage than it did me. We both breathed heavily, the blood catching in my throat made sickening gurgling sounds.

Lisa pinned me down with her knees on my arms. I had no strength left; my eyes were puffing up from where I had been hit.

I said: "Let me go." Lisa stared.

"Let me go," I said. I added lamely, "If you let me go, then we can still be friends."

No response.

"Let me go," I demanded.

At last she spoke. "It's not even about you, you dummy," she was half laughing and half crying. I had no idea what she was talking about.

"Listen love," I tried to placate Lisa, "just let me go and we can sort this whole thing out."

She stopped to consider.

"I'll let you go for one thing," she said.

"Yes," I encouraged.

She held my face and spoke directly into it, "I know about you," she said, "I know about Molex."

"What about her?" What the fuck did Molex have to do with Lisa?

She whispered, "I'll let you free for an introduction to Molex; it's her I really want."

She couldn't have said anything more bizarre if she'd tried. What the fuck is it about Molex that drives everyone round the fucking bend trying to get close to her! I stopped my nicey-nicey approach and laughed incredulously. "Fuck you!"

She continued: "I'll let you free if you tell me who she is."

"Dream on."

Lisa was sweating; the balance of power was shifting and she knew it. "I'll let you free for a kiss," she offered.

She was weakening whilst I was getting stronger. "Let me go right now," I commanded. It worked.

Lisa's hands shook as she struggled to get off me, "You'd better fucking..." she trailed off. "You'd better..."

I rolled on to my hands and knees. I was beyond ache, beyond pain. I stood up like a newborn foal. Then Lisa watched me in open-mouthed silence as I reached into her jacket pocket, pulled out her keys and a handful of money, unlocked the door, walked out of that place, down the stairs and out to my freedom.

I was numb. Maybe I was still hallucinating. There was nobody about. Gravel and stones on the pavement punctured my bare feet, but I started to run anyway. The air hurt my lungs, but I did not stop. At first I felt hollow – an automaton, but single-minded like The Terminator. There was no pain in my legs; I could barely feel my feet hitting the ground; I just had this sensation of flying, and a strong feeling of being alive.

I got to a phone box. I wanted to call Suzanne, but I was too far gone to shock from my beating to remember her number. I have called Suzanne a hundred thousand times, but this time I could not remember anything.

"Shit, shit, what is it," I panted, "it's three-two, three-two-seven-nine. Shit. Fuck."

A tiny memory switched on in my head: Suzanne writing her number on the corner of a beer mat and telling me to call her.

I remembered the number. I was so pleased with myself that I started laughing. My chuckle grew into a belly laugh and I couldn't stop. I was gulping down air and crying. I could barely speak when Suzanne answered the phone.

"It's me," I managed to squeeze it out.

"Ramona, where are you?" she shouted into the receiver. "Where are you? Tell me, I will come and get you."

I laughed and laughed.

"Ramona! Where are you? Tell me now!"

"Stratford."

"Are you at home? I'm coming over now."

"No, Stratford High Street," I wheezed, "by the sewer bank. I will hide by the gate. I am scared. Please come and get me."

"I'm coming baby, don't move, I will find you."

I hung up and slouched out of the phone box. The sewer bank was a long stretch of pathway above the old pumping station. Its gates were locked, but the chain was loose and I squeezed through. The air smelled of shit. It was that late time of the day when the sun and the moon share the same sky. I found a patch of long grass, through which I could see intermittent traffic.

Suzanne was the one who found me. I was afraid she would get stuck in the gates in her eagerness to reach me through them. In the end she gave them a karate-style kick and they bent open enough for her to crawl through. She looked funny, like a clumsy and unconventional superhero, and I would have laughed had I not already been in such a state.

"Oh my God," she wailed as she ran towards me with her arms open. "I thought you were gone." She grabbed me and held me tight.

Suzanne smelled so good and clean, and she looked so honest and loving that I couldn't laugh any more. "I don't think I can stand," I told her in a tiny voice.

"Hey, wait! Come and help me, I've found her!" I didn't know who she was gesturing to, someone by the side of the road. I thought it might be Lisa, come to finish me off, so I bundled myself into a tight little ball to stop her from hurting me too much. Later Suzanne said that she was calling over to the minicab driver who had brought her to find me.

They both bundled me into the car and then they took me to the hospital.

Shortly after Suzanne found me, my life became more of a blur than before. Blood was taken, forms were filled, conversations were held about me. I didn't think much about anything; I just let people get on with it; I endured the probing and tried to keep the hope alive that one day I would be able to tuck myself up into my own bed and sleep without anyone's intervention.

Suzanne explained all the hospital stuff to me a long time after it happened. She told me about the night I was admitted.

The duty nurse told her: "I'm sorry, we can only allow family visitors in with the patient."

Suzanne said, "I'm her family."

The nurse had no idea; she kept on, "I mean like a mum or a dad, or an aunt or siblings," she continued, "you know, blood relatives."

"I'm her only family."

"But the supervisor says..."

"I'm her family," Suzanne snarled.

The nurse went to get her manager. A woman in a cardigan and glasses took one look at Suzanne and buzzed her in through the security doors.

I lay in a curtained-off area for two hours waiting to be seen. Suzanne sat by me and held my hand. I don't remember this, but she said that I was very quiet, that I just waited. She said that it spooked her to see me so passive, and that she was creeped out when I muttered, "I'm frightened they'll think I'm mad."

"Don't worry baby," she stroked my fingers, "don't worry." Then I started to cry again.

The doctor was very brusque. It was hard to describe what had happened. He condensed everything I told him into notes in a file.

"X-rays indicate fractured nose and ribs. There is severe bruising to face and lacerations over body. Patient is disorientated, indicating moderate to severe shock. Possible chemical dependency. Psychiatrist's report pending. Police to interview."

He patched me up and I was kept in hospital for observation. They put me in a room by myself. They took me there in a wheelchair. The hospital porter made jokes, he was "just trying to cheer me up". I had a drip and one of those comedy hospital robes that show your arse. I was frightened of being left alone so Suzanne stayed with me on a fold-out bed. She never let go of me.

"Where's Billy?" I had vision of him crying by himself.

"At his nan's," Suzanne replied.

"Oh no!" The idea of more crazies shocked me out of my rest.

"Yeah, I know, " laughed Suzanne, "I think he'll be okay for a short while. You'll have to help me deprogramme him when he comes back."

I stared.

"That's a joke, babe." She smiled and nudged me gently.

We stayed there together that night; it was so peaceful. The next day Suzanne brought me some flowers and read to me from the papers. I could hear traffic outside and was glad the world continued to spin.

The psychiatrist wanted Suzanne to leave whilst he interviewed me, but we both insisted that she stayed, so he swallowed uncomfortably and got down to work. I never saw his report. The guy spoke to me in a patronising way. He said really obvious things like, "It will take you a while to come to terms with your experiences," and "You might like to join a support group, or get some counselling." Fuck that, it was the medication part of this healing process that interested me the most. The bastard said that he would be scheduling a meeting with my GP to discuss my long-term drug use and that any final decision about medication would have to wait until then.

Suzanne and I both made V-signs behind his back as he left and the door swung closed.

Later that day, I told two policewomen what had happened. They were okay. I even told them about the drugs and they said that considering the circumstances it was unlikely that I would be prosecuted, although they would recommend that I undertook a treatment programme.

They picked up Lisa and arrested her for unlawful imprisonment, or something like that, plus various assault and drug charges too. There is still stuff going on about what happened. I'm not going to go into it though; it's a long story; it's too complicated for me; I want to move on.

That evening Suzanne went to call her parents to ask them to hold on to Billy for one more night. They bitched about her "wasting time looking after that homosexual drug addict friend of yours," but she ignored them.

When she returned to my room, we both cuddled up together on my bed. It was time to talk.

Suzanne said: "I called you and called you. When you never answered, I started to get scared. I thought I would never see you again."

I replied, "I didn't think anyone had noticed that I was missing. It was only a few days."

"How could you think that? I haven't seen you for so fucking long. I called you every day. I went round to your place. I went to the police. I went to a couple of those fucking stupid A-Dyke places where you used to hang out. I even went to see your scuzzfuck landlord. I knew something was wrong."

"Thank you."

"I thought you were dealing; I thought someone had attacked you; I thought you were out on the streets somewhere; I never stopped trying to find you. I've been so frightened and I thought you were dead;

I thought you had run away from me." Her voice turned into a squeak.

I was crying.

"When I found you," she said, "you looked so small; I've never seen you so vulnerable. You looked bad before, the last time I saw you, but this time you looked almost broken." She continued, "You were a mess, thank fuck it was mainly bruising, but with the blood and everything, it was hard to tell. I wanted to kill whoever had done this to you. Worse than kill, I wanted to annihilate them."

Suzanne dug into her jeans pocket, "I need to show you something," she said. In her hand was a small crumpled plastic baggie, the kind of thing you usually find with a gram of whizz in it. She held it up to show me. Inside was something dark and bristly, "Do you know what this is?" she said.

"It looks like hair."

"Yes, it's your hair. I saved it. Do you remember when I shaved your head that first time? I picked some up after you had gone and I saved it. I wanted to remember you as my friend before you went out in the world and changed, in case I couldn't recognise you any more, which is what happened."

I was really bawling now. "Oh Suzanne, I'm so sorry, I'm a stupid arse." Well, that's what I wanted to say, but it came out much more messily and stammered than that.

"I never gave up," she could hardly say it through the tears, "I never stopped."

What did come out more clearly was the next thing. "Thank you," I said, "I love you."

I got the all-clear and Suzanne took me home.

My place stank. We had to call in the exterminator to get rid of a community of cockroaches who had set up home on the piles of trash in my kitchen. Suzanne found some bin-liners and we stuffed them with everything that was mouldering, rank and foetid. I was too weak to do much more, so I slept whilst Suzanne mopped and polished and swept the place clean again.

When I awoke she had filled my fridge with food and run me a bath. I choked guiltily on the times that I had called her a domestic drudge as I lowered myself into the tub gingerly.

Suzanne peed then stayed sitting on the toilet as we chatted about nothing in particular. Her face was red and tired; she had stupid sticking-up hair. She looked fantastic.

After I had washed and soaked for a while, she helped me out and dried me down.

"It seems a shame to waste all that lovely water," she said, and hopped in. I scrubbed her back and helped her rinse her hair.

Afterwards we lazed together on my settee and admired her housework.

Suzanne wore one of my old T-shirts for modesty's sake. She had her hair wrapped in a towel. Two familiar wet patches appeared on her front.

"Er, Suzanne..." I hesitated.

"Yes?" she beamed, "what is it?"

"You're leaking again, babe."

"What?"

"Your milk is leaking." I pointed to her chest.

"Oh fuck!" She pulled the towel off her head, lifted the shirt and pressed it to herself. "What a div," she blushed, "that hasn't happened for ages." Suzanne explained that there must have been a build-up because she hadn't seen Billy for a few days. "I'm trying to wean him off," she said, "but he loves my tits."

"Yeah, me too!" It slipped out of my mouth before I could stop. Suzanne said nothing, but I knew she had heard me. I didn't want to imagine what she might have thought. "Can I see?" I was trying to do something to neutralise the situation, I didn't want to freak her out, but I can see now that this question probably didn't help.

"Yes."

I prised the towel away from her breast and we both looked down at her nipples. They were big, dark and shiny, and they both oozed tiny droplets of pale milk. Suzanne's tits were full and heavy. Fine hairs covered the tops of them, and they stood erect in the cool room.

I passed my finger over one of her nipples.

"See with your eyes, Miss Ramona," she admonished me, "not with your hands."

"I'm sorry," I smiled, wiping the finger on the arm of the settee.

She said, "There's plenty in there."

"Can I have a go?"

"Yes."

I shifted on to my side and lay my head on Suzanne's lap. She propped me up with some cushions until I was at the right level. We both tittered nervously. She offered her breast to me and I took it in my mouth.

Suzanne's milk was rich and creamy. It tasted of her; it was delicious, like liquid love. I sucked and swallowed it down greedily. It made me feel drunk and full. Suzanne stroked my cheek whilst I suckled on one breast and then the other. I rested my hand on her heart; her warmth made me feel happy and secure.

In the corner of my eye I saw Suzanne with her head back – she was zonked and looked glazed, like one of those opium eaters you see crashed out in old photographs.

When I had finished, we lay there for a few moments.

I said, "I love you Suzanne, this is real." Then I said what I was really thinking: "I want to have sex with you."

"I know you do." She smiled.

"So?"

She sighed, "I don't know."

"What's the matter?"

"I don't know how to have sex with a woman; I've never done it; I don't think I'd know what to do."

"That doesn't matter, it's not like you've never had sex with anyone before."

"I'm a lot out of practice," she replied, "I haven't fucked anyone since Billy's dad, and that was long enough ago for me to have forgotten how to do it."

"Just relax, it'll be lovely."

"Babe, I'm scared." Suzanne said: "There are so many things that could fuck it up. I don't want to hurt you; there's still a lot of damage on your body. And you've been through a terrible thing – you're vulnerable." She continued, "And I don't want to be a lezbo. I'm not like you; I think you might laugh at me for being square."

Suzanne added, "If we fuck, what will happen afterwards?"

"I don't know," I said.

"I don't know either."

"Do you love me?" I asked.

"Yes."

"I love you too. Do you fancy me?"

"A bit, yes, I think so, I'm not sure."

"I fancy the arse off you."

Suzanne reconsidered. "We can always stop if I don't like it."

"Yes," I answered, "that's true."

"Shall we risk it?" She laughed.

"Yes," I said, "Kiss me."

She brought her lips to mine and we closed our eyes and would have slipped into the number-one romantic moment of the century had we not accidentally bumped our teeth together. Suzanne snorted with laughter so violently that she blew a snot bubble in my face, which then set me off.

"It's bizarre kissing you; it feels like incest or something," I snorted.

"Come here, little sister," Suzanne leered at me.

"Ew! No! You're wrong!"

She grabbed me and started tickling and biting me enthusiastically. She was very quick, jabbing my armpit and then tweaking my nipple before I'd had any chance to retaliate. In the end I had to use my superior size to pacify her, so I dove down in a Big Daddy style splash.

"Oof!" was Suzanne's response as I winded her triumphantly. "Get off me, you dirty fat lez!" She heaved me off her with all her strength and I flew off the settee and on to the floor.

"That's no way to treat a lady," I sang as I staggered back to where Suzanne sat. "Ow ow ow," I cried, rubbing my rump, "I hope you haven't added to my bruise collection."

"Poor baby," she pouted sarcastically, "Let me have a look." She rubbed the bump and kissed it better, but her kiss was not a maternal peck – she lingered, and I felt her nose and lips nuzzling up against the small of my back and down to my arse cleavage.

It was startling to be in her focus like this, as though she was acting, or as though I was waiting for a punchline. I held still to give us both some time to get into it and then I turned around. Suzanne kissed my belly and pressed her face against my bush. Then she paused.

"I don't know what to do," she said. "I'm sorry."

I lay her back on the settee. We both had stopped joking. I hovered above her, her face vulnerable and expectant; she was radiant, shining. When I looked into her eyes I wanted to cry with happiness, but that would have been very uncool, so I kept the little internal earth-quake that she had set off inside of me to myself. Actually, that's not entirely true, I did exclaim "Wow!" and "Fuck!" a couple of times; I didn't want her to think that I wasn't enthralled by her beauty and loveliness.

My best friend was laid out and ready for me.

I kissed her again and this time we didn't fuck it up. It was the best kiss of my life and even now I can only describe it in terms of shoot-ing stars in the clear night sky, flowers growing towards the sun, and such other romantic corniness. I was throbbing with plump red love-hearts, and I'm pretty sure that Suzanne was doing the same.

I looked away and blinked back some wussy tears. "Babe," I said gently, "I'm going to feel you and then I'm going to put my fingers in-side you."

"Yes," she glowed, and I would not have this memory any other way.

I trailed my hands down her body, past Billy's stretchmarks, down through her pubic hair, down the familiar pathway until I found what I was looking for.

Suzanne's cunt was wet and open. I thought of fresh snow that was about to be played in and messed around. I wanted to keep this mo-ment.

Suzanne noticed my hesitation and she flexed her spine and opened her legs further for me. I slipped in my index finger, twisted it around and pulled it out again. Suzanne exhaled, letting the tension go.

I ran my wet finger around her clit, pushing against it, tickling its tip and then rubbing it firmly.

Suzanne sighed, "Fuck me, baby; I want to feel you."

I had the heel of my palm against her clit; I pushed more fingers inside her and started to fuck. She was smooth and big and gorgeous inside, like wet baby sealskin.

"That's nice," she murmured, smiling with her eyes closed. She had her arms out like branches of a sapling swaying in the breeze. She smoothed her hands down her sides, as though she were doing a little shimmy for me, then she reached out to touch my tits, cupping them and stroking them; she tugged on them and pressed them against me.

"I feel like a kid in a sweetie shop," she chuckled.

My lips were engorged and I felt sweat beads forming on my face.

"Oh my beautiful girl," sighed Suzanne, opening her eyes, hooking her hands around my neck and pulling me down to kiss her.

"How are you doing, baby?"

"I want to come."

I fucked her vigorously and licked her clit like a hungry beast. She pushed the back of my head down into her snatch and humped my face. She came without a sound, she held her breath and screwed up her face with concentration, and then it was gone and she had collapsed.

"I popped your cherry," I whispered bashfully.

"You certainly did! That was a knockout."

"Do you want another one?"

"No, no," she panted, "let me get my breath back." She motioned "C'mere" and I crept on to her lap. She whispered, "It's my turn to sort you out."

"Just hold me," I said, my voice wavering with emotion. We both knew that this was my first time since, well, since the whole thing with Lisa happened. "I'm scared," I said.

"I've got you."

I sat between her legs, facing out into the room, the heat from her cunt warming me. Suzanne held me in her arms and the milky dampness of her breasts pressing into my back was comforting.

"Tell me what you want," she said.

I swallowed and shut my eyes. "I want you to be here," I said, "flying with me like we're ghosts; I want us to be together, twirling and swooping; I want you to shoot though me, to disappear up my hole and out through my mouth. I want to feel you vibrating with loveliness through my veins and my bones and my nerves."

"I'm here," she said, "I'm right inside you. I will never go away; I will always love you."

My cunt was hurting as it swelled and became moist.

"Hold me," I said. Suzanne tightened her grip.

I put both my hands between my legs and clamped my thighs tightly. I squirmed, feeling the edges of my fingers and knuckles against my ragged pussy and libidinous clitoris. I shifted and humped a little. My cunt was a battlefield in which pleasure and pain struggled for supremacy. Suzanne stroked my breasts and I pressed my fingers against my clit. I was afraid it wouldn't feel good, so I touched it lightly in order to blunt my disappointment. My clit was erect and hard; it twitched when I increased the pressure and fizzed with sparkles of sweet bliss as I stroked and fingered in my old familiar way.

Suzanne hugged me to her; she whispered love words and kissed me as I came in her arms. Then we both had a little blub, and just as soon dried our eyes and joked away our earnestness.

"Thank you, Suzanne," I said, after we had come back down to Earth.

"Call me Dipper," she smiled, "okay?"

Dipper went for a piss. "Er babe," she called from the hallway, "there's a letter for you here. It looks like something from the dole office."

The letter was only a Giro. Only accompanied by a computerised form saying that there had been a mistake in calculating my benefit whilst a new system was being installed. Only backdated for two – count them – two whole fucking years. Only advising me that I would be eligible for increased backdated benefit and housing assistance. It was a big motherfucker of a cheque, so weighty that it had been personally authorised by the head of the East London Employment Franchise, and it was all for me.

You're wrong if you think that's where it ends.

The Dipper and I continue to love the shit out of each other, but we did not run off into the sunset holding hands because life isn't like that.

I went and had counselling, which I hated and resisted with all my might, although I agreed that my taste for nose candy had got out of hand, and they helped me deal with all that.

Basically life went on as before. I stayed in my little flat and Dipper continued to be a mother to Billy, although that first shag we had was definitely not our last. Both child and lover got fat on her milk and later threw tantrums when she weaned us off it.

Being a modern kind of gal, she said that we could go off and fuck others if we wanted to, although that remained a largely theoretical concept for a long time because of the fallout from what we now call "that incident with Lisa". But eventually it did happen, and it was okay, and I don't know about her but as far as I am concerned few came close to my beautiful Dip.

And then there was Molex. Yes folks, we get some closure at last!

About a month after my rescue, I went to the library to check my messages on the computer. Lighting up the inbox was one from Molex. It was the last thing I expected. I swallowed and my heart started thumping and my insides churned. I had no idea what she might want with me; I was afraid it wouldn't be good and played with the idea of deleting it immediately. Ah, but you know I couldn't do that.

The message went: "I have an apology to make. It was wrong of me to ignore you.

A lot of people have funny ideas about me and I do not want to encourage them. I have had trouble in the past with some of your young lesbian friends which I did not want to reignite. It was easier for me to leave you to them, but this was not, I realise now, such a kind thing to do to you.

I hear that you have just come through an extremely harrowing episode, one which involves my name to some extent. I am so sorry that I have not been able to offer you support, and ashamed that people get fucked up around me. But I'm very proud that you, as one of my friends, have shown yourself to be a true and courageous survivor.

With this in mind, I would like to hold a small gathering in your honour. I understand that you may not wish to come, but my home is always open to you and I hope that you will take advantage of my hospitality, even if it is just to share a pot of tea."

She left me her phone number. Fuck, let me say this for extra effect: Molex left me her phone number. I was astounded, so shocked and thrilled that I paid the outrageous 50p fee to get the library staff to print it out for me – after all, I could now afford such fripperies. And I have to say "Bollocks!" to anyone who dares to call me a doormat for letting her into my life again after the way that she abandoned me, but she's not the kind of woman that you drop when the wind changes and, you know, I surrendered completely to her charming message.

I almost missed a second note blinking at me to open it. It said: "Are you going? Call me, I miss you. Love, Alex."

At first Dipper was reticent at the idea of meeting more of my "weird lesbetarian friends," but she changed her tune when I said that there might be some sex involved.

"I want to see how the others fuck," she said, "just so that I know you're not having a laugh with me," she added, referring to our still-nascent sex life.

"Molex and her friends are quite hardcore," I said.

"Goody!" squealed the Dipper, "I can't wait."

Molex hugged the air out of us both when she answered the door to me and my girl.

"I'm so glad you came," she beamed. "Come through," she added, "it's a small gathering, but I hope you'll be pleased to see some of the faces here."

I was very pleased indeed.

Iris was sitting on Alex's knee. They turned to wave at me, and then Iris counted in, "One-two-three," and they both harmonised: "Hel-lo Ra-mo-naa, we love you!" It was too fucking cute.

Alba and Jane were there, like weird twins; they turned and smiled at me. "We remember you," said Jane.

"I still have your undies in a pocket somewhere," I laughed.

The final guest made me stop and stare.

"Look who I found," said Molex. Sometimes I think that Molex has some weird magic power or something, because she is able to root out bits of your life that you don't even know that she knows about. No wonder people have funny ideas about her; it's like she's omnipotent. I guess it all adds to her mythology.

This time she had found Tina. Maybe she had done a little investigating of her own when I disappeared, who knows. None of that mattered to me as Tina stood awkwardly.

"Tina, I'm so sorry," I blurted.

"It's okay," she replied. "I know what happened; it's really okay." She brightened and began to laugh. I held her with gratitude. "It's really okay!"

I sniggered to myself despite this touching moment because Dipper looked enthralled by these friends. "They're fabulous," she gushed later, "not like that bloody Nicky!"

Molex poured out some champagne and raised a toast. She said that she had an announcement to make.

"Before the night begins properly, a decision has to be made. I am happy to host a civil gathering of friends; I have some good champagne and lots of stories to tell you. On the other hand," she grinned, "I don't think you could find a better bunch of sick and sexy degenerates." Molex said: "I would like to suggest a big family fuck, the others would also like this, but we would hate to impose it on you Ramona, and Dipper, if you would prefer a more sedate evening."

I looked at Dipper; she nodded enthusiastically at me and mouthed a silent expletive.

"Let's fuck!" I yelled to a room full of cheers.

This was no time to be inhibited. Clothes were ripped off and thrown to the sides. Molex put on some music, loud grinding electric guitars, a total sonic attack of lecherous noise.

Alba and Jane chased Tina around the room. They pirouetted and minced as Tina teased them, always just out of their reach. Alba snapped at Tina like a padlocked dog. Jane ran round the other way and they cornered Tina and closed in on her. Tina was screeching with joy.

Alba pressed her body against Tina's, pinning her to the wall. Jane pressed her fingers into Tina's mouth and she sucked them hard like a happy little pig. Alba licked her face, she and Jane whispering dirty talk into Tina's ears.

In the middle of the room, Iris made space on Alex's lap and Dipper came to join them. Iris bit her neck, much to Dipper's surprise, and Alex chastised them both. Dipper reached out to pet Iris' breast with one hand and undo Alex's fly with the other. Alex scratched soft red welts into her back and Iris, thrilled to be the focus of so much attention, giggled like an idiot.

Molex grabbed a fistful of my hair and pushed me down over a chair. The shock of her gesture was exhilarating. She was a strong motherfucker, I could not squirm out of her grip, and neither did I want to. Molex was the only one of us who had remained relatively clothed. She wore leathers. I could feel her hips pressing up against my arse, and I knew she had a hard-on. The thought of her cock made me wet.

Alba and Jane had Tina on the floor. They were rolling around together in a ball like a human puzzle. Tina would try to get free and the others would pounce and assimilate her into the whole. Fingers flicked and dug and probed, and bodies curled together.

Molex forced open my legs and drew the side of her hand up against my slit. She did it gently. Her hand was hard, an edge against which I could push.

Dipper was snogging Iris and Alex had his hands on her snatch. She was jigging backwards and forwards, like a fidgety kid. Alex pulled out his cock, rolled down a rubber and masturbated himself shamelessly.

Tina was stretched out between Alba and Jane. Jane was eating her arsehole and Alba had her fingers in Tina's mouth. Tina's eyes were closed; she was dribbling and her hair was messed up.

Gently, Dipper and Alex helped Iris on to his cock. She faced outwards and her legs strained to balance. Alex had his hands on Iris' waist to steady her. Dipper knelt in front and played with Iris' clit, and her own too. Iris humped and flexed her hips. She looked blank and imperious. Her movements were deep and steady. She sang along to the music.

Jane had eased her fist into Tina's tight cunt. Alba had opened her legs for Tina. Tina was chowing down.

As usual, Iris wanted it harder. Alex and Dipper swapped places. Because Iris was small, it was easy for the Dipper to hold her weight whilst Alex pumped into her from behind. Iris inched her fingers into Dipper and, before my girl really understood what was going on, she had hooked up her legs and was getting fucked hard by that mean angel-winged harridan.

I was oozing sex juice and was very ready for Molex to get inside me. This was going to be a no-frills fuck. Molex threw me down and climbed on top of me. Her dick was big. I shifted myself so that she could enter me more easily. I pulled myself open for her. I could see the effort in her face as she plunged right in, veins standing out on her neck; she was sweating like a hog.

The room filled with groans and the music clicked off.

Molex looked me straight in the face as she fucked me. She had wicked eyes. I was passive, like a dutiful wife. I opened my mouth to gasp for air and Molex dripped a long line of saliva into the back of my throat, which I swallowed gladly. The effort of fucking me made her snort and breathe heavily. I could feel my spine compacting with her thrusts, my whole body shuddering as she withdrew and then slammed it into me again. It was not hard to come in these circumstances. She pulled out and fell backwards.

I expected to lie for a while and then join in with the others, but Molex whistled through her teeth and everybody closed in around me. Their faces glowed and sparkled with sex.

"Welcome home, Ramona," smiled Iris.

Every hand was on me, rolling me around, tickling, pinching, making gentle slaps, rubbing, stroking. I stretched and purred like a randy fat tomcat. I'm sure Dipper would have liked to have said something sarcastic, but she was too dumbfounded to formulate it.

Some hands held my tits; others raked their nails down my sides. There were mouths sucking my toes, my nipples. Lips teasing my clit, tongues in my holes. Dipper kissing me deeply, no, it was Molex, no, it was Tina.

My own hands wandered and flailed, catching a cock, then someone's hip, soft flesh and hard. Alba had climbed on to my face and was teasing me, just out of reach, making me strain, then rewarding me for my good work. I could feel seven, eight, three, fingers sliding into my cunt – sometimes many, stretching me further than I thought I could go; sometimes only a few, tempting me and making me hungry again.

There was only one place I could go and I decided that I was going to be the one in charge of the trip.

"Hands off!" I snarled. Everybody but Iris removed their hands from me.

"I said hands off!" Iris reluctantly left me alone.

I wet my index and middle fingers in my mouth and dragged them down my body to the wet spot. My cunt was tired.

I let my mind empty and smoothed my fingers across my soft lips and hard clit. I circled the bump and let my senses focus on the darts of pleasure shooting through my thighs and belly. Before long, my breathing had become laboured and my legs bent open at strange angles. Involuntary facial twitches and spasms crossed my body, and then the atom bomb bright explosion of goodness spread up and outwards from the epicentre of my cunt, and I was wetter than ever and so glad to be alive here, amongst my friends. And, as I came, I felt wind rushing past me, like being catapulted, like a bullet from a gun or a blood cell whooshing through an artery. The sound metamorphosed into the whoops and laughs and claps and kisses of those around me. I will never forget it.

Fingers and hands scooped me up and lifted me high into the air like a sacrificial virgin, or a king. They paraded me around Molex's front room, laughing, hooting and stamping whilst I gurgled with pleasure. Then Iris wanted a turn, so we carried her for a while, and then everybody wanted a ride and, when no one was looking, I picked up my clothes and slipped out the door and went to find myself another dyke cherry to pop.

More new erotic fiction from Red Hot Diva

Scarlet Thirst
Crin Claxton

For once, the lesbian vampire novel is not just a metaphor: this novel is as up-front about sex as it is about biting into beautiful young necks. They're butch, they're femme, they're out for blood.

RRP £8.99 ISBN 1-873741-74-X Out in September 2002

The Fox Tales
Astrid Fox

A truly omnisexual collection of Astrid Fox's erotic short stories, which have been published in diverse anthologies ranging from *Viscera* to *Best Bisexual Women's Erotica* to Black Lace. *The Fox Tales* combines unapologetic West Coast lust with the darker tones of Angela Carter-style magic realism.

RRP £8.99 ISBN 1-873741-79-0 Out in October 2002

d Hot Diva Books are available from bookshops or direct from Diva's mail er service on the net at www.divamag.co.uk or on freephone 0800 45 45 (international: +44 20 8340 8644). Please add P&P (single item £1.75,) or more £3.45, all overseas £5) and quote the following codes: rlet Thirst SCA74X, The Fox Tales FOX790, Cherry CHE731.